THE SIN AND THE SINNERS

THE SIN AND THE SINNERS

by

Frederick E. Smith

Dales Large Print Books
Long Preston, North Yorkshire,
BD23 4ND, England.

British Library Cataloguing in Publication Data.

Smith, Frederick E.
    The sin and the sinners.

    A catalogue record of this book is
    available from the British Library

    ISBN   978-1-84262-556-9 pbk

First published in Great Britain in 1958
by Jarrolds Publishing (London) Ltd.

Copyright © Frederick E. Smith 1958

Cover illustration by arrangement with Alison Eldred

The moral right of the author has been asserted

Published in Large Print 2009 by arrangement with
Frederick E. Smith

Dales Large Print is an imprint of Library Magna Books Ltd.

Printed and bound in Great Britain by
T.J. (International) Ltd., Cornwall, PL28 8RW

To

STEWART & PEGGY

1

The small, ragged boy broke cover from the alley opposite the Law Courts. With face screwed up into an anxious grimace and with shirt-tails flying in the wind, he fled along the pavement, dodging people emerging from the brightly lit shops with an almost miraculous agility. He swerved round a pram without checking his pace, leapt over the leash of a dog that stretched halfway across the pavement, and turned the chattering of two women into gasps of indignation as he tore between them. In all, he left as much confusion in his wake as a star rugby player making a burst for the line.

He reached the end of the block of shops and turned sharply right. The road that stretched ahead of him now was less crowded with pedestrians, and after a quick glance over his shoulder he fled down it like a hare.

At that moment, unknown to the boy, a tall, slim girl was stepping from a car in a side street some eighty yards ahead of him. She was wearing a black raglan coat with matching hat that set off her blonde curls admirably and added a fetching paleness to

9

her attractive features. Over her left arm she was carrying an open-topped shopping bag. High-heeled, black suède shoes, gloves, and a handbag to match completed her *ensemble:* one that made her look as well groomed, fashionable, and expensive as the car she had just left.

She started up the street. She was making for the shops that had just witnessed the meteoric passage of the boy. Although it was barely four-thirty, the afternoon was dusky and sombre, and a draughty east wind was playing down the street. The busy northern industrial city of Lidsborough made a practice of commencing its winters early, and was making no exception this year.

Along the road raced the small, grubby boy; up the side street walked the girl, a picture of stylish young womanhood. The boy was considerably farther from the street corner than the girl, but he was also moving considerably faster, and a set of celestial vectors would have established them to be approaching it at the same relative speed. Fate, then, had ordained a collision between this ill-assorted pair, with results, for the girl at least, that were to change her whole life.

The girl was Beris Carnes, the only daughter of Victor Carnes, a wealthy Lidsborough manufacturer. Brought up by her father – her mother had died when she was a child – she had been denied nothing money could buy. For education she had first attended a private school and then gone to the type of boarding school (which, if one seeks them, still exist in certain sequestered parts of England) where young ladies are taught it is more important to be respectable than to be human. She had elected to return home instead of going on to university, and since then to her present age of twenty-four – thanks to the competent housekeeper her father employed – she had enjoyed a life of the utmost leisure.

The consequence of this upbringing can be easily imagined. She knew next to nothing about the less-savoury side of life, and although basically she was a kind-hearted girl, her upbringing had done nothing to make her tolerant to those who lived in its shadows. She had a quick mind and a receptive one, but like a camera it had only been allowed to click its shutters on certain prescribed pictures. Now Fate was to start clicking that camera about in the rudest possible way.

On she walked, on raced the small grubby boy. A distant ship's siren let out a hoot of warning but neither took the slightest notice, and the vectors shrank and shrank... Beris reached the corner of the street and turned right, the boy reached the corner and dived left. There was a shrill yell from the boy, a startled gasp from Beris, and two distinct bumps as both lost their balance and fell. The catch of Beris's handbag snapped open as it hit the pavement, scattering its contents in all directions.

The boy was the first to regain his feet. Catching hold of Beris's arm he tried to pull her up.

'Sorry, miss,' he panted. 'Didn't see you… Awfully sorry.'

Beris was winded and her ribs were sore where the boy's shoulder had struck her. In addition her coat was soiled and one of her nylons laddered. She told the grimy boy in no uncertain terms what she thought of his conduct as he helped her to pick up the contents of her handbag

He stood before her with downcast head when she had finished. 'Sorry, miss. I didn't mean t' do it.'

Beris eyed him with some distaste. 'Why were you charging along like that? What had you been doing?'

The boy started and threw an anxious glance back over his shoulder at her words.

'You aren't in any trouble with the police, are you?' Beris asked suspiciously.

The boy suddenly looked frightened. 'No, miss. I haven't done anything – honest I haven't.'

Beris gazed down the road but could see no one who appeared interested in the boy. She turned back to him.

'I don't know what you've done, but in the future don't go flying round corners like that. If I'd been an old man or old woman you might have hurt me seriously.'

With that she started down the road. She had not gone ten paces before she heard a shout.

'Hey, miss. Wait a minute.'

Turning, she saw the boy running towards her. He held a two-shilling piece out in a grimy hand. 'It rolled into the gutter, miss – that's why I didn't spot it when I picked up the other things. Sorry.'

Beris felt instant shame. For the first time since colliding with the boy she paid attention to his appearance. Through its coating of grime a young-old face stared up at her, a face both serious and wise with its puckered blue eyes, snub nose, and thin cheeks. It was a plain face – there was no denying that – and yet to her surprise Beris found there was something rather attractive about it.

'That's very honest of you. What's your name?'

'Tommy, miss. Tommy Fowler.'

Beris pushed the florin back into the boy's hand. 'You can keep it, Tommy. It's a reward for being so honest.'

The boy's eyes brightened like those of a bird, only to cloud over as if he had suddenly remembered something. 'No, miss.

He'd be mad with me if he found out.'

'Who would be angry? Your father?'

'No, miss. Mr MacTaggit.'

'Who's Mr MacTaggit?' Beris asked curiously.

The boy's face turned sullen and he stared down at the pavement. 'He's the chap who looks after me.'

'Well, I won't tell him, whoever he is. I don't know him. Come on, take it.'

Tommy shook his head stubbornly. 'I can't, miss. He made me promise.'

A passer-by stared at them curiously and Beris suddenly felt the incongruity of the argument. Her voice became impatient.

'Don't be such a stubborn little thing. You did me a favour and I want to reward you for it. There's nothing wrong with that.'

Tommy, as quick as a ragged sparrow in his movements, jerked his head up sharply. 'Do y' mean it, miss? Do you really want t' reward me?'

'Of course I do.'

'Then, miss'– Tommy's shrill voice was suddenly excited – 'won't you rather go and tell Mr MacTaggit what I've done?'

Puzzled, Beris stared down at him. 'You mean tell him you returned the two-shilling piece to me?'

'That's it, miss. Then maybe he won't be so mad wi' me when he finds out about the kid opposite...'

'You have been up to some mischief,' Beris said accusingly.

Tommy stared around to reassure himself, then drew confidentially closer. 'It isn't nothing serious, miss. It's the kid who lives over the tobacconist shop across the road... Every time I come to see Mr MacTaggit he yells things at me. I've stuck it for weeks, miss, honest I have, but this time I couldn't stand it any longer...'

'You hit him!'

Tommy nodded contritely. 'He ran in howlin' and his old man came out of the shop with a stick. I hid in the alley for a while, then belted down the road. Now I'm scared he tells Mr MacTaggit what I did.'

Beris could not hide her smile. 'And you think this might help to even things up? All right. Give me Mr MacTaggit's address and I'll tell him. But I can't go today – I've too much to do.'

Tommy's face brightened. 'Thanks, miss. That's super.' He pointed to where the massive bulk of the Law Courts towered over the surrounding buildings. 'He's in there, in room number 214.'

Puzzled, Beris took down the address. 'What is he – a lawyer?'

'No, miss. He's the chap who looks after me. You'll find him easy enough in there. Room 214.'

'All right; I'll go. Probably tomorrow.'

Beris held out the two-shilling piece again. 'You can take this now. I'll explain everything to Mr MacTaggit, whoever he is, when I see him.'

One last hesitation, then Tommy's small, dirty hand closed over the coin. 'Thanks, miss. It's super of you. You won't forget about MacTaggit though, will you?'

'I won't forget, Tommy. Good-bye.'

'Good-bye, miss.'

And that was the undramatic encounter that was to prove the turning point in Beris Carnes's life. If anyone had told her such a thing at the time she would have thought them mad.

2

By the time Beris had finished her shopping the nightly exodus of cars to the suburbs was in full flood. Breaking clear of the city centre she edged her car into the stream of traffic down Markham Road and let it sweep her out to Deanwood, Lidsborough's most fashionable suburb.

Markham Road flowed by her, neon lights, garages, a darkened park, blocks of lighted shops, gloomy side streets, a typical English thoroughfare in a typical English industrial city. She drove for fifteen minutes before the flanking shops thinned out and rows of cramped houses took their place. She passed under a railway bridge, slowed down at a roundabout, and took the road to the left.

Here the side streets were wider and lined with ornamental trees; the houses of better quality and mostly semi-detached. She passed a red-brick church, a nursing home, and then the entrance of Crescent Avenue appeared on her left.

Crescent Avenue was as provincial as a Sunday Suit or lace curtains in the Front Room. Its very name indicated its unpretentious background, for it was in fact a crescent, marching purposefully behind a small wooded park and emerging somewhat sheepishly a few hundred yards farther down the road. In the daylight its respectability could be seen at its best: its detached houses, prim and lace-curtained behind their privet hedges, looking as corseted and inviolable as two ranks of school matrons.

Victor Carnes lived at the purposeful end of the avenue in a large house directly opposite a thick clump of elms in the park. His car was already standing outside the house when Beris drew up. Vaguely surprised that he was home so early, she turned her car up the side drive and parked it in the double garage. As she turned towards the house the

17

side door opened, throwing a yellow oblong of light across the drive.

Mrs Morrison, the housekeeper, with hands still white with flour from her industry in the kitchen, was waiting at the door to receive her. She eyed Beris with both excitement and anxiety as the girl approached.

'Hello, dearie. Have you heard the news?'

Beris stared at her. 'What news?'

Mrs Morrison stood aside for her to pass by. 'Come out of the cold, dearie, and I'll tell you. It's been a real shock to me, I don't mind admittin' it.'

Mrs Morrison, known to Beris as Morrie, was a big, grey-haired, homely north-country woman. She had been a widow when she had come to Victor Carnes after his wife's death, and had been with him ever since. She was a woman with an outsize maternal instinct, and the irresponsible death of her husband before fulfilling his primary role of child-giver had left her lost and frustrated. The post of housekeeper to the rising young industrialist and his baby daughter had come as a godsend to her: like a broody hen without eggs she had fluttered eagerly over to this new nest and sunk her warm body on it with a cluck of profound relief.

That her eggs had hatched out into a different specie, with mannerisms, accents and outlooks quite different from her own, had strengthened rather than weakened her loyalty to the family. She respected their 'class' as she put it, and was very proud of Carnes's status in Lidsborough. It was a measure of her position in the family that on his return home Carnes had told her what he had discovered that afternoon – news she was now about to impart to Beris.

She ushered Beris into the house and closed the door against the cold wind. Beris eyed her curiously.

'What has been a shock to you? What's happened?'

It was not often Mrs Morrison had the edge on Beris in such matters and she made the most of the moment. She shook her head mournfully. 'I always said it was a mistake. An' time has proved me right. After all we did, too... But I did think we'd heard the last of it.'

'Heard the last of what?' Beris asked impatiently.

Mrs Morrison made her strike. 'It's Danny. He's back in town.'

Beris's face turned pale. 'Danny! Who says so?'

'Your father. He met him in King George Street today.'

Beris stared down the empty corridor, then turned back to Mrs Morrison. 'Where is Daddy?'

'He's in his study. I think he's phoning

your Aunt Cecilia about it.'

Beris flung her hat and coat on to the hallstand. 'Did he speak to him?'

'Yes. He asked him what he'd come back for and he wouldn't say anythin'. Just sneered, and then walked off.' Mrs Morrison touched Beris's arm anxiously. 'Won't it be horrible if he comes round here to see us? What will the neighbours say if they find out?'

Beris shook her hand away impatiently. 'Stop making the worst of it, for heaven's sake. I'm going to see Daddy.'

She started down the corridor towards her father's study. The sound of his voice speaking on the telephone made her pause. She glanced back along the corridor, to see Mrs Morrison bustle around and make a great show of going back to the kitchen. A moment more and the phone bell tinkled as the receiver was replaced. She knocked and entered.

Victor Carnes was sitting at his desk. He was a man who had passed few of his physical characteristics on to his daughter, being broad and stocky in build. He was in his middle fifties, halfway to baldness, with shrewd deep-set blue eyes and an aggressive chin well covered with flesh.

He was a man who liked company, and as his behaviour towards Beris suggested, a man who could be excessively generous to those near to his heart. Against this he had a fiery, bellicose temper which was often directed against those in disagreement with him. He was completely sure of himself (or thought he was sure, which is, perhaps, a flea of a different itch), having decided many years ago that for a man to keep vacillating and changing his concepts was nothing but sinful weakness. The result of this confidence – no doubt because the world values a man on his own valuation of himself – had won Carnes considerable distinction in Lidsborough.

He was a first-rate twentieth-century businessman with all that that implies. Thirty-five years ago he had worked with his father and two employees in a converted shed, making burglar guards for shops. Today he owned a factory employing two hundred men and turning out every conceivable article made of wire, from rolls of chicken netting to lamp shades.

With his boundless energy he had found time for other activities. For a long time he had been an active layman in the Unitarian churches, had served on many church committees, and given many a down-to-earth sermon attacking the low level of present-day morality (Carnes was a great moralist). Of late, possibly driven on by the same crusading spirit, he had turned his attention to politics, and at the moment was serving on a number of committees.

It is true there were some in Lidsborough who thought him too overbearing in his confidence and too uncompromising in his rectitude, but to such critics Carnes paid little attention, believing, with every justification, that any man worth his salt has enemies, and that the bigger the lion the greater the howl from the jackals around him.

When Beris entered the study he was frowning down heavily at the telephone. On seeing her his face cleared at once. He rose to his feet.

'Hello, darling. I didn't know you were back. Had a nice afternoon in town?' Unlike Beris he had a faint trace of the local accent in his voice.

She offered him her cheek to kiss. 'What's this I hear about Danny being back in town?'

He started, then gave a brittle, resigned laugh. 'Mrs Morrison, eh? I might have guessed she'd spring it on you as soon as you came in. Yes; I ran into him as he was coming out of the Black Boy, the pub in King George Street. Apparently he'd just arrived in town today and had booked a room there.' He walked over to the fireplace and selected a cigar from a box on the mantelpiece. 'He's had his name changed by deed poll. He's called Meadows now.'

Beris drew closer to him. 'What did he say to you? Has he come back for money?'

Carnes shrugged his heavy shoulders. 'He said no – that he wanted nothing from us. When I asked him what else he'd come back for, he wouldn't tell me. He said he'd come back to stay here, and that was all I could get out of him.'

Beris showed her dismay. 'To stay! But if he's here for long, things might come out. And that'd be awful.'

Carnes had struck a match and was lighting his cigar. He paused, staring at her through the smoke with his shrewd, narrowed eyes. 'What do you mean – awful?'

She paused, confused. 'Well, I know none of it was our fault, but you know how people gossip and twist things. It would be bound to cause a lot of scandal.'

Behind the smoke Carnes's face set. The dead match snapped between his blunt fingers as he ground it into an ashtray. He stared bleakly across the room for a moment, then said slowly: 'He probably has no intention of staying long: you know what a liar he is. He'll be back in London before the weekend – there's nothing in Lidsborough to appeal to a person like him.'

'But that's just it – he must have come because of us or why would he have come at all? So what is it he wants?'

Carnes turned abruptly away without

speaking. Watching him Beris realized he was at least as worried as she herself. He stared down at the log fire for a moment, then swung impatiently round again. His face was aggressive now, his heavy jaw thrust forward.

'All I know is this – he isn't likely to come around here or to go to the factory – not after what I told him. And if he doesn't come to see us, there's no reason why people should find anything out. So let's not worry about things that may never happen.'

'You're worrying yourself,' she accused. 'You're only talking this way to cheer me up.'

'Nonsense,' he scoffed. 'What have I to worry about? Even if people did find out, they couldn't blame me for what happened, could they?' He patted her cheek affection-ately. 'Stop fretting about it, Beeda. Every-thing will be all right.'

Beeda had been Danny's name for her in the days when they had both been tiny, lisping children, and her father, probably forgetting its origin, often used it as a term of affection. This time, for some obscure reason, it touched her emotionally.

Her father's efforts to reassure her only served to underline the anxiety she sensed in him. Moving restlessly by him she took a log and threw it in the fire. She straight-ened, dusted her hands, tried to keep her voice casual.

'How did he look?'

'Pretty down-and-out. Shabby clothes, old mackintosh, and he looked seedy – you know, pale and thin. Too much drinking and smoking, I expect.'

'He didn't say what he'd been doing these last six years?'

'He didn't have to,' Carnes said dryly. 'I've a pretty good idea.'

'Did he … mention me at all?'

'He asked how you were.' Carnes' voice became aggressive again. 'I warned him what to expect if he tries to see you. I don't think it's likely.' A short, tight silence followed, then he laid a hand on her arm. 'That's enough about him – let's talk of something pleasant now. How about a drink before dinner? I bought a bottle of that favourite sherry of yours today.'

She turned towards him; for a second his eyes were unguarded, and she realized with a shock that it was he who needed the change of conversation. Something more than mere anxiety about local gossip was worrying him, and her anxiety deepened. She was extremely fond of her father.

She made herself smile. 'I'd love a drink. Where is it?'

He looked around, then gave a frown. 'Stupid of me – I must have left it in the car.'

It was unlike him: he had an excellent

memory. She caught his arm as he started for the door. 'I'll fetch it. You sit down and enjoy your cigar.'

Carnes sank back into an armchair. Smoke rose from his cigar, spreading a blue screen before him on which he saw again the events of that afternoon. Danny, thin-faced, derisive ... refusing to say why he had returned to Lidsborough ... jibing at his curiosity. Nothing about him appeared to have changed – if anything the bad streak in him seemed more conspicuous than ever.

The industrialist's heavy face turned thoughtful as he recollected his movements after Danny had gone. Worried about the significance of the boy's return, urgently requiring to know whether he intended making trouble, he had been unable to think of any other way of finding out than by employing a private detective agency. Knowing nothing of such agencies, he had considered phoning his friend in the C.I.D., Inspector Greaves, for advice until he realized such a request would be certain to make Greaves curious, and curiosity over his affairs now that Danny was back was the last thing he wanted. As a result he had been compelled to pick an agency at random, and his choice had been the Foley Investigation Company, chosen because its address had been conveniently near King George Street.

Carnes frowned at the memory of his visit

there. He had been interviewed by a man in a grey, pin-stripe suit called Clinton – a chap with a fair moustache and receding hair, probably still in his thirties but already running to seed. He had been attentive enough, but Carnes had inwardly summed him up as the type that is unctuous in front of authority and derogatory away from it … the type that needs firm handling. He was not the kind of person Carnes would have chosen to confide in about Danny, yet there had been no alternative, and – as Carnes tried to reassure himself – the fellows couldn't stay in business if they gave their clients' secrets away. And Clinton would know who he was, would know his influence in the city... He would know better than to talk.

Carnes wondered if he ought to tell Beris what he had done, then decided against it. Without her knowing his real reasons, it could only alarm her further. And – although in this case Carnes felt complete justification in employing the use of such an agency – he was uncomfortably aware of the general odium such agencies had in the circles where Beris had received her upbringing. Better by far she were told nothing about it, he decided.

The sound of her approaching the study door brought Carnes back to the present. Lifting his stocky body from the armchair he went over to a cocktail cabinet and took from it a corkscrew and two wineglasses.

Beris handed him the bottle. She lit a cigarette, then turned to him apologetically. 'I'm sorry to bring it up again, but two things have just occurred to me. What about Morrie? You don't think she'll talk, do you?'

Carnes was bending over the bottle, removing the cork. He looked up sharply, then shook his head. 'She hasn't said anything for seven years – I don't see she's likely to start now. I know she's an old busybody, but she does consider herself part of the family. But I'll have a word with her to be on the safe side.'

'Then there's Richard,' she reminded him. Richard was her fiancé. 'Should I tell him or not? He's coming round tonight after dinner.'

Carnes looked thoughtful. 'Richard, eh? How do you feel? Do you want to tell him?'

'I think so,' she said after a short pause. 'It didn't seem to matter before – I never thought we'd see Danny again – but now I'd feel happier if he knew. I'm sure he won't talk about it.'

Carnes turned slightly away to hide the cynical amusement in his eyes. 'I'm just as sure of that, m' dear. All right; tell him if you like. You say he's coming tonight?'

'Yes. About eight.'

Carnes handed her a glass of sherry. 'Then you'll have the house to yourselves. Mrs

Morrison is going out and I've a committee meeting in town at 8.30.' Seeing she was still looking concerned he gave a frown. 'You aren't worrying about telling Richard, are you?'

Nothing had been further from Beris's mind – she was sure of Richard. 'Oh, no. I wish he knew, of course, but I'm not worrying about how he'll take it.'

'I should hope not,' Carnes growled. 'He's the luckiest young chap in Lidsborough and I hope he knows it.'

Beris reached forward and touched his cheek affectionately. 'It's you I'm anxious about. I can't help feeling you're more worried than you'll admit.'

The industrialist gave a hearty laugh. 'Me! Worried? It'd take a lot more than a whippersnapper like that to worry me. There'll be no trouble from him, but if there is, you can rely on me to handle it. Now drink up and let's go and see how Morrie's getting on with the dinner. I'm starving tonight.'

This was the man she had always known, confident, aggressive, as sturdy as an oaktree. It was easy to imagine she had exaggerated her fears as she followed him from the study.

3

It began raining heavily just after dinner. Beris's father drove off to his committee meeting just before eight, and a few minutes later, prompt as always, Richard arrived in his small saloon car.

'Hello, darling,' he greeted as she opened the front door. 'What a filthy night.'

Rain was coming down in pencil-straight lines and rebounding from the path. Shivering, she closed the door. After Richard had removed his coat she led him into the sitting-room.

'How about a drop of whisky to warm you up?' she asked, smiling at him.

'Good idea.' He gave her a kiss, then paused. 'Where's your father? In his study?'

'No; he's gone to a committee meeting tonight.' Beris was feeling a certain constraint. It was a difficult story she had to tell, and Richard was bound to wonder why it had not been told before. It would not be difficult, she thought with sudden resentment, if he were not such a prig.

Richard was an accountant, sharing a business with a friend, a business that had greatly prospered since his engagement to

Beris, for Carnes had seen to it that a good deal of work flowed his way. In appearance he was quite a presentable young man, nearly six feet tall, with good features and dark-brown hair. It was true he had rather a sullen mouth, and the cow-lick of hair that kept swinging down towards it did nothing to improve its petulance, but the girls of his own age seemed to find the effect pleasing enough – no doubt thinking it gave him a look of refined arrogance.

Certainly his social behaviour left nothing to be desired for he had attended St Martin's College – the only school in Lidsborough where Rugby Union football was played. St Martin's was an educational matrix that turned out young men as plumb and precise as wireless sets on a conveyer belt. All had the same accent, the same standards, and the same political opinions – indeed, they uttered the clichés of their middle-class, mass-circulation, daily newspaper with a fidelity that was astonishing. If such a body of nice young men had an abhorrence at all, it was for the intellectual crank who spoilt a good conversation by dropping an original remark into it. As if any chap could think and talk at the same time...

Richard, a prime product of St Martin's, was never guilty of such bad taste. He had two interests in life, money and rugby football, which he still played. Sometimes his walk suggested he had succeeded in amalgamating the two, for he carried his briefcase under his arm exactly like a rugby ball. With such a glut of virtues to his credit it would be unworthy not to forgive Richard for being a snob.

Beris was perfectly aware he was one, and she waited for the double whisky to sink into him before beginning her story. She also let him kiss her a few times, thinking it might also help to soften him up. Inwardly she was irritated at the need for these precautions, although she was forced to admit the fault was partly her own for not telling him sooner. The net result of these mixed emotions created a perverse imp inside her which almost looked forward to shocking him.

After fifteen minutes she took the bit in her teeth. 'I want to tell you about someone my father met in town today,' she said abruptly. 'A man called Danny. I should have told you about him before, but he seemed to have gone right out of our lives and I wanted to forget the whole thing. But now he's back I feel you ought to know about him.'

Richard stared at her. 'Danny! Who's he? An ex-boy-friend of yours?'

Her irritation and discomfort grew, sharpening her voice. 'Don't be silly, of course he wasn't. In any case I haven't seen him since

I was seventeen.'

The sulkiness, never far from Richard's mouth, promptly took station. 'Sorry. But what's all the mystery about then?'

'The mystery,' Beris said with deliberation, 'is this. Danny is my brother.'

Her perverse imp took real satisfaction from Richard's astonishment. 'Your brother! But I didn't know you had any brothers.'

'Well, I have. Not a real brother – an adopted one. And he's back here in Lidsborough.'

Richard looked puzzled. 'But why shouldn't he come back here if he wants to? What's so strange about that?'

Beris took a deep breath. 'Because he's a thief. That's why.'

Richard gaped – no other verb could describe his expression.

'A thief! What on earth are you talking about?'

'I said my foster brother, Danny, is a thief. He's been in prison. And now he's come back to Lidsborough.' Richard looked so bewildered now that Beris suddenly felt sorry for him. 'I'm sorry to blurt it out like this without any warning, but it isn't the kind of thing one can break easily.'

'But how on earth did your father come to adopt anyone like that?' Richard asked, coming to the surface again.

Her irritation returned with a rush. 'You

don't think Daddy knew what he was like then, do you? He was only a child of four at the time. His bad streak didn't come out until years later.'

'What made your father adopt him in the first place? Did he want a son?'

Beris shook her head emphatically. 'No. He did it for me. Apparently I was a neurotic child after Mother died – lonely, I expect – and the doctor advised Daddy to get a companion for me – to adopt a brother or sister. I asked for a brother and that was how we got Danny.'

'How old were you at this time?'

'The same age as Danny, between four and five. Daddy chose him because he was my age.'

'Did your father know his parents?'

'No. Now he wishes he had known them.'

'When did you first find out he had this bad streak in him?'

'Not until he was over ten.' For a moment, unknown to her, Beris's eyes held a nostalgic expression. 'Until then he'd seemed very nice. We weren't evacuated during the war, you know, and we had lots of fun together. But two months before he went to boarding school Daddy caught him stealing money from one of his suits. You can imagine the shock it gave Daddy – you know how honest he is. He gave Danny a terrible thrashing' – she gave a shudder – 'I'll never forget it. He thought it had cured him, but just before he went off to boarding school he stole some money again.'

'Did he know at this time that he'd been adopted?'

'Yes; that's what made it seem worse. Daddy had told him some years earlier, when he'd been misbehaving over something or other. Of course, after this Daddy didn't have much to do with him – didn't see much of him when he came home on vacations and that sort of thing. And he kept me away from him as much as possible too. Danny tried to make up to me, but I couldn't feel the same towards him either.'

'I should think you couldn't.'

'That wasn't the worst of it, however. Just before Danny's fourteenth birthday Father was asked to go up to his school and the headmaster told him Danny had been caught stealing from one of the teachers. I don't know exactly what happened – Daddy didn't say much about it – but it seems he was given a last chance. But he did something similar a few months later and this time he was expelled. That was the end of his education – Daddy couldn't find another boarding school that would take him – and so he was found work in an office.'

'Your father didn't put him in his own business?'

'No. He wouldn't have him there.'

'Don't blame him. Was Danny living with you all this time?'

'Yes and no. He'd been put in a room at the back of the house where he ate and slept. Of course, I was away at school in those days, but Mrs Morrison said he must have been up to all kinds of mischief during this time because he went out every evening and sometimes stayed out all night. No one knew where he went.'

'Jolly good job you were at school,' Richard remarked.

'I was at home when the police came for him, though. He'd been caught stealing money at work and the secretary had told the police. Daddy was frantic, but couldn't do anything. Danny was tried in a juvenile court and sent to a remand home for observation. When he returned after three weeks, the court put him on a year's probation.'

'What did that mean?'

'Oh; it was horrible. He came under the supervision of a probation officer who had the right to enter our house and enquire about his living conditions there. I never met him, but it seems he was always asking questions about how Danny had been treated in his earlier days, and that kind of thing. Of course there never was any suggestion that it was our fault, but it was horrible for Daddy just the same. He's never forgiven Danny for it.'

Richard nodded warmly. 'I should think not. What happened then?'

'Daddy decided to move to the other side of town. Of course he wasn't anything like as well known as he is today, but you know what neighbours make of things like that. Before we left Danny got into more trouble. It seemed he hated the job the probation officer had found for him, and after a month of it he struck the foreman in charge of him. This time he was sent to an approved school. Before he went Daddy told him he'd had his last chance, and that he never wanted to hear from him or see him again.'

'Not before time, by Jove.'

'We received reports from the school until he was discharged and then nothing more for nearly a year. Then we heard he'd been arrested with two other men for selling stolen goods in the Black Market. He got a month's hard labour for that. Since then we've heard nothing more of him for six years, not until Daddy ran into him in King George Street this afternoon.'

'What has he come back for? Have you any idea?'

Beris shook her head. 'Daddy asked him, but he wouldn't say.'

Perplexed, Richard stared down at his highly polished shoes. 'It's odd – his appearing out of the blue like that. What does your father think he wants?'

'He seems very worried. It's upsetting, of course – I was upset myself when I heard it – but Daddy seems more than just uneasy. And I can't think why – he isn't the type to let people worry him.'

'He'll be thinking of the business,' was Richard's instant comment. 'Things like this can affect one's credit if they become known. Not that any of it is his fault,' he continued hastily, seeing Beris's expression. 'But you know what people are.'

She nodded moodily. 'I suppose it could be that, although I wouldn't have thought gossip could have affected a business as firmly established as his.'

'Then it's probably just the scandal he's thinking of. After all, he's on church committees and goodness knows what else. He doesn't want it to get known. That's natural enough.'

Beris, although neither pleased nor satisfied with the explanation, had hardly expected anything more sagacious from Richard. 'I suppose that's all it is. And yet he seems so … oh, I don't know. Probably it's just my imagination, but I can't help feeling it's something more than that.'

A thought struck Richard, making his voice uneasy. 'You don't think your father's afraid he's come back here to–' He paused awkwardly.

'To what?' Beris asked sharply.

'Well, to do a job, as they say. To commit a robbery or something like that. That would set off a fearful scandal.'

With Beris anxious and consequently fretful, his tone and suggestion touched her on the raw. Her reply was half mocking, half biting.

'You see now the kind of family you've got yourself mixed up with. Are you sure you wouldn't like to pull out before it's too late?'

He stared at her sullenly, not knowing whether to take her seriously or not. He decided to play safe, muttering: 'There's no need to take it that way. It's not your fault he's got a bad streak in him, and anyway, he's not your real brother.'

'Let's talk of something more pleasant,' she said abruptly, unconsciously following the line of retreat her father had taken earlier in the evening. 'You've heard all there is to hear about him – now your guess is as good as mine. So let's drop it now.'

This they endeavoured to do, and although the evening was more pleasant as a result, Beris was unable to forget her concern for her father. Before falling asleep that night she decided to pay a call on her Aunt Cecilia the following day. Aunt Cecilia was her father's sister – if anyone knew a reason for his anxiety she should be the person.

With one resolution made, she was

reminded of another. From the gathering mists of sleep a small ragged figure ran up to her and lifted a grimy, anxious face to her own. She must not forget Tommy, the small boy: he had been so earnest. She little knew the importance of that second resolution in the light of what was to follow.

That same evening at eight o'clock, Danny, the object of all this concern and speculation, came downstairs from his room in the Black Boy and entered the saloon bar. He was a man of twenty-four years, slightly built, of average height, and with a thin, pale face and black hair. His features were sensitive and well formed, and if it had not been for a certain sullenness about his mouth and eyes he might have been considered good-looking. He was wearing grey flannels and a somewhat shabby sports coat.

Because it was mid-week and comparatively early in the evening, the saloon of the Black Boy was quiet. Two middle-aged men and their wives occupied a table in the centre of the room; a bus driver and his conductor, just off duty, chatted in low tones at one end of the bar; and in a corner near the door through which Danny had just entered a man was sitting alone at a table. He was pretending to read a newspaper, but as Danny entered his eyes lifted over it, examined Danny, then shifted enquiringly to the bald, rotund proprietor behind the bar, who gave him an almost imperceptible nod in return.

He was a man in his middle thirties, although a tendency to self-indulgence, showing in a thickening waist-line and florid cheeks, made him appear older. He had a smooth round face, his receding fair hair was well slicked back with brilliantine, and he wore a neatly trimmed moustache. He sat hidden behind his newspaper, listening.

Danny, his watchful eyes examining the occupants of the room, approached the bar. He laid two shillings on it.

'A pint of bitter, please.' His voice was well spoken although with a morose edge to it.

The proprietor hesitated, then drew the glass of beer. As he pushed it towards Danny he leaned across the counter.

'I shan't be able to let you stay more than one night, lad – you'll have to take your things out tomorrow. Sorry.'

Danny, eyes still busy on the other occupants, turned on him sharply.

'Tomorrow. Why?'

The proprietor's eyes shifted. 'I've got a party of people wanting rooms. I had a phone call this afternoon.'

'You told me this morning your rooms were hardly ever used – that the hotels got all the business.'

The proprietor, a choleric man at the best

of times, took umbrage at his tone. 'I'm not going to argue with you, lad. I want you out in the morning, and that's the end of it. So don't let's have any trouble.'

Danny's eyes had narrowed. 'Someone's been talking to you, haven't they?' He spun round on his heels, gazing suspiciously around the saloon. The man in the corner was staring down at his paper. Danny swung back. 'Who was it? Who's been saying things against me?'

'Now look, lad, don't start making trouble or I'll phone the police. And you wouldn't like that, would you–' The proprietor broke off at the expression that came on the younger man's face. He recoiled a step.

Danny's voice was strangled with anger. 'Who's been talking to you? Tell me.'

The two men at the end of the bar were now staring at him. Reassured by their nearness, the proprietor recovered himself. 'I'm not having you talk to me like that,' he blustered. 'Get your things packed and get out. If you aren't off the premises before ten, I'll call the police. I'm not having people like you in my place.'

For a moment it seemed Danny would strike him. Then he turned and made for the door. As he reached his table the solitary man with the newspaper touched his arm. 'Just a minute, kid. I'd like a word with you.'

Danny moved like a startled cat in turning

to face him. His voice was brittle with sus-picion. 'Who are you?'

The man grinned. 'All right, kid, not so fierce... I'm on your side.' He motioned towards the angry-faced proprietor. 'I couldn't help hearing what old sour-puss over there said to you and it seems pretty hard, turning you out on a night like this. Have you got anywhere to go?'

'I'll find somewhere,' Danny muttered, turning to the door.

'Wait a minute, kid. You won't get into a hotel tonight – they're always full this time of the year. And they're expensive, too.'

'I'm all right. I don't want any help.'

'You're not very sociable, are you, kid? I'm trying to help. I know a place where you can have a decent bed and warm fire – you can pay a few bob for it if you want to feel independent – and you can keep it a day or two until you find something more perma-nent. Now what's wrong with that?'

Slowly Danny relaxed. The man pushed a chair towards him. 'That's better, kid. Sit down and let's talk about it. What about a drink? Wait a minute – that drink you paid for is still on the counter. I'll fetch it over.'

He went across to the bar, giving the proprietor a sly wink as he picked up the glass. He returned with it to Danny. 'Here you are, kid. All the best to you.'

Danny eyed him sullenly. 'What's this

room you're talking about?'

'Well, it's this way. Me and a friend of mine, Johnnie Preston, share a flat not far from here. Johnnie's going to stay with his mother at the other side of town for a few days – he was talking of going either today or tomorrow. I can easily fix it so he goes tonight and you can have his room until he comes back or until you find something more permanent. How's it sound?'

'It sounds all right,' Danny muttered. 'But what about Johnnie? Isn't it too late to ask him to move tonight?'

'No; he won't mind. You stay here while I run down and have a talk with him. He's playing in a darts match in a pub not far away. I can fix things up and be back in less than half an hour – I've got a car outside. All right?'

Suspicion still lurked in Danny's wary eyes. 'I don't see why you should be doing this for me.'

'Don't be like that, kid. It'd be a poor world if we couldn't do one another a good turn now and then. I'll hurry back, then we can move you in and get better acquainted. Stay in here, kid, or I might miss you.'

On his way out the man turned back. 'By the way, kid – what's your name?'

'Meadows. Danny Meadows.'

'Mine's Jack Clinton. See you in half an hour, kid.'

Danny remained at the table, his brooding eyes settling every now and then on the rotund proprietor. As the minutes passed a few more customers began drifting into the saloon. One of these was a girl, bare-headed and wearing a green mackintosh splashed with rain. In a bold, handsome way she was attractive, her black hair and high cheek-bones giving her a slight look of the gypsy. She took in the occupants of the room in a glance, her eyes pausing a moment on the solitary figure of Danny in the corner. She bought herself a gin at the bar and then made her way towards a table near him. His eyes followed her, pulling quickly away when she glanced at him. She pulled a packet of cigarettes from her handbag, put one between her rouged lips, and then searched for matches. Apparently finding none, she rose and approached Danny's table.

'Can you give a girl a light?' Her voice had a trace of the Lidsborough accent but was not unpleasant.

Danny nodded and struck a match for her. His eyes shifted away as she stared at him boldly. 'Thanks.' She inhaled deeply, then nodded at the saloon around them. 'Is it always as quiet in here at nights? It's like a blinking mortuary, isn't it?'

He shook his head. 'I've never been in here before.'

'You're like me,' she said. 'I'm right out of my usual stamping grounds tonight. Had to work overtime, felt like a drink, and this was the nearest place.' She motioned to the empty chair opposite Danny. 'Mind if I take the weight off my legs or are you waiting for somebody?'

He started uneasily, then nodded. 'Sit down if you want to.'

She fetched her glass from the other table. 'It seems daft for people to sit alone staring at one another, doesn't it?' she said, slipping off her mackintosh. 'My name's Madge. Madge Edwards.'

He saw now that she was not as young as he had at first thought – she was nearer thirty than twenty. But the tight woollen frock she was wearing under the mackintosh showed her figure to be attractive. She put her elbows on the table, smiled at him.

'You don't talk as if you come from these parts. Are you new here?'

'Yes. I arrived this morning.'

'Where from?'

'London.'

She gave a wry grimace. 'You've picked a dump to come to from London. The pubs close at ten, and the last buses are at eleven. If you're seen in the streets after that you're practically a police suspect. What've you come on – business?'

'You could call it that,' he muttered,

looking away.

She shrugged her unconcern. 'You don't have to give anything away, dear, if you don't want to – I'm not nosey. In any case, I like a man with a bit of mystery about him. Where are you putting up, or is that a secret too?'

'I've just met a chap who thinks he can get me a room for the night. I'm waiting for him now.'

'You've left it a bit late, haven't you? It's raining cats-and-dogs outside.'

'I think it'll be all right.' He motioned to her empty glass. 'Would you like another drink?'

'Why, thanks. That's very sweet of you.'

They talked for another twenty minutes before she looked regretfully down at her watch. 'I'm afraid I'll have to be going, dear.'

After his initial hesitation his sullenness had diminished and he looked disappointed at her words. 'Wouldn't you like another drink before you go?'

'I'd love one, dear, but I promised to be home early tonight. Another time, perhaps.'

'When?' he asked.

She slanted a glance at him. 'That's up to you, dear. I'm pretty booked this week, but could make a night next week, if you like. How about Tuesday?'

His face brightened. 'All right. Where shall I meet you?'

She thought for a moment. 'What about outside here at eight-thirty? I can't make it earlier because of this damned overtime.'

He nodded eagerly. 'Fine. I'll be here.'

She touched his sleeve with her hand, a caressing gesture. Then she picked up her handbag, waving him back as he moved to accompany her to the door. 'I'm going to run, dear – I'm late already. See you next Tuesday, and between you and me I'm looking forward to it.'

At the door she turned and waved to him before going out, bringing a flush of plea-sure to his pale cheeks. His face appeared younger, more relaxed, as he sat waiting for Clinton.

It was another ten minutes before Clinton appeared. 'Sorry, kid,' he said apologetically as he approached Danny's table. 'It took a bit longer than I thought. But it's all fixed now – you can move straight in. I'll give you a hand with your things, if you like.'

Danny led Clinton up to his room. His personal effects were quickly packed, a single suitcase containing them all, and in less than ten minutes he was following Clin-ton through the rain to a somewhat battered car that stood outside. Clinton threw open a door and waved him inside.

'We haven't far to go, kid. Only a few minutes by car.'

Two hundred yards down the rain-swept

King George Street Clinton turned to the right. Here was the old town, a labyrinth of narrow, cobbled streets and Georgian houses. It lay between the city centre and the eastern perimeter of Darntown, the huge industrial area that ran alongside the docks. Most of its Georgian houses had been converted into offices, and in the daytime if one peered through the grilled, dust-covered windows, a yellow unreal world straight from Dickens could be seen.

Tonight the old town was dark and dismal, with the rain dripping from the eaves and running in tiny sluices down the cobbled streets. After threading his way into it for a few minutes Clinton turned into a dark *cul-de-sac* and pulled up outside a row of garages.

'Here we are, kid. Johnnie and me live above 'em. Couldn't be handier, could it?'

He put his car into one of the garages, then led Danny into the flat upstairs. It consisted of two bedrooms and a small kitchen. Clinton led Danny into the second of these bedrooms, a room so neat and well decorated it could have belonged to a woman.

'How will this do you, kid? Pretty smart, isn't it? Johnnie likes his things nice and tidy. Get your things unpacked and make yourself at home.'

After a moment's hesitation Danny took off his mackintosh and opened his suitcase. Turning to find somewhere on which to lay his things he caught sight of a knotted stick lying across the chair alongside his bed. Clinton, who had been watching him approvingly, gave a laugh.

'That's Johnnie's shillelagh. He's scared of burglars, is Johnnie, and always has it at his bedside. Throw it under the bed if it's in your way.'

Danny picked it up, gazed at it for a moment, then slid it under the bed. Clinton took off his overcoat, hung it up in the other bedroom, then returned to Danny. 'What about something to eat, kid? Are you hungry?'

Seeing Danny's hesitation he spoke before Danny had time to refuse. 'I thought so. I'll put something on the stove while you're finishing unpacking.' He pointed to a cabinet across the room. 'You'll find a bottle and some glasses in there. Pour us both a drink when you've finished and bring mine through into the kitchen.'

His voice came back through the kitchen door. 'You must tell me what your plans are after supper, kid. If you aren't fixed up with a job yet, maybe I can help you.'

4

Beris's first mission the following morning was to keep her promise to the small boy, Tommy, and just after ten o'clock she jumped from her car and made her way into the Law Courts.

According to the policeman on duty in the hall, room 214 was on the second floor, and Beris took the lift up to it. There she walked along a long corridor lined with doors. Alongside room 214 was a door bearing the word *Enquiries*. She knocked on it and entered.

A smartly dressed girl of about her own age looked up from a desk. 'Good morning.'

'Good morning. May I see Mr MacTaggit, please? My name is Beris Carnes.'

'Have you an appointment, Miss Carnes?'

'Why, no. I'm afraid I haven't.' Beris hesitated, then went on: 'I've come about a boy called Tommy Fowler.'

The girl rose. 'Wait here, please. I'll ask Mr MacTaggit if he can see you.'

Somewhat mystified, Beris waited while the girl went into the adjoining room. She returned a minute later.

'It's all right, Miss Carnes. Mr MacTaggit

will see you. Go straight through, please.'

Beris went through the door into the next room. A small man, sitting at a desk before a pile of files, turned his head sharply towards her as she entered. He was a man of indeterminate age, neither young nor old, with sharp features and crinkly, sandy-brown hair. There was something both irascible and mischievous about his sharp face with its small, bright eyes and bushy, bleached eyebrows. He resembled a curious squirrel that had leapt on to the chair to investigate the contents of the desk and was now caught in the act.

'Are you Mr MacTaggit?' Beris asked as she approached his desk.

'Aye; I'm the man. Take a seat, Miss Carnes, and tell me what I can do for you.'

MacTaggit's voice, sharp and peppery, suited his appearance. Beris was trying to place his accent. She had expected Scotch or Irish, but it was neither. There was a faint flavour of Yorkshire about some of the vowels, the rest had a pleasant individuality of their own.

He pulled a chair out for her, then seated himself. Sweeping aside the pile of files he planted his elbows on the desk and fixed his sharp gaze on her.

'My secretary tells me it has something to do with Tommy Fowler. What's that little rascal been up to now?'

'He hasn't done anything wrong,' Beris said quickly, sensing at once that Tommy's standing in these quarters was not all it might be. 'Quite the opposite, in fact.' She went on to explain what had happened, finishing: 'I wanted him to keep the two-shilling piece, but for some reason or other he said you wouldn't approve. Apparently' – and she had difficulty in suppressing a smile as she recalled the incident – 'he'd been in a little trouble earlier on and thought this might help to square things up with you.'

MacTaggit gave a sharp bark – the sound could not be described in any other way. 'A little trouble is one way of putting it, I suppose. He only gave a lad who lives near here a black eye and a bloody nose, and caused that lad's father, who completely misunderstands my authority over Tommy, to come here and nearly do the same for me. Just a little trouble, as you say. Go on, Miss Carnes.'

'Tommy did say the boy had been teasing him for weeks. And it was honest of him to return the money, wasn't it?'

MacTaggit scowled. 'The little rascal seems to have found himself a champion.' He leaned over his desk accusingly. 'Do you know something, Miss Carnes? That lad's father was nearly twice my size. If he'd hit me they'd be screwing me down in a wooden box this morning. That Tommy wants his bottom spanking until he can't sit down.'

The mock fierceness faded from his face as he saw Beris's bewildered expression. He gave a low chuckle. 'Don't take me too seriously, Miss Carnes. Tommy's not a bad little lad – I know that. In fact, if I hadn't defended him yesterday, the other lad's father wouldn't have threatened to hit me. It's good to hear this news about him and nice of you to come and tell me.'

His dry voice and quizzical expression brought a relieved smile from Beris. 'I promised him I'd come.'

'Aye, but it isn't everyone who'd keep a promise to a lad like that. Thanks again, Miss Carnes.'

Beris's eyes were roving curiously around the office. She turned them back to him with some embarrassment. 'This will sound a stupid question, but what exactly is your relationship with Tommy? He told me you were the "man who looks after him", but that was all. What did he mean?'

MacTaggit looked surprised. 'You didn't know who I was when you came?'

'No. All I had was your name and room number.'

MacTaggit let out another dry chuckle. 'You obviously didn't see the notice board down the corridor, either. I'm a probation officer.'

'A probation officer!'

'Aye, that's how Tommy and me come to know one another.'

'I never thought of that,' Beris muttered.

MacTaggit's shrewd eyes were taking note of her every change of expression. 'You're disappointed in the lad now, aren't you?'

'Yes,' she admitted, lifting her head. 'I am, rather. I didn't think he was a delinquent.'

MacTaggit leaned forward across his desk again. 'He isn't a delinquent. He's the boy who returned a two-shilling piece to you yesterday. The rest's all over, at least I'm hoping it is.'

'What did he do to be put on probation?'

'Nothing you or I mightn't have done if we'd had the same upbringing,' MacTaggit said dryly. 'I'd tell you the story if I wasn't supposed to keep their affairs secret.'

Beris gave a disappointed nod of her head and glanced at her watch. 'I shall have to be going. My father has a political meeting at eleven and I promised to do an errand for him before he goes.'

MacTaggit suddenly snapped his fingers. 'That's it. I've been trying to place you ever since you came in. You're Victor Carnes's daughter, aren't you?'

'Yes. Do you know my father?'

She imagined a look of caution came into his shrewd eyes. His voice was non-committal. 'I've met him once or twice in the past. Nothing more.'

'I must tell him. Where was it?'

'He won't remember me, Miss Carnes. It's a long time back.'

His obvious reluctance to talk more about her father added fuel to her sudden suspicion. Her throat felt dry, constricted. 'It wasn't seven years back, was it?'

He gave a slow, reluctant nod. 'Aye, it could have been as far back as that.'

She knew now her guess was right. 'It was you who saw my father about my foster brother, wasn't it? You were the probation officer in charge of the case.'

His eyes, grave now and oddly watchful, met her own. 'Yes, it was me. You were away at school at the time, I remember. There was just your father, a housekeeper, and the boy. I remember the whole case very well.'

There was a short, tight silence. Mac-Taggit broke it first. 'How is the boy?'

'I don't know.'

'Haven't you heard anything about him at all?'

'Only that he went to jail for a month soon after he left the approved school.'

MacTaggit frowned. 'Yes; I heard about that. It was a great pity. I remember that lad well, and there was a lot of good in him.'

'You don't have to white-wash him for my sake,' she said bitterly. 'I know the bad that was in him too.'

He threw one of his sharp, bird-like glances

at her, but made no comment. Watching him Beris felt a sudden temptation. She knew her father would strongly disapprove, yet there was some quality in Mr MacTaggit that made her feel he was trustworthy.

His next words decided her. 'If you ever do hear anything more about him, let me know. I'd like to hear how he's getting on.'

She took the plunge. 'He's back in Lidsborough. My father ran into him yesterday. He's called Meadows now – he's had his name changed by deed poll.'

MacTaggit showed immediate interest. 'Back here? That's interesting.'

'He wouldn't tell Daddy why he's come back and we're rather worried. I can't see the slightest reason why he should leave London to come here unless it's to cause mischief. What do you think his reason could be? You must have got to know him pretty well–'

'What does your father think?' MacTaggit interrupted.

She bit her lips. 'He won't admit it, but he seems very worried. All I can think is that, like me, he's afraid Danny has come back to make things unpleasant for us.'

'You mean by letting people know of his relationship with you?'

'I suppose so, yes.'

'Would that matter to you?'

Beris flushed. 'I can't say I'd look forward

to everyone finding out we have a thief in the family. And I'm afraid it might do Daddy's business some harm.'

MacTaggit pushed his feet against the desk, rocked his chair backwards, and frowned at the ceiling. He was silent for a moment, then shook his head. 'I can't see him coming back purely out of malice. It is just possible, of course – bitterness can do strange things to people, and I haven't seen him for seven years to judge how it has affected him – but I think it's highly unlikely.' He dropped his feet from the desk and a brought a pair of quizzical eyes to bear on Beris again. 'Couldn't it be just that he felt like coming home?'

Beris looked puzzled. 'I don't follow you.'

'It's simple enough. He spent all his childhood and adolescence in this town, and they say there's no place like home.'

'I can't believe that. He couldn't expect us to receive him, and what else is there here to leave London for? In any case, Danny's not the sentimental type. Look what he did.'

MacTaggit's voice was dry. 'Delinquents can have their sentiments too, Miss Carnes.'

She was disappointed with his suggestion. 'Not people like Danny. No; it's something much more concrete than that.'

His quizzical expression grew. 'If you want to know so badly why don't you look him up and ask him? He might tell you.'

'Ask him?'

'Aye, why not? No doubt he'd be delighted to see you. If you like I could make a few enquiries to find out where he's staying. I don't doubt I could have his address for you by next week.'

Beris was very much on her dignity now. 'I wouldn't dream of doing such a thing. I never want to see him again.'

MacTaggit gave a grunt of impatience. 'Then you aren't likely to get your curiosity satisfied.' He paused, then said suddenly: 'You've really got your knife in this lad, haven't you? Why?'

The unexpected allegation caught Beris completely by surprise. She stared at him almost flabbergasted. 'Have you forgotten what he did?'

'Not a thing. I remember his case very well indeed.'

'Then why do you ask such a silly question? You don't expect me to approve of him, do you?'

Mocking lights danced in MacTaggit's eyes. 'I don't expect you to bear malice towards him for the rest of your life, either. We're supposed to forgive those that trespass against us, aren't we, not to condemn them for evermore.'

Beris rose sharply to her feet. 'If you'll excuse me I'll go now.'

MacTaggit eased himself forward. 'What's

the matter, lassie?' he asked softly. 'Can't you take it?'

Her cheeks were pale with anger. 'I'm not used to being spoken to in this way, Mr MacTaggit.'

'Obviously,' he said dryly. 'And when it happens you run away.'

'I'm not running away. I'm just not going to listen to such nonsense. You can't expect decent people to welcome thieves back into their families.'

His reply was like a sharp slap across the face, making her gasp. 'What exactly are decent people, Miss Carnes? Those who have charity in their hearts or those that haven't?'

She had tears of anger in her eyes as she turned for the door. His sharp voice checked her.

'Just one moment, lassie. There's something else I'd like to say to you before you go.'

There was an odd fascination about his treatment of her that made her hesitate and turn towards him. 'More insults?' she asked coldly.

He gave a mischievous grin. 'No more insults, lassie. Some facts this time. I've decided to tell you something about young Tommy's life. Would you care to hear it?'

'Tommy's life! What has that to do with Danny?'

He grinned again, wickedly. 'I'd rather not

be the one to say. Anyway, sit down and listen. It'll only take a few minutes.'

To save her pride she refused the chair. He pressed his feet against the desk again, leaned back. 'Little Tommy's life,' he told her. 'In a nutshell. To begin with he never had an adult mother. She'd never properly grown up and all she wanted from marriage was a baby girl she could go on playing dolls with. So when poor little Tommy came along he wasn't very popular, particularly when eighteen months later his mother had the baby girl she wanted.

'But the first six years weren't too bad because Tommy's father, who was a labourer on the docks, idolized him and helped make up for his mother's neglect. But one day, just on four years ago, the whole bottom dropped right out of Tommy's world. His father was killed in a dock accident.

'Now put yourself in the lad's shoes. He was left entirely in the care of the woman who had always grumbled at every penny spent on him, although she had spoilt her daughter to death. She was the woman who Tommy had so often heard quarrelling with his father – in fact his childish mind probably blamed her for his father's disappearance. And to make things worse he had to live with his spoilt brat of a sister who was now being favoured more than ever.'

MacTaggit stabbed a sharp forefinger at

61

Beris. 'What do you think that sort of environment does to a child?'

She shook her head coldly. 'How should I know?'

'Quite,' MacTaggit said dryly. 'How should you? Well, I'll explain. Deep down in their minds, children start growing bitter. Without even knowing why, they start doing things to get their own back on people who've been unfair to them. If they are very young they may start wetting the bed. As they grow older they may break cups, saucers, windows, anything around them. And very often they being to steal.'

Beris gave a start. 'Steal!'

'Yes. Take the money from the mantelpiece, steal the change after running an errand, even take money from their mother's purse. It sounds nasty, doesn't it, until you know the real reason.'

Beris stared at him incredulously. 'You're telling me this because you believe Danny was one of those children, aren't you?'

MacTaggit shrugged. 'I'm telling you a true story about Tommy. What you care to make of it is your business. Tommy's mother put him out on a newspaper round ten months ago. He ended up by stealing money from the newsagent. You'll ask why he did that. Because when someone gets an infection it often goes on spreading unless a doctor is called in. Tommy couldn't analyse his own bitterness, he didn't even know its cause. Children like that grow up to hate everything and everybody, and if they aren't helped in time they become enemies of society. But they aren't criminals. Tommy was nothing but a heart-sick, lonely boy when I got him, needing only kindness to cure him. Now that he's living with a foster mother who gives him that kindness, he's well on the way to being cured.'

Tight-lipped, Beris shook her head. 'I don't believe a word of it. Some children are born with a bad streak and there's nothing anybody can do about it.' Her voice rose indignantly as MacTaggit shook his head. 'Danny didn't have an upbringing like that. He had a good home, good food, good education. What excuse have you got for him?'

MacTaggit did not answer, but she found something very disconcerting in his shrewd, steady eyes. 'You're suggesting my father made a favourite of me at his expense, aren't you? That's what you mean.'

He gave one of his exasperating shrugs and rose to his feet. 'I've hardly said a word about Danny, lassie. You've done all the talking about him.'

'But that's what you think, isn't it? That's why that look came into your eyes when I first mentioned him. You think we're to blame for his conduct.'

He gave a low chuckle, took her by the

arm, and led her to the door. 'Are you sure you're not getting my looks mixed up? It was probably the one I always get when a pretty girl enters my office.'

'It's nothing to laugh at,' she said coldly. 'It's a terrible thing to suggest my father showed any favouritism, particularly at the expense of a boy he adopted. If Danny didn't get everything I got, it was his fault, not my father's.'

His voice surprised her with its sudden gentleness. 'Aye, well, lassie; there's nothing wrong in having loyalty to your parents. And now I'll have to say bye-bye as I'm already late for an appointment.'

To her astonishment she found herself shaking hands with him. 'Don't forget that offer of mine,' he said, his bright eyes very friendly now. 'As I remember it, you and the lad were the best of friends until his first offence. Let's see – how long a period would that be?'

'Six years,' she said quickly, then bit her lip.

'There you are. Six years as children playing together – you'll have a lot of happy memories to talk about if you meet him.'

She shook her head. 'I couldn't do it – it's quite impossible.'

He pulled a comical face at her. 'I think you ought to. Anyway, if you change your mind, let me know. Oh, and drop in again soon and have another chat with me. I've enjoyed your company.'

She felt completely bewildered as she went down the long corridor.

5

When Beris left MacTaggit it was too late for her to perform the errand for her father: all she could do was phone him in the hope he had not yet left for the meeting. Fortunately he had not, and as always he accepted her apology without recrimination. She purposefully left her excuse vague, preferring to tell him about her meeting with MacTaggit at her leisure that evening.

Her next call was on her aunt. Aunt Cecilia lived down Springfield Road, one of the many side streets that ran off Markham Road before it burst into the glory of Deanwood. It consisted of two long rows of attached houses, each one as similar to its neighbour as human ingenuity could make it. Each row shared the same grey-slate roof that ran the full length of the street; each house had the inevitable lace curtains at the window of the front room. Aunt Cecilia lived in number 43, one of the few houses that had no television aerial attached to its chimney stack. Beris pulled up outside it, crossed the tiny front garden, and rang the bell.

A dog barked inside the house, there was a pause, then the sound of a latch being drawn.

Aunt Cecilia looked mildly surprised to see Beris. 'Hello, my dear. How very nice to see you. Now don't jump up, Roger. You might tear Beris's stockings.'

Her admonition was addressed to a fussy old spaniel who was making a great show of welcoming Beris. With tail wagging like an agitated metronome, he followed her and his mistress into the back room where Aunt Cecilia lived. It was a small room and made to appear smaller by the heavy mahogany pieces of furniture that cluttered it. From a birdcage in the window that overlooked the small back garden a budgerigar chirruped enquiringly at Beris. A hide settee and two armchairs were grouped around an old-fashioned cooking range in which a coal fire was burning.

Aunt Cecilia ushered Beris into the more comfortable of the two armchairs. 'This is a nice surprise, dear. Make yourself comfortable while I go and put the kettle on. I was just feeling like a cup of tea myself: you couldn't have come at a better time.'

Aunt Cecilia, four years older than her only brother, Victor, had remained a spinster after her twenty-two-year-old fiancé, David Pearson, had been killed in the Somme shambles of 1916. Mutual grief had brought David's brother, James, and herself together; and in 1919, to help James build up his import agency, she had gone to work for him on a part-time, unpaid basis. Later she had accepted full-time paid employment and eventually became his private secretary.

With all the prejudice of his time, Cecilia's father had been shocked at his daughter going out to work, but in those days Carnes' Wireworks had not been a prosperous concern and he had soon discovered the advantages of having a salary-earning daughter. Financially, however, the situation had rapidly changed once Victor Carnes had taken over the business, and in the early thirties he had offered Cecilia a far more remunerative post, which, to his great surprise and disgust, she had refused. Her stubbornness in not making the change had been a perennial puzzle to him – he had never guessed, and she had never hinted, that the real reason was the contrasting business methods of the two men. Pearson, quiet, gentle, with nineteenth-century habits, was as different from the high-powered Carnes as a hansom cab from a Cadillac.

Death had severed Cecilia's second loyalty – Pearson dying of heart attack in 1950.

This could have meant disaster for Cecilia, for in thirty years she had been able to save only a few hundred pounds from her salary. However, although Pearson had paid the price of his courteous business career by dying a comparatively poor man, he had not forgotten Cecilia, leaving her a small annuity. With this annuity, augmented by drawings from her savings, Cecilia was able to retire into her small house in Springfield Road, where, with her dog and bird, she lived in genteel poverty, refusing with the utmost graciousness the annual offer of help made by the impatient Carnes.

She was, then, almost the antithesis of her successful brother. In appearance she was nondescript, being plump and faded and also, perhaps because of her indigence, inclined to be dowdy. Her one good physical feature was her mouth. It had a curve of extraordinary sweetness, and was the one thing about her face Beris could readily call to memory. This was not surprising because in a normal year it was unusual if she and her aunt met more than three or four times. Christmas was the only certain occasion, when her father collected Cecilia and brought her round to Crescent Avenue for the day.

Beris waited somewhat impatiently for her aunt to return from the kitchen.

'Daddy phoned you yesterday, didn't he?

Did he tell you about Danny?'

Aunt Cecilia's mild face showed no surprise at the question. 'Yes, dear. He said he had seen him in town.'

'It gave me an awful shock when I heard it. Aunt Cecilia, you knew Danny quite well in the old days. What do you think he can want here?'

Aunt Cecilia shook her head. 'How should I know, dear? Your father asked me the same question yesterday.'

'Daddy seems terribly worried about it. That's why I came to see you. Do you know any reason why he should be so worried?'

Aunt Cecilia gave a faint sigh. 'He has told me, but I'm not sure I ought to say any-thing. You see, part of it is to be a surprise for you.'

Beris leaned forward pleadingly. 'It's so unlike him to be worried. Please tell me what it is, otherwise I shall imagine all kinds of things. I won't tell him I know – I promise.'

There was no mistaking her anxiety. Aunt Cecilia hesitated, then sighed. 'If you're as worried as that, dear, then I suppose you'd better know. Very well–'

At that moment, to Beris's disgust, the kettle in the kitchen let out a high-pitched scream for attention, and it was some minutes before order was restored. Aunt Cecilia handed Beris a cup of tea, offered her a biscuit, then sank back on the settee.

'Now, dear, where were we? Oh yes; I was going to explain your father's present anxieties. As far as I can gather they started at a political tea party in Merriby five years ago. Your father raised twenty pounds that afternoon for the Fighting Fund and was invited to be chairman of the West Lidsborough Association. Since then he has gone on so many political committees he has hardly any time for his business affairs.'

Beris nodded, listening closely.

'Well, it appears that Prime Ministers reward people who work for their parties by giving them awards in the New Year and Queen's Birthday Lists. I was astonished when I first heard this, dear, it sounds such an if-you-help-me-I'll-help-you sort of thing! The recipients get letters behind their names or knighthoods or peerages. Well, apart from the other work your father has done for his party, it seems he has also raised a good deal of money to help it fight the general election next year. They seem very pleased with him, and he has been tentatively approached to see if he would accept a knighthood in the New Year. He's terribly thrilled about it; although for the life of me I can't think what he wants such a thing for.'

Beris's eyes were shining. 'A knighthood! You mean he'll become Sir Victor Carnes?'

Aunt Cecilia gave her gentle smile and nodded.

'Daddy, a knight! Why, that's wonderful! Aren't you proud of him?'

'Of course, dear. He's very clever.'

'I think it's marvellous. It's absolutely the last thing I expected.' Then Beris remembered the point of her visit and sobered down. 'But what has Danny's coming back here to do with it?'

'Well, dear, it seems there are two reasons for that, although he has only talked to me openly about one of them. It is that people who accept these awards are supposed to have absolutely clean family records. Without being uncharitable it's difficult to believe they all have, but there it is...'

Beris stiffened with indignation. 'You mean they wouldn't give it to him if they found out about Danny? But that would be dreadfully unfair. It wasn't his fault Danny turned out the way he did. And, in any case, he wasn't Daddy's real son.'

'Nevertheless, that is the position, dear, and your father is worried that in some way Danny has found out and come to spoil things for him. I told him not to be so suspicious and silly. As if Danny, or anyone else for that matter, could be so malicious.'

Beris sprang to her father's defence immediately. 'I think it's quite possible. You should have heard the things he said to

71

Daddy before he left home.'

'There were things said on both sides, dear,' her aunt reminded her gently. 'But they were said seven long years ago.'

'I don't suppose for a moment that he's changed,' Beris said sullenly. 'Anyway, what's the second thing that's worrying Daddy?'

'I'm only guessing this from the things he has said – he hasn't openly admitted it's worrying him. Nevertheless, I feel certain the fear is there at the back of his mind. You see, dear, under the sponsorship of the Earl of Beverley, a very valuable collection of gold plate and candelabra belonging to a wealthy American collector called Delmont is being shown around certain cultural centres in this country. Of course nobody even thought of Lidsborough until your father offered to show it here and guaranteed minimum takings of £400. It's an absurd figure – who in Lidsborough is interested in a lot of old plate? – but if your father is silly enough to give away his own money, others will obviously take it. He has been given permission to display it, and so in about eight weeks' time he'll find himself personally responsible for thousands of pounds' worth of gold antiques.'

Beris looked puzzled. 'But Daddy's never been interested in antiques. Why has he offered to do it?'

Her aunt gave her gentle smile. 'The Earl

of Beverley is a very influential member of your father's political party, dear.'

Beris nodded doubtfully. 'Oh; I see.' A pause, then: 'He's afraid Danny has heard of this. Is that what you mean?'

'Yes. You see, if your father were to lose any of the antiques it would put him in extreme disfavour with the Earl, and that would almost certainly cost him his knighthood. So I think he's afraid Danny may have come back to steal them and ruin him. Did you ever hear anything so preposterous?'

'I don't think it's preposterous at all,' Beris protested. 'Danny's a thief and he hates Father... It's just the kind of thing he might do.'

Aunt Cecilia shook her head gently. 'Your father takes himself too seriously, my dear. I can't see anyone caring a hoot whether he gets a knighthood or not, and certainly not travelling hundreds of miles and committing a crime to prevent it. Let's keep things in their perspective, dear. Even if Danny were so malicious, how could he find out all these things about your father?'

'The itinerary of the collection might have appeared in the newspapers down south.'

Her aunt was silent.

'And don't forget the antiques are gold. He wouldn't only be ruining Daddy, he'd be making a fortune for himself at the same time.'

Aunt Cecilia lifted a plump hand in protest. 'My dear; don't you think we ought to be more charitable-minded? As far as we know the boy hasn't committed a single crime in six years. That's a very long time. Perhaps he is an entirely different person now.'

'*As far as we know* he hasn't committed a crime,' Beris reminded her grimly. 'On the other hand, he might have been too clever for the police.'

Her aunt gave a deep, resigned sigh and reached down to give a biscuit to the spaniel. Beris watched her for a moment, then said suddenly, 'What would you do if Danny came round to visit you?'

Even at that moment the sweet curve of her aunt's lips attracted her eyes.

'I should invite him in for a cup of tea or a meal, dear. What else could I do?'

'You wouldn't be afraid of the neighbours finding out who he was?'

'Good gracious, no. Why should I worry about them? But he won't come – I'm quite sure of that.'

'He always seemed to like you. Why are you so sure?'

'Because of the neighbours,' Aunt Cecilia said, giving her a sweet smile again.

The phone box at the corner of Springfield Road had an acrid smell of stale tobacco. The directory was badly torn, but after some searching Beris found the number she wanted.

'Hello, I'd like to speak to Mr MacTaggit, please. My name is Carnes, Beris Carnes.'

MacTaggit's peppery voice came on almost immediately. 'Hello, Miss Carnes. What is it? Danny again?'

'Yes, I'd like to take you up on that offer, if it's still open.'

'It's still open, lassie. How shall I get in touch with you?'

'Phone me at home. But whatever you do, don't let my father find out.'

6

A high, blustering wind rose that evening, and as Beris sat in the window bay waiting for her father to return home, she could hear the commotion it was causing in the elms opposite. There was a book on her knee, but her eyes lifted from it each time a car came down the avenue. She was anxious to talk to her father, and he was already half an hour late.

Her restlessness stemmed directly from the things told her that day, first by Mac-Taggit, then by her aunt. If her father's fears proved justified, there was no knowing what scandal might explode during the next few weeks.

But, for the moment at least, the doubt that MacTaggit had raised in her mind – that Danny's delinquency could have resulted from her father's treatment of him and not from a fundamental defect in his character – was so startling and revolutionary that it overshadowed everything else.

Memories, long buried, came back to her now. How, on leaving for work in the morning, her father had kissed her, and never even waved at Danny who had stood waiting near by... How, on his return home at night, he had always picked her up and put her on his knee ... and left Danny waiting until she was free to play with him again. How, when going by car on business to nearby towns, he had sometimes taken her with him, leaving Danny in Mrs Morrison's care. A sudden flush of heat ran through her as she remembered more and more such incidents.

Then outraged loyalty to her father rose and crushed her insubordinate thoughts. He was her natural father – therefore it was natural he had been more demonstrative with her. Danny, knowing he was an adopted child, would have expected slightly different treatment. In matters of importance, such as food, clothing, toys, and education, they had been complete equals – her father had never shown any favouritism there. So on any count Danny had been infinitely better off than if he had been left in an orphanage…

Nevertheless, she was greatly relieved when headlights glowed momentarily through the brocade curtains. Pulling the curtains aside she saw her father's large car half-turned into the entrance of the drive and his shadowy figure busy opening the gate. A moment later the car disappeared round the side of the house.

She sat waiting for him. She heard the side door open, heard Mrs Morrison's welcoming voice; there was a pause while he removed his overcoat, then the heavy tread of his feet down the corridor. She turned to face the door.

He was wearing a dark grey suit and an impeccable white collar. He was too stocky to wear clothes well, but he looked strong, aggressive, and reliable. After her disloyal thoughts the sight of him brought her a rush of affection that blurred her eyes for a moment.

'You're late home tonight,' she said.

He crossed the room, bent down and kissed her. 'Yes; old Simons came round and asked me to read the lesson on Sunday. You know what an old gas-bag he is – kept me talking over half an hour. Had a good day?'

She held his arm a little longer than usual. 'Yes, thanks. I'm sorry about this morning.'

'Oh; it wasn't important. Forget about it.'

'I really couldn't help it. You'll never guess where I was.'

'No. What happened?'

She told him about her encounter with Tommy the previous day. 'He was such a funny little thing, and so serious about this "man in charge" of him. I couldn't make head or tail of it until I met Mr MacTaggit this morning.' Her voice suddenly faltered at his expression. It had grown suddenly alert, sensing danger. 'I found he was the same probation officer who handled Danny's case seven years ago. Wasn't it a coincidence?'

'Quite a coincidence,' Carnes said grimly. 'And what did you do when you found out – tell him Danny was back?'

It was not easy to lie to him – she tried and failed. 'I did tell him in confidence, yes. I thought he might have some views on it.'

He frowned and shook his head, a gesture of exasperation. 'You shouldn't have done that, Beeda. You mustn't tell anybody. People talk.'

'He won't tell anybody – I'm sure of that. In any case, from what I gathered this morning, he didn't seem to think too badly of Danny.'

Carnes gave a grunt. 'Did he have any ideas why he'd come back?'

'He didn't seem to think there was any special reason. He suggested it might be

78

homesickness, a desire to return to the town where he was born.'

Carnes gave a contemptuous laugh. 'Danny – homesick. That's a good one.'

She was only too eager to hear MacTaggit detracted. She was relying on her father to simplify life again, to assure her that things really were black and white as she had always believed them to be.

She made herself laugh with him. 'He's the oddest person I've ever met. You should hear his views on delinquency. For example, he blames the mother for everything that this boy, Tommy, has done.' She went on to give an account of Tommy's history, finishing: 'MacTaggit seems to think that almost any crime a child commits can be blamed on its environment, not on the child itself.'

She was watching her father closely, and saw from his resentful face that MacTaggit's purpose in relating Tommy's life-story was not lost on him. His eyes were bleak, un-forgiving.

'I remember MacTaggit well – a crank if ever there was one – full of this modern psychological rubbish and daft ideas of his own thrown in as well. I wouldn't listen to the fool when he started gabbling at me.'

MacTaggit had spoken to him, then. She wondered what had been said... She tried to strike the right note of impersonal curiosity in her question. 'Do you think it's possible that a child who felt unwanted could be driven into theft and crimes like that?'

'Never on your life,' he grunted. 'It's absolute bunkum. People are born that way, not made. It's an excuse for crime, not a reason for it. The world's full of unhappy people, but they don't go along taking it out of the innocent ones. My God, if one followed the argument to its logical conclusion, there wouldn't be any sinners in the world – they'd all be just unfortunate victims of their environment. It's poppycock – one of those decadent modern views that could tear the whole foundations of society apart. If all probation officers are like MacTaggit, it's no wonder we're becoming a nation of Teddy Boys.'

'Then you don't believe one should forgive them for what they do?'

'I don't know what you mean by forgive. These people are born that way, and you don't alter 'em a scrap whether you forgive them or not. Far better to think about the decent people who're their victims. There'll always be evil in the world, and the only way you can stop it spreading is to be ruthless with it – in fact, it's your Christian duty to be ruthless. Once you start feeling sorry for criminals, start making excuses for the things they do, your own standards start going down and down. It's like a disease – if you don't isolate it, it spreads to you and others. You've got to fight evil, not condone it. It's something you can't compromise on.'

She nodded slowly. 'I suppose you're right, but it seems a little hard, somehow.'

'It's not hard at all, it's commonsense. If you started forgiving 'em, you'd stop punishing 'em, and then what would happen? Think what a world it would be if you had no prisons, if all the riff-raff and scoundrels were running loose. Why, there'd be anarchy, girl, chaos.'

Her smooth forehead furrowed. 'I hadn't thought of that.'

His voice rose, hearty, confident. 'No, Beeda, cranks like MacTaggit run away from realities. They imagine people as they would like them, not as they really are. They live in a little world of their own, hiding their eyes to the facts of life. I've no time for any of 'em.'

There it was, the kind of talk she had always heard from him, confident, clear-cut, black and white. She could not understand how the smallest doubt could possibly remain in her mind.

7

It was a week before Beris heard from Mac-
Taggit. He phoned her in the middle of the
afternoon, just after she had finished helping Mrs Morrison to lay a new carpet in her
father's study.

'Hello, Miss Carnes. Sorry I've been so
long in getting in touch with you, but my
contacts had a bit of trouble tracing the lad.
He's got a room at 121 Spiller Street, in
Darntown. It looks as if he is pretty short of
money – it's a tough district. Would you like
me to go along with you?'

She was tempted but decided otherwise. 'I
think it would be better if I went alone.'

'Do you mind a little word of advice
before you go?'

'Of course not.'

'Then go easy with him. He'll be touchy at
first; in fact he may be downright hostile.
Don't lose your temper with him if he says
things that sting – just give him that nice
smile of yours and gradually he'll come
round.'

'I'm not trying to bring him back into the
family fold,' she said impatiently. 'All I want
is to find out why he's come back here.'

MacTaggit snorted. 'Give him a smile or two – you don't have to pay for them. And come round to my office after you've seen him, will you, and let me know what's happened?'

'I'll do that,' she promised. 'Thank you for the trouble you've taken.'

'Not a bit, lassie. Good luck.'

After deciding the best time to catch Danny home would be between five-thirty and six-thirty, Beris found the remainder of the afternoon something of a strain. The very fact of meeting him again after seven years made her extremely nervous. In addition, anxious as she was for reassurance that his return did not signify mischief for her father, she had no way of knowing she was taking the right step, and her mind was not eased at the thought of the intense opposition her father would raise if he heard of her plan.

She left before he returned home, leaving a message with Mrs Morrison that she had gone out to dine with a friend. Fifteen minutes later she was in Darntown, driving along the busy Barferry Road that ran parallel to the docks.

Although it was an integral part of Lidsborough, and although her father's factory was in the heart of it, Darntown was as little known to Beris as it was to most girls of her upbringing. It was a district of smoking chimneys, screaming cranes, and ships' derricks; of humming factories and busy warehouses; of public houses, fish-and-chip shops, cheap stores, and tenement houses, of blowzy women gossiping on their doorsteps and half-wild children playing in the litter-strewn alleys. A vulgar, dirty, boisterous district, packed with more vitality than the rest of Lidsborough put together, Darntown was the place where men like Carnes made enough money to ensure their daughters need never go near it.

It had been dark when Beris left home but the darkness of Darntown had a very different quality from that of Crescent Avenue. In the winter a mist always seemed part of it, a mist that drew its being from the great oily river that flowed past Lidsborough. It wreathed itself around street lamps, draining their light, and crept into the squalid alleys to lie cold against each door and window.

Spiller Street proved to be a gloomy side street with a gasworks at the corner. Beris turned into it and drove slowly down, trying to read the house numbers from the car. Finding it impossible she pulled up a hundred yards down the street and jumped out. The night air was raw and carried on it the mournful wail of a ship's siren. Shivering, she put up her coat collar and peered at the house alongside her … it was number

89. Leaving the car, she made her way down the apparently deserted street. Long gaps, overgrown with weeds and littered with bricks, gaped among the tenement houses, reminders of the fierce air-raids suffered by Darntown during the war.

She found number 121 standing in the centre of one of these sites, an incongruous house whose double-frontage and ruined portico gave silent testimony to its one-time gentility. Patches of grey mist lay like cobwebs on the waste ground around it. From a side window a single yellow light shone balefully. As she approached the broken front path a cat leapt from the tangled bushes alongside her and fled round the side of the house. For a moment she paused, heart hammering with shock. Then she climbed the three stone steps, found an old-fashioned bell knob, and pulled it nervously.

A faint tinkle reached her from somewhere deep inside the house. A long silence followed, then the sound of loose slippers flop-flopping towards the door.

A hand fumbled with the catch and the door swung open. A slatternly woman, with matted hair hanging down over her shoulders, peered out at Beris. Her breath was sour with the smell of gin.

'Hello, dearie. What d'you want?'

Beris tried to calm herself. 'Does a Mr Meadows live here, please?'

The woman nodded. 'Aye. 'E came four days ago.'

'May I see him, please?'

The woman stared at her dubiously, then drew aside. 'I suppose so, if he's in. Come on inside, I'll show you 'is room.'

She led Beris across the darkened hall and up a carpetless flight of stairs, her slippers flopping grotesquely on each bare step. There was a damp chill about the house that seemed to sink through Beris's coat more readily than the mist outside. On the first landing the woman turned on a light switch. The naked electric bulb above was as unkind to the house as early-morning light to a raddled woman, showing the bareness of the landing and the flaked plaster of the walls. A draught, stealing up the staircase, sent a whirl of dust scurrying ahead of them like a frightened mouse.

'You'll be lucky if you catch 'im in,' the woman muttered hoarsely, pausing for breath. 'He stayed out all last night an' was out half the night before that. I can't make out what 'e wants a room for at all. Still, I suppose it ain't for me to ask questions just as long as 'e pays his rent.' She was about to start up the second flight of stairs when she paused. 'There ain't no need for me to go any further, is there, dearie? Turn right at the top and his room's the second on the left.'

Beris thanked her and continued up the stairs. She turned down a corridor and paused outside the second door. Her heart was hammering so fast she found herself out of breath. She waited a full minute for it to slow down, but the moment she tapped on the door it began racing faster than ever.

A chair creaked, footsteps approached the door, and she braced herself. The door appeared to open slowly – for a few seconds time became a slow-motion film, holding her in a refinement of suspense. A glimpse of an illuminated strip of distempered wall, then a wardrobe, then a window bay. Only then did Danny enter her vision.

His surprise was of such magnitude that it took time to register. His expression changed to one of pure astonishment and her childhood name came involuntarily to his lips.

'Beeda!'

She had been expecting anything but that nostalgic name, with all its associations. It burst in her mind like a tiny grenade, scattering into a thousand disconnected words all the sentences she had so carefully prepared. It tore time apart, and through the gap she saw a laughing, chubby face, the Danny of her earlier memories. White-faced and helpless she stood staring at him.

Then his face thinned as the bitter years came back between them. His voice, harsh now, completed the destruction of the vision. 'What do you what? What have you come here for?'

She moved uncertainly forward. 'May I come in? There's something I want to ask you.'

He moved aside, more out of bewilderment than desire, and she entered the bedroom. It was a cheerless place furnished with an old-fashioned high bedstead, a mahogany wardrobe, a single chair, and the inevitable marble-topped washstand. Its distempered walls were pock-marked and scratched, and apart from a single thin carpet alongside the bed, the floor boards were bare.

He closed the door and turned slowly round, following her movements. 'How did you know I was here?'

She was able to take in his appearance now. He was wearing a threadbare pair of grey flannels and a long-sleeved pullover well darned at the elbows. His black hair, a contrast to the pallor of his face, was awry as if he had just risen from the bed. With the initial shock of recognition past she saw now the changes in him: the thinning of the mouth, the hollow cheeks, the sullen eyes. Something inside her began to ache like a deep-seated bruise.

Her voice was shaky. 'Do you mind if I smoke?'

He stared at her, then gave a quick

impatient shake of his head. She pulled her cigarette case from her handbag and held it out to him, conscious of the violent tremor of her hand.

He waved her offer aside brusquely. 'I've got my own, thanks.'

She took as long as possible to light her cigarette, for the expression in his eyes disturbed her. Without knowing why, she had a sudden vision of Jack, their big retriever and childhood playmate, lying on the pavement after being run over by a car. With eyes blood-rimmed, he had snapped at everyone around him, and yet behind those same agonized eyes had been a mute pleading for forgiveness that, even as a child, she had recognized and sobbed over.

She tried to check her memory at that point, but it ran on rebelliously, reminding her of the sequel of the accident. How, after she and Danny had cried together for hours, he had stumbled away, to return with an absurd little brooch he had bought to comfort her.

Emotion evoked by the memories confused her intentions, and she was grateful for his harshness as he repeated his question.

'How did you know I was here?'

'A friend of mine traced you. He did it as a favour. I wanted a few words with you.'

'Who is he?'

The sharpness of the question, the suspicions prompting it, made her flinch. 'No one that means you any harm.'

The intensity of his eyes, the indefinable expression in them, seemed to grow. 'Why do you want a word with me? Why have you come?'

'I wanted to know why you had come back. I couldn't understand it and thought I'd ask you.'

The expression in his eyes died and was gone, leaving them as bleak as a winter sky. 'So you're just like your father, are you – curious about it? Why didn't you bring him in with you? Or is he waiting outside?'

'Of course he isn't. He doesn't know I've come.'

'Things have changed a bit since I was here last, haven't they?' he jeered. 'In those days you couldn't go a hundred yards without Daddy.'

The bruise inside her was hurting badly now, but the sudden increase in his hostility was almost a relief, simplifying matters as it did. His tone towards her father also helped to harden her heart.

'He wouldn't have let me come if he'd known,' she told him.

'Of course not – in case you got corrupted. He hasn't changed, has he? I suppose he told you all about our meeting in town last week?'

'Yes, of course. He said you wouldn't tell him why you'd come back. So I thought I'd ask you myself.'

'Why the sudden concern over my movements?' he sneered. 'You haven't worried about them for the last seven years. It wouldn't be because you're both afraid of a bit of scandal, would it?'

She tried to hide her apprehension. 'I haven't come to quarrel with you, or to rake up the past. I just thought you might tell me if I asked. Naturally we'd both like to know your reasons.'

'So it seems, from the trouble you're taking.' His eyes were watching her closely. 'Why is it so important you find out?'

The danger that he did not yet know the power he possessed to hurt her father, and that her visit might alert him of the possibilities, had always been inherent in her visit. His next words alarmed her still further.

'It is important – I know that from the way he behaved. Did you know he offered me money to leave town?'

She could not help giving a slight start. 'No, I didn't. When was that?'

'When he met me – in King George Street. He offered me a cheque for fifty pounds down, and another fifty on my return to London.' He dropped on his bed, lay back on his elbows and eyed her mockingly. 'So he's pretty keen to get rid of me, all right. I wonder why?'

Not knowing whether he was ignorant of the reason or was merely mocking her, she could only hope for the best and let him continue believing what he already knew. 'It's the scandal, Danny. He doesn't want it all coming up again. That's the only reason.'

'And you both think I've come to stir up mischief.' He gave a mocking laugh. 'I see you think as highly of me as ever.'

'I'm not saying that's your reason. But you must admit it seems strange you should come back here after all this time and after all that happened.' In her efforts to defend her father she made a bad mistake. 'You can't blame Daddy being a little anxious. He has a different standing in the city than when you left.'

His lips twisted. 'Oh, yes; he's quite a person in Lidsborough these days, isn't he? I've been hearing all about him… President of this council, chairman of that… The great Victor Carnes. He does a bit of Bible-punching in his spare time too, doesn't he?'

She bit her lips, did not reply. He gave another jeering laugh. 'So he's worried, is he? I'll lay odds it's on account of this political work of his.' Seeing her start he laughed again. 'Poor Daddy – afraid his political ambitions will be ruined by the return of his prodigal son. What's he hoping to get out of it – is he going to sit for Parliament next year? Or is there money in it somewhere?'

Here at least it appeared there was something he did not know. She remained silent.

'There'll be a reward in it somewhere,' he gibed. 'I've never known him do anything for nothing yet.'

That stung her to retaliation. 'He took you out of an orphanage for nothing. He fed you, clothed you, and educated you for twelve years for nothing. How dare you say such things about him?'

Her words were a spark, exploding an intense charge of emotion inside him. He rose from the bed, face distorted. 'For nothing, did you say? You know better than that. He took me because he wanted a toy for his brat of a daughter. And after she'd grown tired of me I'd to be put away like a toy until her next play-time... Took me for nothing! My God – don't give me humbug like that.'

Her eyes faltered before his burning, resentful gaze. 'I'm not denying the reason he took you. But you still got all the advantages of adoption. I don't see that the reason mattered so much.'

Two weeks earlier she could have said the words and meant them. Now she was uncertain. His bitter reply undermined her confidence even further.

'You wouldn't see. You're a product of your father.'

93

She was almost surprised to find herself give a little ground. 'I'm not saying he didn't show some favouritism to me, and perhaps that was thoughtless of him. But it was no excuse for what you did later, and you know it.'

'No excuse for stealing his money, you mean.' He almost spat the words out. 'No excuse for the bad streak that turned me into a thief. Go on – why don't you say it?'

'You're saying it, not I, but it's the truth.' In her mind she was challenging MacTaggit as well as him. 'You're the last person in the world who can blame Daddy for those things. If you hadn't done them you'd have gone on to university and been someone in the world today.'

For a moment his eyes defied her. Then they dropped and he turned away. He stood motionless a moment, his back to her, then lit himself a cigarette. There was something abandoned in the way he flicked the dead match across the room. In the silence Beris heard the tiny click as it landed on the bare boards.

She made a last appeal. 'You can't bear malice all your life, Danny. If you've come back for an innocent reason, why make such a mystery of it? Why not tell us so that we don't have to worry any more?'

'It might be a mystery, and it might not,' he said, deliberately tantalizing her. 'But there's something I will tell you, and you can chew on it on your way home. Last week, when I arrived in town, I took a room in a pub in town for the night. The landlord was all smiles and said I could stay as long as I liked. That was in the morning. When I saw him in the evening he told me to get out or he'd call in the police. Do you see the point now?'

'No; I don't. What has this to do with Daddy?'

He mimicked her cruelly: 'What has this to do with Daddy? I'll tell you. Someone had been telling that landlord things about me to cause trouble – I could tell that from the way he spoke. Your father knew I was staying the night there. Now do you understand why I prefer to keep my affairs to myself?'

His suspicions astonished her. 'You surely don't think Daddy would go around discussing you with landlords of public houses!'

'He doesn't have to do it himself. Your father has money, you know.'

'He wouldn't pay anyone to do such a thing, either. You've let everything grow out of proportion in the last seven years. I've never heard of anything so absurd.'

He nodded cynically. 'You've seen one side of your father and I've seen the other – that's the big difference between us.'

'There isn't another side – not to those

who play the game with him.'

'Still the same dear little Beris. Dear Daddy is always right, isn't he?'

She bit her lip. 'Why must you bear malice like this?'

He gave a loud, bitter laugh: 'That's lovely. You and your father have completely for-given me, of course. That's why he threat-ened me with police action the other day if I paid you a visit. But it's convenient to forget these things when you want something, isn't it?'

They were far apart now, much farther than strangers. She hesitated a moment more, then moved towards the door. 'I'll be going... I'm sorry to have bothered you.'

His bleak eyes took on a semblance of regard and he took his jacket from the chair. 'Have you come by car?'

'Yes; it's down the road. There's no need for you to come,' she added quickly, seeing his intentions.

He ignored her and led the way down the staircase. Their footsteps had a hollow, unreal sound. As they reached the hall the slatternly woman emerged from a side door and peered at Beris.

'So you got hold of him all right, did you, dearie?' She turned her attention to Danny. 'Are you going out tonight, luv, or not?'

'Yes. Why?'

'Will you be coming back or stayin' out

the night like you did last night? If you're coming back late, you'd better 'ave a key.'

'I'll be coming back, but I may be late,' he muttered. 'I'll get the key from you later.'

They descended the stone steps into the street. The cold air stung Beris's face. Over the bombed site the mist had grown denser. The rumble of traffic and machinery sounded in the distance, accentuating their loneliness as they started up the street.

His sudden question startled her. 'I forgot to ask you. Are you married yet? Or engaged?'

'I'm engaged,' she told him.

He seemed about to question her further, then stared moodily ahead again. His jacket collar was turned up and his thin shoulders hunched against the cold. She suddenly thought how wan and ill-nourished he looked, somehow inadequate for his harsh surroundings.

'You'd better go back,' she told him. 'You might catch cold without a coat on.'

He seemed to resent her concern. 'Don't worry about me. I'm all right.'

Against her will his stubbornness reminded her of the dark winter evenings of long ago when, no matter what the weather, he had always met and escorted her back from her music lessons. Although her own age, he had always shown an odd protective attitude towards her.

They reached the car and she unlocked the door. Without meeting her eyes he tucked in a fold of her coat before closing the door after her. Something about the gesture made her eyes ache with tears. His white face stared at her through the window, and a sudden impulse made her lower it.

'Danny; let's meet again somewhere. We've got so much to talk about ... all the things we did together...'

A street lamp made dark pools of his eyes. She wished she were able to read the expression in them.

'Let's meet somewhere, Danny. We can have a long talk, and perhaps I can help you a little...'

The sudden stiffening of his body warned her of her clumsiness. He shook his head brusquely. 'No. It wouldn't do either of us any good.'

'But I'd like it, Danny. Please...'

'No; you wouldn't. We're in two different worlds – you wouldn't like mine when you knew it. Good-bye, Beeda.'

When she looked back at the street corner she could still see him, a motionless, hazy figure under the street lamp.

On her return she drove straight into the garage, parking her car alongside her father's. As she entered the side door of the house, Mrs Morrison came bustling out from the kitchen. Her flushed appearance told Beris something was amiss before a word was spoken.

'Hello, dearie. You're back early. Have you had dinner or will you be wanting something to eat?'

Removing her coat, Beris shook her head wearily. 'No; I don't want anything, thank you.'

'You're looking as off-colour as your father did when he came in,' Mrs Morrison commented, unable to contain herself a moment longer. 'Have you seen the evening paper too, dearie?'

Beris turned on her in surprise: 'Evening paper! Why, no. What's in it?'

Mrs Morrison's voice dropped a full tone. 'Then you won't have heard about the burglary in Mason Street last night?'

Beris shook her head, puzzled: 'No; I haven't, but why should it upset Daddy? He hasn't any property there, has he?'

'It was an auctioneer that was robbed,' Mrs Morrison told her. 'He'd had a sale yesterday afternoon – too late to get the money to the bank afterwards. So he'd put it into an old safe like he's done for years. But this morning he found the safe lying open and all the money gone. Over two hundred pounds of it, dearie, all in banknotes.'

'But why should it be worrying Daddy? Has he said anything to you about it?'

Mrs Morrison gave a sniff of disgust: 'He hasn't, but I've got eyes, you know. It's right on the front page, an' when I gave the paper to him I saw him go as white as death. It gave me a turn, I can tell you. I thought for a moment he was going to be ill.'

Beris realized now the trend of Mrs Morrison's gossip and felt a vague resentment: 'But we've had burglaries before in Lidsborough. Why should he suspect Danny?'

Mrs Morrison's homely face took on a triumphant expression. 'Not burglaries like this one, dearie.'

'Why not?'

'You'll see when you read the article. It says the police believe the job was done by someone from out of town. I can't quite follow it, but apparently they know the way the local burglars work, and this job was done differently. Now do you see why your father's worried?'

Beris felt sick. 'When do you say it took place?'

'Some time during last night, dearie.'

8

That same evening, two hours after Beris's visit, Danny took a bus to the city centre where he was to meet Madge Edwards. He was early, and after making certain the girl was not already inside the Black Boy, he passed the time gazing into the brightly lit shops of King George Street.

A quarter of an hour passed before she came into sight, a slim figure in her green mackintosh emerging from a side street. She waved a gloved hand at him as she hurried along the pavement.

'Hello, dear. Why didn't you wait inside for me where it's warm?' When he made no reply she went on: 'Sorry if I'm a bit late, but we had a load of work on today.'

He sounded a trifle self-conscious as he answered her: 'It's all right. I haven't been here long, and anyway I was early. What do you want to do tonight?'

'I'd have liked to have gone to a show, but I suppose it's too late now. That's the worst of this damned overtime – it wrecks your evenings. All we can do is have a drink and a talk, I suppose, unless you feel like...' She paused, then shook her head. 'No; we'd better not go there.'

'Where?' he asked curiously.

'There's a new place opened not far from here called the Erebus. It's a bit like those small places in the West End – you know, a bar for those who just want a drink and a small room for meals and dancing. It has a bit of a floor show, too. I was taken there a few weeks ago and it's not bad at all.'

'Would you like to go there?'

'Well, we could have a dance or two, couldn't we? The only trouble is it might be a bit expensive.' She squeezed his arm. 'I'll tell you what – let's go there and we'll share the bill. What do you say to that?'

'We'll go if you want to,' he muttered. 'Where is it?'

She squeezed his arm again. 'You're a sport, dear. It's just what I need after that damned office. Come on – we can walk there.'

He followed her into the labyrinth of the old town. After five minutes she caught his arm and led him down a gloomy street paved with cobble stones. Alongside a darkened, crooked shop window filled with compasses, sextants, and other mariner's instruments, she stopped him.

'Here we are, dear. Don't let the outside put you off. The inside's all right, and that's what matters.'

The building before them appeared in

darkness but Danny could hear the stifled sound of music issuing from it. Madge led him down a flight of stone steps and rang a bell on the door. A woman in evening dress opened it for them. Somewhat hesitantly Danny followed Madge inside.

She pressed his hand. 'Wait for me here, dear. I won't be a moment.'

He removed his coat in the dimly lit hall, handed it to the attendant, and waited for Madge. She was back within a few minutes, looking attractive in a blue, square-necked frock. A pair of pendant ear-rings, swinging by her high cheek-bones, accentuated her gypsy-like appearance. She took his arm and led him towards the right-hand room. A blare of music met them as they entered it.

It was a small hall, surrounded by perhaps thirty tables and with a raised dais at the farthermost end containing a tiny, three-piece band. The décor and lighting were bizarre: the paintings on the walls representing scenes from hell with satyrs, harpies and furies stabbing their pitchforks in democratic concord, while flames from hidden lamps leapt up redly around their victims. Here and there, from alcoves in the walls, phosphorous skulls grinned out at the guests, reminding them of their mortality and encouraging them to make the best of it. The total effect was one of contrived decadence.

As they were being shown to a table by a

waiter whose flattened nose and cauliflower ears betrayed his origin, Madge nudged Danny's arm: 'Just order a bottle of wine. You need only have meals on Saturdays.'

As time passed the few empty tables began filling up. The band grew louder and the floor more crowded. Madge, dancing with Danny, pressed her cheek against his. 'Do you like dancing with me, dear?'

Her company and the wine had taken the sullen lines from his face. 'Yes. You dance very well.'

'I'm glad you came to Lidsborough,' she murmured. 'You're not going back to London, are you?'

He shook his head. 'No; I'm staying here.'

Back at their table she noticed how his eyes ceaselessly watched guests entering and leaving the room. 'Why do you watch everyone the way you do?' she asked curiously. 'I've noticed it before. Who are you looking for?'

His eyes jerked guiltily back to her. 'Nobody – it's just a habit of mine.' He hesitated, then motioned towards the door. 'What is there upstairs? Where do they all keep going to?'

She shrugged: 'I don't know. Another bar, perhaps.' Leaning forward she touched his hand. 'What about another dance? I love waltzes.'

'Just a moment,' he muttered, rising to his

feet. 'There's something I want to find out. I won't be long.'

She watched him walk over to one of the waiters who was standing by the door. After a moment the waiter led him outside. On his return, five minutes later, she could see at once that something was amiss. He reached her side, a tight alarmed expression in his eyes. 'Get your coat, please,' he muttered. 'I want to be going.'

She stared up at him. 'But why? What's happened?'

He jerked his head in the direction of the door. 'Everyone's pretty tight-lipped – I suppose only regular clients are supposed to know about it – but a chap in the bar says they have gambling tables upstairs.'

She relaxed. 'For the moment I thought the place was on fire. That's nothing to get alarmed about, dear, even if it's true. The place has been open nearly six months and nothing's ever happened.'

The familiar sullen look had returned to his face: 'I can't help that. I don't want to stay.'

She opened her mouth to protest further, then gave a resigned sigh: 'All right, if that's the way you feel. I don't know where we'll go now … it's after ten – everywhere else will be closed. This isn't London, you know.'

'I can't help it. I don't want to stay.'

She shrugged and rose. 'All right; but give

me five minutes to powder my nose. Or can't you wait for that?'

He flushed at her mild sarcasm. 'Don't be long, please.'

He sat at the table waiting for her, his eyes watching the door anxiously. More than once he stiffened as if a suspicious sound had reached him through the blare of the band. After five minutes he rose, went to the door and stared out. There was no sign of Madge. Noticing a waiter's eye on him he returned to the table. As he was about to light himself another cigarette she entered the room.

'Did you think I was never coming, dear? Sorry, but there was a bit of a queue out there.' She looked longingly at the floor. 'Won't you give me just one more dance before we go? Go on, dear – don't be too hard on a girl.'

Relief that she had returned coupled with the knowledge he was spoiling her evening made him hesitate. She caught his arm and pulled him forward. 'Just a couple of times round. Then we'll go.'

He danced mechanically, clearly without enjoyment. She pressed his arm. 'Be a bit sociable, dear. It's not my fault what they do here.'

The band were making too much noise for them to hear the loud rapping that suddenly sounded on the hall door. It was a woman across the room that gave the first warning, letting out a scream: 'Look out! It's a raid!'

Instant panic followed, drowning the authoritative voice that was shouting orders to the raiding police. Danny swung round to face Madge, his eyes brilliant with alarm. 'I must get out,' he panted. 'I mustn't be caught here.'

Madge, after giving an initial start, had herself under control again. 'Don't get excited, dear. They'll only take your name.'

He caught her shoulder, shook her. 'Will you be all right if I go without you? I mustn't be caught here.'

'But what have you done?'

'Will you be all right?' he shouted.

'Of course I will. They can't arrest me...'

He waited to hear no more, fighting his way through the panic-stricken dancers towards a door he had noticed behind the dais. He was within a few yards of it when a hand grabbed his shoulder, pulling him back.

'Just a minute, sonnie. Where d'you think you're goin'?'

He found himself face to face with a burly policeman. 'Let me go,' he panted. 'I haven't done anything.'

'Nobody said you had, sonnie. All we want is your name. You won't come to any harm as long as you stay where you are and act sensible-like.'

Danny jerked his shoulder away. The constable immediately grabbed his arm. 'I said behave yourself.'

Danny swung round, aiming a blow at the constable's face. His arm was twisted back, bringing a gasp of pain from him. 'Let me go,' he sobbed, struggling vainly to free himself.

'What's the matter, Garton? You having trouble?'

The constable turned to the police officer who had come up alongside him. 'This young feller tried to get out the back way, sir. Took a swing at me when I stopped him.'

'All right, put him in the van and we'll check on him at the station. Don't forget to collect his things from the cloakroom.'

'Right, sir.' The constable swung the sobbing Danny round and bunched him forward with his knee. Seeing Danny's frantic efforts to break loose, a second constable took his other arm. Between them they dragged him outside and threw him into the waiting van.

9

Before going to see MacTaggit the following afternoon as she had planned, Beris first called on her father. A heavy, cream envelope with a London postmark had arrived for him in the midday post and, guessing its origin, Beris decided to take it to him. His town offices and showrooms were at the bottom end of Lantengate Street, a busy road near King George Street and less than five minutes from the Law Courts.

Her father had an office for himself and another for his private secretary, a Miss Ainsworth, on the third floor. Beris took the lift up and thrust a head into Miss Ainsworth's office.

'Hello,' she said. 'Is anyone with my father at the moment?'

Miss Ainsworth, a pleasant, efficient girl with whom Beris was on excellent terms, smiled back at her. 'No; he's alone at the moment, Miss Carnes.'

'Oh, good. I won't keep him long.' On her way out she called back over her shoulder: 'He'll have had lunch by this time, I suppose?'

Miss Ainsworth shook her head. 'He says

he won't be going out for lunch today.'

Beris turned in surprise. 'You mean he's not going to have anything to eat? Why? Isn't he well?'

'I went into his office half an hour ago and he looked very pale. I told him he ought to see a doctor but he wouldn't take any notice of me.'

Beris nodded. 'I'll find out what's wrong.'

She knocked on her father's door and entered. She saw at once something was amiss. His usual ruddy colour was absent and there was a hunted expression in his eyes. He looked as if he had received bad news and had not yet recovered from the shock.

She hurried across to his desk. 'What's the matter? You're pale. Don't you feel well?'

His eyes had lightened on seeing her and he managed a smile. 'Who said anything was wrong?' he said, trying to bluff. 'Why shouldn't I be well?'

'Miss Ainsworth says you haven't had lunch today. And anyway you're looking ill. Have you had bad news about something?'

He stared at her heavily, then nodded his head: 'You'll have to hear about it, I suppose. Danny's in trouble. A friend of mine at the police station – Inspector Greaves whom I sometimes play golf with – phoned me this morning about him. He was arrested just after ten-thirty last night.'

110

The news was like a blow in the face, stunning her for a moment. 'Last night. That's impossible.'

'It's true, I'm afraid. Someone had tipped the police off that the new night club, the Erebus, allows a bit of gambling on its premises. They raided it just after ten-thirty. Danny was there with some girl he must have picked up. Instead of letting them take his name with the rest of 'em, the young fool tried to make a break for it – guilty conscience, I suppose. He struck a policeman and was arrested. When they got him to the station they found fifty pounds in banknotes in his mackintosh pocket. I don't have to tell you what the police believe now.'

She could do nothing but stare at him flabbergasted.

'He's going in front of the magistrate this morning,' Carnes went on, looking down at his watch. 'It should be over by this. I'm waiting to hear the result. Greaves promised to phone me.'

'But I don't understand. What has the fifty pounds to do with it?'

'It's made the police quite certain he is the chap who broke into the auctioneer's the other night. They know all the methods the crooks of the town use to break into buildings – they have them filed. That's how they can thin a search down to a handful of men. In this case, as the papers said last night, the method used was foreign to the town. Now they've found the banknotes on Danny, and have looked up his record, they're quite positive he's the man.'

'But that means he'll be sent to jail, doesn't it?'

Carnes's face was grim. 'Not yet, although it's only a matter of time. You see, they can't prove the money isn't his. All they can pin on him is a charge for striking a police officer. But you can imagine how they'll watch him in the future.'

'But couldn't it be his own money?'

'Is it likely? When I saw him he didn't look as if he had the money for a box of matches.'

She remembered the condition of Danny's clothes, the room he was staying in. She bit her lips, fought back her panic.

Carnes's voice ran on, a dull, hopeless monotone. 'The police are thinking what I've been thinking ever since I knew he was back. He's been away seven years learning his trade. Now he's come here to practise it.'

Her eyes were bright with fear. 'What do you mean?'

His heavy-cheeked, resentful face stared at her. 'What would you do if you were a professional cracksman – where would you sooner work? In your home town, of course – the one you know best. It stands to reason – you know the conditions, the right shops and businesses, and the hide-outs. That auctioneer was his first job. There'll be more to follow unless the police get him first.'

She knew his hidden fear and wished she had not promised her aunt to keep the knowledge secret. 'Will everything be in the papers tonight?' she asked hesitantly.

He drew in a deep, steadying breath. 'I don't think our connection with him will be mentioned – Greaves promised to do all he could there. But if he goes on like this, it's only a question of time.'

She remembered the letter she had brought, and handed it to him. His expression, a mixture of satisfaction and despair, told her it contained news that he wanted. He read it again, then his hand suddenly clenched, crushing the letter to a ball.

'My God,' he muttered. 'Why had the brute to come back? After seven years he has to come now, of all times...'

His breathing was uneven and there was sweat on his forehead. Alarmed, she ran round the desk and caught hold of his arm.

'Don't take it so badly, Daddy – it's not the end of the world. And you don't know for certain he did it – the money could be his own.'

He recovered quickly, patting her on the cheek and giving a short, embarrassed laugh. 'Sorry, darling. I am making too much of a fuss about it, I know. I suppose it's caught me off balance a bit.'

She did not know what she would have said, what admissions she might have made, if the office intercommunication had not buzzed at that moment. Carnes, looking relieved himself at the interruption, leaned over his desk and clicked the switch.

'Yes, Miss Ainsworth. What is it?'

'There's a Mr Storey of the National Electrical Company to see you, Mr Carnes. I haven't the appointment in my book, but he says you arranged it with him over lunch last week.'

Carnes frowned. 'That's right, and I forgot to tell you. All right. Give me two minutes, and then bring him in.'

He turned apologetically to Beris. 'Sorry, darling. That's the second appointment I've forgotten to give her this week – I must be slipping.' Pulling out his wallet he handed her a five-pound note. 'Go and buy yourself something, and try to forget all about this business for a while.'

Shopping was the last thing she felt like doing, but she took the note to please him. 'You say you expect to hear from Inspector Greaves at any time?'

He nodded. 'He should have phoned already.'

'I'll be home in just over an hour. Phone me, will you, and let me know what's happened?'

'I will,' he said, kissing her. 'Now run

along and try not to think about it. I'll be home as early as I can.'

Seeing he had fully recovered she said good-bye and left him. As she emerged into the busy street below, her mind was sealed up in a tight, lonely cell of its own, trying to digest all she had just heard, trying to resolve it with what she had seen and heard the previous evening. Suddenly she remembered MacTaggit and almost ran to a kiosk to phone him.

'Hello. Beris Carnes here. How soon can I come round to see you?'

'You can come as soon as you like, lassie. I'm pretty free until four o'clock.'

'Then I'll be round in five minutes.'

She was shown straight into his office on arrival. His sharp, keen face showed his pleasure at her visit. 'It's good to see you again, Miss Carnes. Make yourself comfortable.' With characteristic quick movements, he gave her a chair, offered her a cigarette, then settled himself at his desk. At first she believed he had not heard the latest news about Danny, but as his shrewd eyes settled on her she saw her mistake.

'You've heard about Danny being arrested, haven't you?'

He nodded. 'As a matter of fact he was sitting in that same chair not twenty minutes ago.'

She gave a start. 'In here?'

'Yes. The magistrate sent him up to me both before and after the trial. I had a long chat with him the second time.'

Her voice shook a little. 'What happened to him?'

'He was fined ten pounds and bound over for a year – the maximum sentence they could give him apart from imprisonment.'

'What about the fifty pounds? Was that brought up?'

His bushy eyebrows lifted. 'Now how have you heard about that?'

'I've just seen my father. A friend of his at the police station has told him all about it.'

He was leaning forward across his desk. 'Tell me something – did he mention anything about that fifty pounds last night?'

She shook her head.

'And nothing was said that could give you a clue?'

'No. He looked pretty down-and-out – I wouldn't have thought he had so much money on him.' While talking she remembered what the slatternly landlady had said about Danny having been out all the previous night. About to tell MacTaggit, she suddenly thought of her father, and went on instead: 'It seems impossible he could have done a burglary only the previous night, and yet my father says the police are convinced it was him. What do you think?'

He avoided her question, asking one of his

own instead. 'Tell me about last night. Was he glad to see you?'

Her brow furrowed. 'At first I thought he was. But then he began saying things against my father, and ... oh, we became so bitter towards one another there was no point in staying.'

'He didn't tell you why he'd come back?' MacTaggit interrupted.

'No. I think he enjoys the idea of keeping Father worried, although he makes out it's because he can't trust him.' She went on to give an account of Danny's suspicions of her father. When she had finished MacTaggit gave a non-committal nod.

'Lads with his background are always suspicious. It doesn't mean much one way or the other.'

She eyed him anxiously. 'What did he say to you? Did you mention the fifty pounds to him?'

MacTaggit squinted at her under his bushy eyebrows: 'Aye; and what do you think he told me? – in confidence, of course. He said the money had been planted on him.'

'Planted! I don't understand.'

'He contends that, unknown to him, someone put the money into his coat pocket.'

'But why on earth should anyone do that?'

MacTaggit shrugged. 'If someone in the club had the stolen money on them when the police arrived, they might have lost their heads and stuffed it into the nearest mack-intosh pocket. I've known such things happen.'

'Why didn't he tell the police that?'

'The lad isn't a fool. He knew a story like that would only make them more suspicious than ever. The only thing he could say was that the money was his.'

She again asked him the question he had avoided earlier. 'What do you think? Do you believe he stole the money?'

He picked up a ruler from his desk and scowled down at it. 'He might have done,' he grunted, after a pause. 'There's no deny-ing that. But after my chat with him today my feelings are that he didn't. I can't give a single concrete reason – perhaps it's sheer prejudice. But this time, anyway, I'm giving him the benefit of the doubt.'

'Has it changed your feelings towards him at all?' she asked curiously.

His eyes lifted from the ruler to her face, and the expression in them made her flush. 'If my feelings towards my charges changed every time there was a possibility they'd left the straight and narrow path, I wouldn't be much use in my job, would I? It's not my job to condemn people; it's my job to help them sort themselves out.'

'But Danny's not in your charge any more.'

His reply was meant to sting her and it

did. 'You can't write off your responsibilities towards people with a few words or a stroke of the pen. That's what I was trying to tell you the other day. You can't have dealings with them, as you and your father and I have had with Danny, and then, when you see them in trouble later on, walk by with a shrug of your shoulders. I make an effort to follow the lives of my charges to see how they turn out, and for reasons I've already given you, this lad had a special interest for me – although until you came I thought I'd heard the last of him. You know my views on his upbringing – you guessed 'em the last time we had a chat. I think your father, and to a lesser degree you, have a debt to that lad. And candidly, just because your father won't admit that debt, it doesn't mean you should do the same.'

He leaned forward across his desk again. 'When you mentioned him the other day, it all came back to me. All the things he let out – unguarded things because, after all, he was hardly more than a child in those days. And one thing I do know – the lad used to think the very world of you. And that puts a responsibility on you. Maybe not a fair one, yet I don't see how you can morally dodge it. Can you see what I'm driving at?'

She shook her head, almost afraid to listen.

'It's simple enough, lassie. Which is worse

– to receive contempt from someone you dislike or someone you love? You were only a child when he stole for the first time, and so couldn't be blamed for imitating your father's disgust, but it's still a fact that your disgust hurt him far more. Of course the initial damage had already been done by your father's favouritism – let's not get confused here, he was the real culprit – but nevertheless I'm convinced that the biggest single factor in completing the demoralization of his character was your attitude to him. And that's why – now you're a grown-up woman and can understand these things – I suggested last week you went to see him. I didn't know why he's come back – I still don't – but I couldn't think of a better beginning than the two of you becoming friends again. Now, after what's happened,' and he paused for emphasis, face bleak, 'I feel it's about ten times more important.'

'But I went, and what happened?' she protested. 'He wouldn't talk to me, and when I suggested seeing him again he refused, telling me we were living in two different worlds. And only a few hours afterwards he was arrested. What can I do with a person like that?'

'You can do a tremendous amount, lassie. But first you have to understand him. People like Danny are the most vulnerable people in the world. Do you know why?'

She shook her head.

'Because they're desperately lonely. All their bitterness and suspicion makes it hard for them to make friends. Add to that the fact that decent society won't have them back and you see why they usually go from bad to worse. They're so lonely for companionship that it only takes someone to come along and give them a smile or buy them a drink and they're won over. They start doing jobs for a crook, get into the hands of a good-time girl, and the slide gets steeper and steeper... Until one day they're buying a drink for another lonely lad... Take my word for it, lassie – loneliness of that sort is the devil's recruiting officer. It's a hellish thing.'

She was thinking of the dark house in Spiller Street, of the cobwebs of fog floating over the ruins alongside, and a shiver ran through her.

MacTaggit pointed a sharp forefinger at her. 'But think of it now the other way. Suppose someone decent comes along with a smile... Oh; they'll be much more sullen with him – to them he's one of the enemies who threw them out into the wilderness, and anyway you can't cure a chronic disease with a single dose of medicine. But they can't escape their loneliness any more than they can escape their longing to return to the fold. They'll come back eventually –

unless you leave it too late. That's why I want you to keep at him, lassie. That boy used to worship the ground you walked on. And after talking to him today I think he still does. Oh, he puts on a couldn't-care-less act, but it didn't fool me any more than I think it fooled you last night.' His eyes seemed to be reading her most secret thoughts. 'Be honest, lassie. You're a woman – you can feel such things. Wasn't that the impression you got last night?'

There was a tight, swollen ache about her eyes. 'But how can you change people who don't want to be changed, who don't want to see you and are rude when they do?'

'Sink your pride and pester 'em,' he said sharply. 'Make yourself a nuisance if you have to. You'll find you're a good deal tougher than you think, and that rude words don't break bones, anyway. It won't be for long. Have faith in kindness, lassie. It's the magic elixir that changes lead into gold, sinners into saints. It's the only virtue in the world worth a damn – the rest of them are meaningless without it, anyway. Try it on this lad and watch the miracle.'

'It's so difficult,' she muttered. 'I've got my father to think about. He stands to lose something terribly important if it comes out that Danny is his son. And it may come out if I start seeing Danny.'

His answer to that made her start. 'It'll

come out a damn sight more quickly if Danny gets himself into more serious trouble. If that's how things are, you're doing your father a service by helping the lad.'

She realized the truth of his words. 'But how can I see him against his wishes?'

He gave a sudden impish grin. 'I thought of that, lassie. When he was here I had a chat with him about his lodging house. From what I hear it's a pretty grim place.'

She shuddered. 'It's absolutely sinister.'

'I suggested he made a move,' MacTaggit went on. 'He can't afford much, of course, and for some reason wants to stay on the river side of town. That gave me a brainwave. I gave him Tommy's address. I happen to know that his foster mother, Mrs Johnson, has got a spare room at the moment.'

Her puzzled expression showed she did not understand. 'But is it a good idea to put him and Tommy together? I should have thought just the opposite.'

He gave another mischievous grin. 'Not a bit, lassie. It's a case where two wrongs can easily make a right. That was one reason for giving him the address. The other reason was you.'

'I don't understand.'

'It's easy enough. If I'm not mistaken you took a liking to Tommy and it wouldn't need much encouragement to make you kind to the little chap.' MacTaggit's voice was unashamedly insinuative. 'For example, you might think of buying him a present some time and taking it round to his house. Or you might call round to offer him a ride in that snazzy car of yours. Are you getting the idea now?'

She shook her head. 'You're a terrible person, Mr MacTaggit.'

'Aye, I am. But you must admit it looks a good way of killing two birds with one stone.'

'Has Danny agreed to make the move?'

'Yes. In his way he seemed quite keen on it. I promised to fix things up with Mrs Johnson today, and he'll move in on Friday night. So that seems as good as settled.' His keen eyes were watching her closely. 'You've decided to do it, haven't you?' he said suddenly.

She gave a shaky laugh. 'You haven't left me much option. What about this Saturday? Will you ask Tommy if he'd like to go for a drive with me in the afternoon?'

MacTaggit nodded. 'Yes; I'll let Tommy know.' Contradictory as ever, he was looking serious when she would have expected him to look pleased. 'There's just one thing I must say to you, lassie. Your reason for seeing more of Danny mustn't be selfish. If you go to him for your father's sake or to ease your own conscience, he'll see through it and become more bitter than ever. It's very important you do it for his sake, because you care enough about him. Do you think that will be your real reason lassie?'

She hesitated, then said slowly: 'I can't be sure, but I think so. I haven't been able to forget the look in his eyes when he first saw me. And I did feel horribly rich and smug beside him...'

She was surprised to hear how gentle MacTaggit's peppery voice could become. 'Don't be upset about it, lassie. We'll put things right between us.'

Much to his relief, Carnes was able to get rid of the representative of the National Electrical Company in under fifteen minutes. After seeing him to the lift, Carnes collected his coat from his office and went in to see his secretary.

'I have to go out for a while,' he told her. 'I shall be back about four o'clock if anyone wants me.'

With that he took the lift down to the street and made his way to a telephone kiosk on a nearby street corner. His first call was to his friend at the police station, Inspector Greaves.

'Hello, Jack. Have you any news for me yet about the boy?'

'Hello, Vic. Sorry I haven't had a chance to phone you but things have been pretty hectic here today. Yes; I've got the report in front of me. By the way, you don't have to worry about anything coming out. All that has been taken care of...'

After listening to the decision of the court and after thanking Greaves for his help, Carnes made a second call, to Foley Investigations.

'I'd like a word with you right away,' he told Clinton brusquely. 'I'm coming straight round in my car and will pick you up outside the tobacconist near your office.'

Ten minutes later he drew up outside the tobacconist. Clinton, wearing a duffel coat and waiting in the doorway, came forward and jumped into the front seat of the car. With no more than a grunt of greeting Carnes drove off, to swing into a quiet side street where he switched off the engine. He then turned to Clinton.

'Well. What have you to tell me about last night?'

Clinton nodded. 'You've already heard about it, have you, sir?'

Carnes eyed him with some distaste. A man who prided himself on being down-to-earth with no frills, he had a particular aversion to brilliantine, and Clinton brought a strong smell of it into the car. In addition, there was a certain provincial simplicity in Carnes that expected men to look their part in life. If he had thought at all of private detectives in the past, he had visualized them as small, dark creatures with a stealthy, feline appearance. Clinton's sleek hair, plump cheeks, moustache, and somewhat toothy smile certainly reminded him of a cat, but not of the lean and hungry variety.

'I've heard about it, but not from you,' he said testily. 'Why wasn't I told as soon as it happened?'

'I keep him in sight whenever I can, sir, but there are times when I have to be careful or he'd guess my game. He took a girl out last night, so I felt he'd be safe enough. I couldn't guess the police would raid the dance hall, and that he'd have a scrap with them, could I?'

The explanation mollified Carnes somewhat. 'You'll have heard what happened to him in court, I take it?'

'Yes. He was fined ten quid and bound over for a year.'

'But you haven't heard about the fifty pounds in banknotes that was found in his mackintosh pocket?'

Clinton stared at him, then gave a low-pitched whistle. 'Fifty quid! Are you kidding?'

'Of course I'm not. I want to know if you've any knowledge of it. Has he said anything to you about having so much loose money with him?'

Clinton shook his head. 'It's always a hell of a job to get him to talk about himself, but he's always given me the impression he was broke. I'm certain he hadn't fifty quid on him when he arrived in town last week.'

'You can guess what the police are thinking,' Carnes muttered.

'Not half I can't! A kid with a police record comes to town, there's a shop-break a few days afterwards, the kid tries to escape when the police raid a night club, and they find fifty quid in notes on him... It fits like my hand in this glove.'

Carnes had never thought to find himself defending Danny, but prudence made him do so now. 'Let's not jump to conclusions. He could have saved the money.'

Clinton gave a jeering laugh. 'Him – saved fifty quid! Not on your life.' He shook his head admiringly. 'The kids a lot deeper than I thought. I've been wondering why he's been holding out on his reasons for coming back here. He's come back because he knows this town better than any other and intends making it his hunting ground.'

Convinced as he was himself of Danny's intentions, Carnes found it infinitely disturbing to hear Clinton voice the same suspicions. He tried to throw off his feeling of despair, made himself face the problem.

'Do you think you can go on watching him without his growing suspicious?' he asked.

Clinton grinned. 'Why not? We're pals now. He visits me at my flat; we go out together sometimes.'

'But hasn't he ever asked you what you do for a living?'

'I've had that angle covered from the beginning. You see, I've got a part interest in a garage in Darntown and he thinks it's my full-time job. Don't worry; he won't find out who I am.'

Carnes sat silent for a full minute, his brooding eyes staring out through the windscreen. At last he turned to face Clinton again. 'Now listen. I don't have to tell you how the police are going to watch that lad in the future. One false step and they'll be down on him like a ton of bricks. And that'll mean a big court case which I simply can't afford at the moment. Isn't there some way he can be discouraged from wanting to stay on here?'

Clinton pretended not to understand. 'I don't quite follow you, sir.'

Resentment at the need to explain did nothing to improve Carnes's feeling towards the enquiry agent. 'I don't mean any rough stuff, of course. And the last thing I want is for him to get involved with the police. But, damn it, he can't be left to do just as he likes – we can't wait for some old woman to get knocked over the head and lose her life's savings. It's our clear public duty to see things are made uncomfortable enough to drive him back where he came from. Can't you think of anything in that line? I'll see you don't lose by it.'

Clinton kept his face expressionless. 'I can't promise anything, sir – it's a bit off my beat. But I'll see what I can do.'

10

The following evening Richard took Beris to the cinema. Owing to his working overtime they were late and found a queue a hundred yards long outside the cinema of their choice. By the time they obtained seats in a smaller cinema, neither had the faintest idea what the feature film was about.

At first sight it appeared to be purely a war film, and Beris prepared herself to endure it manfully. But when after a few minutes a small Korean boy emerged from the background of devastation and stood pitifully before the camera, she had her first intimation that all was not well. The feeling grew when the small boy was befriended by an American soldier who gave him food and clothing...

The film was not a good one – its pathos was overdone – and normally it would not have touched her deeply. But she watched the unfolding of its plot with a morbid fascination. The boy's love for the soldier grew, as did his dependence on him. The soldier found in the boy all the affection his lonely heart desired. They became like father and son ... like buddies, as the American solider said. Then he was drafted, and the boy stood alone...

Beris had a personal resentment towards the script writer at that moment. She touched Richard's arm and whispered: 'Do you mind if we go? I don't want to see any more of this.'

He turned towards her in surprise. 'Go? It isn't that bad, is it?'

She was not clear what caused her eruption of anger. 'It's morbid and horrible, and I don't want to see any more of it. Are you coming with me or not?'

His face turned sullen at once as he rose to follow her out. By the time she reached the cooler air of the foyer she was feeling penitent.

'I'm sorry I snapped at you like that. But I really couldn't have stood that film a minute longer.'

A thin drizzle was falling. He led her out into it. 'I didn't think it was so bad,' he muttered. 'Anyway, it was better than this. Where can we go now?'

The neon lights of the Manhattan Hotel glowed on the opposite side of the road. A sudden impulse made Beris point to them.

'Let's go in the Manhattan and have a

drink. There's something I want to tell you.'

They went into the cocktail bar, a spectacular room with midnight-blue walls and silver skyscrapers. Beris fortified herself with a dry martini and waited for the second to arrive before giving Richard his second jolt of the evening.

'I went to see my brother, Danny, the other night,' she said abruptly. 'I haven't told my father, but I think you ought to know.'

He gave a violent start of surprise. 'You've been to see *him!* But I thought that was the last thing you intended doing.'

At his shocked expression a door seemed to open and shut inside her, and she knew her demon imp was back, the imp that always kept her company these days when she was with Richard.

'So it was – when I first knew he was back. But since then I've changed my mind. I'm going to see him again at the weekend.'

'But what's happened to change your mind?'

It was not easy to explain – not everything was crystal clear in her own mind yet – but she felt if he could grasp, even vaguely, the sentiments that had prompted her to see Danny again, then a basis for a deeper understanding between them might be found and the demon imp driven away for ever. She told him everything, about her meeting with

Tommy, with MacTaggit, and finally with Danny, watching his face with a hope that faded as his puzzled expression grew.

'I don't follow you,' he muttered. 'What had this ragamuffin Tommy to do with it?'

'Don't you see – he was the odd man out in his family, just as Danny was the odd man in ours. Mr MacTaggit used him as an example to show me that.'

'But you've said yourself that your father gave him the same toys, food, and education he gave you. Then how could he have been the odd man out?'

'I said he got the same material things, but I never said he got the same affection. He didn't – I realise that now.'

Richard shrugged his contempt. 'That doesn't turn a child into a thief. It's a lot of sentimental piffle. The chap obviously had a bad streak in him or he wouldn't have gone that way.'

Less than two weeks ago she would have welcomed the assurance that her father was innocent. Now, coming from Richard, it brought her no comfort.

'I'd have thought you'd have been up in arms about all this,' Richard went on. 'After all, it's a direct attack on your father.'

She shook her head in protest. 'That's too easy a way out. I'm not blaming Daddy – he didn't realize the harm he was doing, so how can I blame him? But that doesn't help

Danny, does it? If Mr MacTaggit is right, we're directly to blame for what happened to him. And in that case surely I must do something to make amends, not sit back and let him sink further down.'

'MacTaggit's not right. The chap's crazy. People don't become thieves and criminals because of things like that. They're born that way. The difference between us and them is that we get down to it and do an honest day's work while they hang around street corners waiting to see what they can pick up.'

She tried to reach him, tried to clarify the problem in her own mind as she was doing so. 'No, Richard. I've learned from Mr Mac-Taggit that nothing is as simple as that. I've been thinking a good deal about it recently. Life makes people what they are, not birth. You and I had firm foundations to build on: a happy childhood, a good education, love from our parents to give us the confidence to face life... How do we know what we'd have become without those things behind us?'

'We'd be no different. Those aren't reasons, they're excuses. I've got on in life because I've worked hard and not moaned and whined about the luck of others.'

His self-satisfaction was too much for her. 'You've got on in life because everything was smoothed out for you. An only child, doted on by your parents, given three thousand pounds by your grandfather when you were twenty-one... Don't sit there telling me what a struggle you've had.'

She regretted the words as soon as they were spoken. 'I'm sorry – I didn't mean to pick you out. Anyway, I'm just as bad; in fact, I'm worse. But don't you see – I've just had my eyes opened. I've discovered how damned smug and self-centred I've been all these years, and now I want to put something back into life instead of always taking out.' Her voice faltered as she noticed his expression. 'There isn't anything wrong with that, is there. Why are you looking at me like that?'

'Where's all this melodrama leading you to? What precisely do you intend doing?'

'I'm going to see Danny again,' she muttered, not certain herself. 'I'm going to try to let him see how sorry I am for what happened...'

'And what will that do? Make a good boy of him?'

'Mr MacTaggit thinks it will do a great deal.'

His exclamation of disgust made her flush. 'MacTaggit! That crank! Why should you apologize to a thief who robbed the man who gave him a home? The only way to talk to a Teddy Boy like that is to give him the thin end of the cane or a look at the inside of a jail. He wouldn't understand you if you tried to be decent to him.'

She realized she might have been listening to her father. 'You're so sure of yourself,' she said dully. 'Everything's black and white to you, isn't it?'

'It's black and white when it comes to ethics. Crime is crime and should be punished, not encouraged, and that's what you'll be doing if you go around making out the fault was yours. In any case, it's dangerous to be seen with him now. After that affair in Mason Street the police will be watching him like a hawk – you've admitted it yourself. You can't continue seeing him – God knows what it might lead to. After all, we are engaged and I have some say in what you do.'

Her reply made him flush resentfully. 'That's more to the point, isn't it, Richard? We mustn't let our precious selves get mixed up in a scandal, must we?' Her eyes moved from him to the adjacent tables where other well-dressed men and women were seated. Her expression made him shift uneasily in his chair.

'What's the matter now?' he muttered.

She looked back at him. 'I was just thinking what a thoroughly unpleasant lot we really are – we who have got everything, I mean. It's funny, isn't it? We get a good education which should teach us to be tolerant. We're brought up to go to a Church that should teach us kindness. And yet at the end of it we seem more bigoted and uncharitable than anyone else in the community.'

He looked genuinely anxious now. 'Are you sure you're feeling all right? You're looking rather pale.'

The futility of reaching him lay like a heavy stone inside her. She finished her martini and rose. 'Shall we go home now?'

He had difficulty in hiding his relief. 'Yes; if you're ready.'

They said little to one another on the way home. As he pulled up outside her home and prepared to leave the car, she laid a hand on his arm.

'Do you mind not coming in tonight? I've got rather a headache and think I'll turn in early.'

'I thought you weren't feeling well,' he said with relief. 'All right. By the way, what time shall I call round on Saturday? Ron Simpson wants to know as I'm collecting him afterwards. We want to leave ourselves plenty of time if we're going to have lunch on the way.'

She suddenly remembered that on Saturday she had promised to accompany Richard to a neighbouring town where his rugby team had an important match. She turned to him apologetically.

'Will you mind very much if I don't go? I'd

forgotten and promised Mr MacTaggit I'd take Tommy out for a drive in the afternoon. He's certain to have told Tommy by this.'

'But you promised me weeks ago.'

'I know, and I'm terribly sorry. But I can't break my word to a little boy, can I? You'll still win without me.'

No schoolboy could have looked more sullen than Richard at that moment. 'It's a bit thick putting a ragamuffin from Darntown before me, isn't it?'

Her voice rose at his pettiness. 'For heaven's sake – you don't want me to disappoint a child just so that I can rah-rah the old Martonians, do you?'

'I don't know what's come over you all of a sudden,' he muttered. 'You've changed so much I don't understand you.'

Suddenly and unhappily, she realized what she must do. She took off her engagement ring and handed it to him. 'I'm sorry. But it's better now than later.'

He sat dumb-founded, staring at her. 'What's the idea? What's this for?'

'I've tried to make you understand, but it's hopeless. We've nothing in common any more, Richard. As you say, I've changed too much.'

'Don't be so absurd. You're just feeling off colour, that's all...'

She pushed him away. 'No; I mean it. I felt it earlier but wasn't certain what it meant.

Now I know. We wouldn't be happy together, Richard. Believe me, we wouldn't.'

He looked down at the ring in his hand, then his face set. 'I'm not letting any ex-convict come between us. I'll speak to your father and see what he has to say about it.'

His words turned her as cold as ice. She turned to face him. 'I don't want this break between us to affect your business. And as things are I shall tell Daddy the fault is entirely mine, so he'll leave his affairs in your hands. But I shall do that only on condition you keep silent on what I've told you tonight.'

His tone changed at once. 'Put the ring on again, and let's have another talk tomorrow. Our tempers will have calmed down by then.'

'It's nothing to do with our tempers – it's our whole outlook on life that's become different. And that's not going to change by tomorrow.'

'Then let me come in for a little while,' he begged as she climbed from the car. 'We can't break it off like this.'

'Not tonight. I'm too tired. Good night, Richard.' She turned and ran for the front door. She did not want him to see she was crying.

Danny ran down the long, uncarpeted staircase into the dimly lit hall where the slatternly woman held out the telephone to him.

'It's some girl or other who wants you,' she muttered. 'You'd better tell 'er you're leavin' tonight. I don't want her pesterin' me after you've gone.'

Danny lifted the receiver. 'Hullo. Who's there?'

'Hello, dear. It's Madge here. I was hoping I'd catch you before you left. How's the packing going? Do you want a hand with anything?'

'No, thanks,' he muttered. 'I'm leaving in a few minutes.'

'What's the matter, dear? – you sound a bit broody. You aren't still fed-up with me for what happened the other night, are you?'

'No; of course not,' he muttered.

'It wasn't my fault the police chose that night of all nights to raid the damn place. And anyway, if you hadn't tried to make a break for it, they'd never have found that money on you.' Her voice turned curious. 'That was a funny business. You haven't got any ideas yet where it can have come from, have you?'

'No. I wish I had.'

She became flippant. 'Anyway, it paid your fine, and you've still got forty quid to play with, so it could have been a lot worse. I wish somebody would stick fifty quid in my hand-bag when I wasn't looking. You wouldn't hear me complain.'

When he did not answer her voice chatted on: 'Roll on the weekend. I'm as fed up as hell of this damned overtime.'

'Isn't it over yet?' he asked.

'No; we've at least another week of it. As a matter of fact it's going to make me ask a little favour of you. But I'll tell you all about it when I see you tomorrow night – I know you're in a hurry to get along now. You're sure you don't want me to help you straighten out things at your new place?'

'No; I'll be all right.'

'O.K., dear. See you tomorrow night, same time, same place. Bye-bye for now...'

Half an hour later Danny heaved his suitcase into a bus heading for the suburb of Stone-fleet. He shoved it into the alcove under the stairs and took a seat from which he could keep his eye on it. After a few minutes Darn-town's congestion of houses and brightly lit shops began to thin out. On the right-hand side of the road they fell away altogether. Here the river and main road drew closer, the half-mile between them being occupied by timber yards, factories, and the dock railway system.

This was familiar territory to Danny, for in his childhood Carnes had lived at the east-ern side of the city and Danny had spent much of his time down by the river. He tried to peer through the opposite window, but his own yellow image obscured his view. Crossing the bus aisle he took the seat opposite. Now, in spite of raindrops that were scurrying over the glass like translucent tadpoles, he was able to discern dark shapes beyond the street lamps at the roadside. Their details were hidden in the darkness, but memory sketched them in for him. The cluster of rounded objects opposite would be the Millsend oil tanks; the line of lights to their left the cement works; the tiny fountain of sparks, twinkling like fireflies, a locomotive shunting timber from the huge yards along the river bank...

Houses and shops suddenly closed in on the road again. The conductor caught Danny's eye. 'Lambert Street next stop, mate. Second on the right.'

The bus pulled up with a jerk. Danny pulled out his suitcase and jumped down on the pavement. The rain was sharp, lancing coldly out of the darkness. He crossed the road and made for Lambert Street.

A hardware shop marked its northern end. It was perhaps two hundred yards along, two parallel lines of houses, built with no apparent geographical reason, that stretched from the main road to the waste land on the river bank. Although older, the small houses were of a similar design to those in Springfield Road, where Beris's Aunt Cecilia lived, each block sharing the same slate roof. Before the houses two lines of street lamps sent pencils of light slanting through the rain.

With nothing to hinder its progress from the river, the wind was fierce, and Danny bent his head to it as he started down the street. He found number 57 easily enough, crossed its tiny front garden, and lowered his suitcase with some relief on the front step. There was no doorbell: only a knocker which he rapped a couple of times. The echoes had barely died away before the door sprang open, releasing a yellow rectangle of light that fell over him. A small, tousle-haired boy in pullover and jeans stared out excitedly at him. The boy was Tommy Fowler.

'Does Mrs Johnson live here?' Danny asked.

Tommy nodded eagerly. 'That's right, mister. Are you the new chap that's comin' to live here?'

'Yes. Is Mrs Johnson in?'

'No, mister – she's had to go across to Mrs Dalton's place. But she said I'd to show you your room if you came before she got back.'

Danny swung his suitcase into the tiny hall. Tommy closed the door behind him, then pointed up the stairs. 'Straight up, mister, an' the first on the left. Wait a bit – I'll go up first an' show you.'

He scampered up the stairs and opened

the door of the back bedroom. 'Here y' are, mister,' he called, switching on the light. 'This one's yours.'

Danny steered his suitcase up the narrow flight of stairs and into the bedroom. Lowering it thankfully, he stared around him. With the memory of his last lodgings still in his mind, his first impression was one of cleanliness. The furniture was of First World War vintage – ornate mahogany with elbow-catching knobs and spirals – but the walls were newly papered and the polished floor well laid with carpets. The bed-linen was clean, and a coal fire winked cheerily from the grate.

Tommy cocked his head on one side like an enquiring sparrow. 'How is it, mister? All right?'

Danny nodded. He looked down at the boy. 'How many of you live here? Just you and your mother?'

'That's all, mister. We did have a girl, but she's gone off to another home.'

Danny, busy draping his wet mackintosh over the end of the bed, paused in surprise. 'Another home? What do you mean?'

'They sent her to another foster mother. Good thing – I can't stand girls, can you, mister? Always bawling over something or other. I didn't think Ma Johnson liked 'em either, but she treated this one all right.'

'Why do you call your mother Ma

Johnson?' Danny asked curiously.

Tommy took on a resigned expression, mute protest at the dullness of adults. 'I've just explained, mister. She's a foster mother. I came here six months ago. Mr MacTaggit sent me.'

'MacTaggit? But how did you get mixed up with him?'

Tommy's gaze dropped to the floor. His voice turned sullen. 'I got into a bit of trouble, an' he was put to look after me. I thought you knew, seeing he arranged for you to come here.'

After his initial start, Danny went on unpacking his clothes and hanging them in the wardrobe. 'No; he didn't say anything to me.'

Seeing his apparent unconcern Tommy's confidence began to return. 'Is he a friend of yours, mister?'

'Who?'

'Mr MacTaggit.'

'I know him fairly well.'

'Funny little geezer, isn't he? But he's all right, though – always took my side at home.' Tommy hesitated, then succumbed to a burst of confidence. 'You see, Ma and me never got on – she always put my sister Polly first. And after Dad was killed things got worse. So Mr MacTaggit arranged it so I could come and live here with Ma Johnson.'

'Do you like it better?'

'Not half I don't. Ma Johnson's all right.' For Tommy, the misogynist, this was praise indeed. 'She gets a bit nattery over little things, like women do, but otherwise she's O.K. I'm glad you've come though,' he went on, face bright with pleasure. 'It'll be super havin' another man about the house.'

Danny nodded and carried his suitcase with the remainder of its contents over to the chest of drawers by the window. He drew a few large sheets of sketching paper from it, taking care not to crease them. Tommy's bright eyes, missing nothing, fell on them at once.

'What are those, mister?'

Danny lay the sheets on the bed. The top sheet was a charcoal sketch of a trawler discharging its cargo of fish. The boy gazed at it, then at Danny with awe.

'Did you do that, mister?'

Danny nodded.

'Gee, that's super... Really super. You didn't do that with a pencil, did you?'

'No; that's done with charcoal,' Danny said, showing him a packet of charcoal sticks.

The boy looked at them, then at the drawing again. 'Gee, I'd like to draw things like that. Could I learn, mister?'

'Anybody can learn, if they're interested enough.'

At that moment there was a heavy bump from somewhere below, followed by a weird moaning sound. Tommy jumped. 'That's Minty. You haven't seen Minty yet, have you, mister?'

'Who's Minty?'

'Minty's my dog. He's super. Wait – I'll show him to you.' With that Tommy spun on his heel and was gone. There followed a wild scamper down the stairs, the sound of a door being thrown back, and the delighted yelp of a dog. The noises then sounded in reverse, culminating in Tommy and the dog bursting into the bedroom together.

'Here he is.' Tommy panted. 'This is Minty.'

Danny rounded the foot of the bed to obtain a better view. Minty, bedraggled from the rain, was one of the ugliest mongrels he had ever seen, with a square head, a broad stubby body, and short bow legs. His small ears stood straight up from his head. His predominant colour was black, although he had one white eye and one red for good measure. He looked like an unhappy cross between a bulldog, a Labrador and an old tom cat. As he bounded round the boy, his stubby tail gyrated like the rear propeller of a helicopter.

Tommy grabbed his two front paws and sat him down on his tail. 'He can do all sorts of tricks,' he told Danny. 'Come here and he'll shake hands with you. Shake hands with the gent, Minty. That's it…'

He gazed proudly at the dog as it held out a wet paw for Danny to shake. 'He can jump through a hoop, play hide-and-seek, and even play cricket. He's super, isn't he?'

Danny nodded. 'Is he yours?'

There was a wealth of pride in the reply. 'Yes, Ma Johnson got him for me on my birthday. He's the finest dog in the world, aren't you, Minty?'

Minty endorsed the sentiment by buzzing his tail even faster. He bounded up at the boy again, his wet body marking the wallpaper. Danny pushed them both out on to the landing.

'You'll get me into trouble – you know the fuss women make over things like that. You'd better take him downstairs and dry him.'

'I suppose you're right.' Tommy agreed reluctantly. He started down the stairs, then glanced back. 'You'll be comin' down at teatime, won't you?'

'Yes, I suppose so.'

'Super. Then we'll see you later. Come on, Minty.' With a whoop and a scamper, boy and dog disappeared downstairs.

11

The following afternoon Beris drove her car slowly down Lambert Street, counting the house numbers as she went. She drew up outside number 57 and gazed at it with some diffidence.

She was given little time to speculate on her nervousness, however, because Tommy, who had been watching out for her from the front bedroom window for the last half-hour, was flying down the stairs before the car wheels stopped rolling. He flung open the front door, raced down the path, only to succumb to an attack of shyness at the garden gate. With feet dragging and eyes focused on the pavement, he slowly approached the car. Minty, far less inhibited, bounded up and tried to lick Beris's face through her side window.

She lowered the window. 'Hello, Tommy. Are you ready to go?'

'I suppose so,' the boy muttered.

Beris noticed how smart he was looking. He was wearing a grey jacket, a newly pressed pair of shorts, chequered stockings and polished brown shoes. His face had been scrubbed until it shone and his hair

149

was well greased down. Clearly Mrs Johnson had been putting him through the mill.

'My goodness, you do look smart,' she told him. His flush of embarrassment made her change her tactics. She turned her attention to Minty.

'Is he yours?'

'Yes.'

'What's his name?'

'Minty.'

'He's a fine dog, isn't he? Are you going to bring him with you this afternoon?'

He stole a quick look at her face to see if she were serious. 'Ma Johnson said you wouldn't want 'im in the car,' he muttered.

'She was thinking of the seats, but I don't mind. You can bring him if you wish.'

That did the trick. With a whoop Tommy turned to the dog. 'You hear that, Minty? You can come too. Gee, thanks, miss. That's super.'

At that moment Beris caught her first glimpse of Mrs Johnson. She was coming down the front path, a massive woman, well over fifteen stone with vital statistics to match her weight. The tight apron she was wearing helped to stress her astonishing mammary development. Below her round, cheerful face a series of chins wobbled and swung like a St Bernard's dewlap. Her age was difficult to guess, but she was probably in her early fifties.

She sailed through the gate like a river barge through a lock, addressing Tommy in a shrill Lidsborough accent. 'You go inside an' get your coat, young feller. I don't want you catching cold.' Then she turned to Beris. 'Hello, miss. I'm Mrs Johnson. It's kind of you to take th' lad out like this, I'm sure. I hope he behaves himself.'

'I'm sure he will,' Beris smiled. 'By the way, I've told him he can bring his dog with him. I hope you don't mind.'

'I don't mind, miss, if you don't. I was only thinking of the mess it'd make.'

From the corner of her eye Beris had been watching the house, hoping to catch a glimpse of Danny. 'Mr MacTaggit says you have a new lodger,' she said, as casually as possible. 'Is he settling down all right?'

Mrs Johnson's chins flopped up and down. 'Aye, a nice young feller from London. He and th' lad seem to be hittin' it off fine. He's a bit shy wi' me yet, but he'll be all right in a day or two.'

Beris hesitated, then went on: 'From what Mr MacTaggit says I think he might be someone I used to know. He isn't at home now, is he?'

To her disappointment Mrs Johnson shook her head. 'No, he ran out a few minutes ago. I don't think he's gone far – to th' shops maybe. But I'll tell you what, miss. What about you havin' a cup of tea with us when you get back? He might be home then.'

'Thank you. I'd like to very much.'

Just then Tommy emerged from the house, looking uncomfortable in a long overcoat that had clearly been bought with an eye to the future. He and Minty, the latter distinctly subdued by Mrs Johnson's presence, jumped in alongside Beris, the dog sitting between Tommy's knees.

Hoping Danny might return, Beris chatted a few minutes more with Mrs Johnson before reluctantly turning the car. She waved back. 'Bye-bye. See you later.'

'Good-bye, miss. See they both behave themselves.'

Beris drove off and turned on to the main road. A hundred yards down it she caught sight of Danny, coming out of a telephone kiosk. Tommy's sharp eyes spotted him at the same time.

'There's Mr Meadows, miss – the new chap that's stayin' with us.'

Beris slowed down. As she did so Danny recognized the car. Resentment came into his look of surprise as he saw Tommy alongside Beris. He hesitated, then approached them.

Beris lowered her side window, her heart thumping nervously. Tommy, unable to contain his pride, leaned in front of her as Danny reached the car.

'We're goin' for a ride, Mr Meadows. Isn't it a super car?'

He gave the boy a nod, then turned his attention on her. 'What are you doing out here?'

'Hasn't Tommy told you?' she said innocently. 'I promised to take him out this afternoon.'

His look of suspicion grew. 'I didn't know it was you. How do you come to know him?'

She threw a nervous smile at the listening boy. 'We ran into one another a couple of weeks ago in town, didn't we, Tommy?'

'MacTaggit has something to do with this, hasn't he?'

She pretended to misinterpret his question. 'Of course he has. He's looking after Tommy's interests, and it was he who gave me his address. But why are you looking so angry? It doesn't affect you in any way, does it?'

He stood back sullenly. 'I suppose not. But I wish I'd known before, that's all.'

During this exchange of words Tommy's sparrow-like eyes had been darting from one to the other of them. Now his shrill voice broke in, 'I didn't know you knew one another.'

She smiled at him. 'Oh yes. Years ago Mr Meadows and I used to play together.'

'You did? Where – in London?'

'No. Here in Lidsborough. We had lots of

fun together at one time. Hadn't we?' she said quietly, turning back to Danny.

He hesitated, then gave a sullen nod. 'Yes.'

Tommy's voice grew even shriller. 'I didn't know that. Why, it's super.' In his excitement he wriggled his small body right in front of Beris, poking his head out through the window. 'Then why don't you come with us this afternoon, mister! We can have marvellous fun together.'

Danny avoided the boy's eager eyes. 'No; I'm meeting someone later on. Sorry.'

'Never mind,' Beris told the disappointed boy. 'Perhaps Mr Meadows will come with us some other time.'

'Will you, mister? Promise?'

'I'll see,' Danny muttered. 'I'll have to be going now. Good-bye.'

She held his eyes for a moment. 'Bye-bye, Danny. Take care of yourself.'

He walked hastily away without looking back. As Tommy wriggled back into his seat Beris fumbled in her handbag. Turning, she pushed five shillings into the astonished boy's hand.

'Take this, go into that sweet shop, and buy yourself anything you like,' she ordered, her eyes bright with affection and gratitude. 'And don't you dare bring a penny back with you.'

Encouraged with this beginning, Beris went

to Lambert Street the following Monday and Wednesday evenings. In so far as seeing Danny went, however, these two visits proved unprofitable. On Monday evening he did not return home for tea (as the evening meal was called in Lidsborough), and although, much to Tommy's delight, Beris delayed her stay until eight-thirty, she eventually had to return home without seeing him. Her Wednesday evening visit proved even more abortive, for this time both he and Tommy were absent. Mrs Johnson, seated in her homely living-room beside a table piled with socks, explained the reason. With her massive bulk completely hiding the stool beneath her, she reminded Beris of a fat, friendly bear she had once seen performing at a circus.

'He's taken th' lad to the pictures, miss. He suggested it while we were havin' tea. 'Course, Tommy didn't know you was comin' round or he wouldn't have gone.'

'I'm very glad they've gone out together,' Beris said, truthfully enough. She wanted to take this opportunity of learning something of Danny's habits, but although she knew Mrs Johnson had been told of Danny's history by MacTaggit, she felt a certain diffidence in asking questions that might bring that history into their conversation.

'Do you know if Danny has got work here?' seemed the most innocuous question.

155

Mrs Johnson, busy darning a sock, nodded. 'I don't think he had when he came from London, but last week he asked if he could 'ave breakfast half an hour earlier, and as he goes out every mornin' at half past eight it looks as if he's found somethin'. I hope so – it's when they're out of work they get into trouble.'

Evidently Mrs Johnson had no inhibitions about discussing Danny's affairs with her. Her matter-of-factness gave Beris courage. She leaned forward in her chair, body tensed.

'What do you think of him, Mrs Johnson? He's been with you over a week now, so you must have formed some opinion of him.'

She had to wait a few seconds for the reply. Mrs Johnson, having completed one sock, was fumbling among the pile on the table for its companion.

'What do I think of him, miss?... Well; he's a quiet, well-mannered lad in the house – I can tell he's had a good education. And he seems grateful for the least thing that's done for him... But for his own sake I wish he'd spend a bit more time at home. He's hardly had one night in since he came. He's never back before eleven or twelve, an' one night it was after two when he let himself in. 'Course, that doesn't mean he's up to any mischief – I'm not sayin' that for a minute. But I'd like him to be home a bit more often.'

'I suppose he must have made some friends. Have you seen any of them?'

'A girl called round here one day – I didn't get a proper look at her, so couldn't say what she was like. I heard him call her Madge. Then there was a chap called Clinton came round for 'im last Sunday in a car. Can't say I was taken up with him – looked a bit of a spiv to me. That's all I've seen.'

None of it sounded very encouraging and Beris tried to reassure herself. 'But you say he behaves well at home? You aren't thinking of giving him notice for coming home so late, or anything like that?'

Mrs Johnson looked up from her sock, an indication of her surprise. 'Notice! Of course not, luv, the boy's not been any trouble. An', in any case, there's Mr MacTaggit to think about. As long as he wants the lad to stay, he stays.'

'You think a lot about Mr MacTaggit, don't you?' Beris said curiously.

This time Mrs Johnson put the sock down on the table. 'Miss, I've never met a finer man in my life, an' that's the truth. The things he does for children in this town – you wouldn't believe it. If he feels sorry for this lad, that's good enough for Florrie Johnson.' Her voice turned curious. 'How do you come to know t' lad, miss? Were you neighbours, or something?'

With her father's interests never far from her mind, Beris handled this question warily. 'Yes; we used to play together sometimes as children. That was a long time ago, of course.' She hesitated, then went on: 'I'd like a chat with him about old times one of these days. I don't suppose you could tell me the best evening to catch him in.'

'I can't, miss. As I say, he's hardly ever in at nights. But why don't you wait for him now? I've got to go across the road to Mrs Dalton's when I've finished these socks – she 'ad a baby last week and I'm helpin' out a bit with the housework – but you're welcome to stay. The first house leaves at eight – they'll be home by half past.'

Beris shook her head regretfully. 'I'd like to, but my father is going away for a few days on Friday, and has some friends coming round tonight. I promised I'd be back to join the party. But I'll come round another night if I may.'

'Come whenever you like, miss. Me and Tommy will always be glad to see you, even if th' lad himself isn't here.'

12

Beris drove her father to the station on Friday morning. She knew the purpose of his visit: to make final arrangements for the exhibition of the Delmont Collection in Lidsborough. It was a cold, blustery morning, and the passengers and their well-wishers were huddled together in tight groups on the platform as she walked with her father to his carriage. A well-known figure in Lidsborough, he drew many a glance and muted whisper from them as he passed by, stocky and powerful in his black overcoat and Homburg.

He pressed a cheque into Beris's hand as he kissed her good-bye. 'Something for you to do while I'm away,' he told her.

She hugged him tightly. 'Take care of yourself and don't be away too long.'

'Only a week – no longer.'

'Don't forget to write me.'

'I'll do better than that – I'll phone. Look after yourself, darling.'

She waved until his carriage swung round the bend out of sight. As always when he went away she felt a strong sense of loneliness. This morning, for some reason she did not understand, it made her think of MacTaggit. After some hesitation she gave in to the desire to call on him and drove round to his office. She had to wait ten minutes before she could see him.

'I'm sorry. I know you are busy in the mornings. But for some reason or other I felt like a talk with you...'

He grinned his pleasure as he drew up a chair for her. 'You're more than welcome, lassie. What news have you got? Have you seen any more of the lad?'

She shook her head. 'Only for a few minutes, a week last Saturday. I've been round twice this week, but he was out both times. Mrs Johnson says he goes out every night.'

'Aye; that's what she tells me. I'd like to know who he spends his time with. Find out all you can about his friends, will you, when you get the chance?'

She pulled a wry face. 'When I get the chance! When will that be if he's always out?'

'See if Tommy can't keep him in for you. You know what a rascal he is. He's capable of anything.'

She laughed. 'He's lovely, isn't he. He seems to have taken a strong liking to Danny. And I think Danny's growing fond of him. It was a splendid idea of yours to put them together.'

'There you are then,' he grinned. 'Things

are still moving along. Danny will be hearing pleasant things about you from Tommy, and that'll be softening him up. It'll work out if you're patient. When are you going round again?'

'I've plenty of time for the next seven days. It has been rather difficult with Father at home – I have to make excuses, pretend I'm going round to friends and that sort of thing. But he's gone away for a week, and as I'm no longer engaged' – she smiled ruefully – 'I'm free almost any night.'

MacTaggit gave a start. 'Broken your engagement, lassie? Not over this business, I hope.'

The measure of his distress surprised her. 'It is in a way, but please don't worry about it. We weren't suited – I've realized that now. And it's much better it happened now than later.' She changed the subject. 'By the way, has Mrs Johnson told you she believes Danny has got a job?'

He nodded. 'Yes; and I'm hoping she's right. But, lassie, what's happened between you and your fiancé? When I asked you to help Danny I didn't want you to ruin your own future in the process.'

She met and held his eyes. 'Honestly, now that it's happened I'm glad. We weren't suited, and it was only a matter of time before we found it out. So don't go getting any stupid ideas it has been your fault.'

At her request he talked of other things, and as always when she was in his company, time passed quickly. His peppery anecdotes gave her glimpses of lives she had never believed existed, and his unconventional theories gave her fascinatingly new viewpoints on them. She thought of inviting him to Crescent Avenue for an evening while her father was away, but she was still conventional enough to fear he might misinterpret such an invitation. When at last his secretary came in to remind him of an appointment, she left with real regret.

She spent the afternoon trying to make up her mind whether or not to visit Lambert Street that evening. She did not want to make herself a nuisance to Mrs Johnson; on the other hand she wanted to take full advantage of her father's absence. Wishing for a concrete excuse to go, she eventually thought of one. During her outing with Tommy in the car she had discovered one of his life's ambitions was to possess a football. She would buy him one and take it round that evening.

Her enthusiasm grew as she made her plans. Dared she take Danny a present too? Might not a gift express her feelings, her self-reproach, far better than words? Or was it too big a step to take yet?

Surely not if she took all three of them a gift. Then it would be less personal. Tommy could have his football; Mrs Johnson a large box of chocolates; Danny... That was more difficult, and she puzzled over it some time before remembering his appearance at their first meeting in Spiller Street. She would buy him a pullover.

These three gifts were lying on the back seat of her car when she pulled up outside number 57 at 6.30 that evening. Taking them out, she knocked on the front door. Minty's enquiring bark sounded from inside the house. There was a scamper in the hall and a few seconds later Tommy stood on the step. His eyes shone like polished gems at seeing her.

'Super! Come in, miss.'

Beris gave a laugh of protest as Minty bounded up against her. 'Catch hold of him or I'll drop these parcels.'

Tommy held the dog's collar as she entered the small living-room. There was no sign of Mrs Johnson. Beris laid the parcels on the table, then turned to the boy. 'Is Mrs Johnson out?'

'Yes, miss. She's over at Mrs Dalton's. Shall I go an' call her?'

'No, don't do that. Just take this and give it to her after I've gone.' Beris handed Tommy the box of chocolates, following it with the spherical bag on which Tommy's eyes had been surreptitiously resting. 'And this is for you.'

'For me?' Tommy tore open the bag, and let out a yell of ecstasy. 'A football! A real leather one! Oh, thanks, miss. It's super. Absolutely super...'

It was a full minute before Beris could bring him and the equally excited Minty down to earth again. She pointed at her third parcel. 'I've got a little present for Mr Meadows too. Is he in his room?'

Although expecting no other reply, she still felt disappointment when Tommy shook his head. 'No, miss. He went out straight after tea – just after six.'

'Did he say what time he would be back?'

'No, miss, but he'll be late. He always is when he goes out early like that.'

Beris bit her lips. 'I would have liked a word with him tonight. He's always out, isn't he?'

Tommy, noticing her disappointment, looked troubled. 'Maybe if I went to tell him, he'd come back,' he muttered.

She turned sharply. 'Do you know where he is?'

He showed alarm at the direction of her question and hesitated before answering her. 'Yes, miss.'

'Where is he? Please tell me.'

The boy's head lowered. 'He made me promise to keep it secret, miss. He doesn't want people to know.'

'I don't understand. Do you mean he isn't

164

out with friends?'

'Oh, no, not to this place, miss. He never takes people there. Nobody else knows about it but me.' A thin thread of pride ran through the boy's troubled voice. 'He showed it to me last Sunday.'

She was intensely curious now and dropped on the settee alongside the boy. 'Why can't you tell me about it?'

'Because he asked me not to tell anyone, miss. He's afraid he might lose it if other people found out. And it's a super den.' The boy's troubled, perplexed face stared at her. 'But you wouldn't say anything, would you, miss? You've known him a long time, haven't you?'

'A very long time, Tommy. Since we were very small children.' She took hold of one of the boy's hands. 'Tommy, please tell me where he is. I promise you faithfully I'll not tell another living soul. But I would like to see him tonight.'

The boy looked down at the football that was tucked tightly under his arm, then up at her face. 'You promise – 'cross your heart?'

'Across my heart, Tommy.'

'All right, then, miss. I'll take you there. But first I'll have to ask Ma Johnson if I can go out.'

She nodded. 'I'll wait here until you come back.'

Chased by Minty, and with his football

and the box of chocolates in his arms, Tommy ran out into the street. He was back a few minutes later.

'It's all right,' he panted. 'I told her I wouldn't be more'n half an hour. She's sorry she can't get over, but says I have to thank you for the chocolates. Shall we go now, miss?'

'What about a key?' Beris asked as the boy prepared to close the front door behind them. 'Can Mrs Johnson get in?'

'It's all right. She told me to leave it off the latch.'

With the football still under his arm, Tommy jumped into the car alongside Beris, followed by his dog. He pointed down the street. 'That way, miss, then follow th' road that goes to the left.'

'But doesn't that lead down to the river?'

'That's where he is, miss. I'll show you when we get down there.'

Puzzled, Beris drove down the street until the houses fell away. Then, on Tommy's instructions, she took an uneven road that led them out into the wasteland alongside the river. To her right she saw the twinkling lights of the docks and huge industries of Darntown, but immediately ahead and around the car was darkness. She switched on her headlights and at once a wilderness of tangled grass and weeds sprang into view. With nothing to obstruct its progress the wind, which had been severe all day, rocked and buffeted the car.

They passed a car graveyard on their left, an ugly expanse of rusted iron plates and broken-down chassis. Another hundred yards and Beris's headlights picked out a wartime pillbox, with weeds sprouting from its every crevice. A rusted railway track came into view and they bumped over it. The grass on either side of them had a muddy, wind-swept appearance now: they were clearly nearing the river. The road was deteriorating fast into ruts and water-filled pot-holes. As the right front wheel of the car sloughed into one, Beris turned to Tommy. 'I don't know where we are going, but I can't take the car much further.'

He nodded. 'You'll have to leave it here, miss, anyway. We're nearly at th' end of the road.'

Her headlights showed her the road ended at an old disused jetty. She switched off the engine. 'Where on earth do we go from here?'

He jumped from the car, followed by Minty. 'This way, miss. It isn't far now.'

Utterly mystified she switched off the lights, collected her parcel, and stepped from the car. Immediately the darkness closed around her, bringing with it an almost over-powering feeling of loneliness. A thousand miles away a goods train let out a mournful whistle. The dark waters of the river, lapping against the jetty, made obscene chucking noises. A gust of wind leapt out of the darkness like a wild animal, buffeted her, and went crashing off among the reeds. In the silence that followed she heard the dismal soughing of the mud at the river's edge.

'This way, miss.' Tommy's beckoning call was a welcome sound. She followed him up a muddy slope, keeping her high-heeled shoes on her feet with the greatest difficulty. They reached a track of pebbles that ran along the river bank. Below them, more felt than seen, were the glutinous mud flats and the lapping waves.

Tommy pointed forward. 'It's not far, miss. Only a few minutes.'

She hesitated. 'You're not playing a trick on me, are you?'

At once his voice sounded hurt. ''Course I'm not. You asked me to bring you.'

'I'm sorry,' she said quickly. 'But it seems such a queer place to find anybody.'

He took her apology with good grace. 'That's why it's such a super den. Just wait till you see it.'

Far away, on the other side of the mile-wide river, car headlights probed the sky for a moment, then dipped away. The wind came again, smelling of salt and seaweed. When it had blustered away Tommy turned to her, his voice troubled this time.

'I hope he's not going to be mad at me for bringing you. You'll tell him why I did it, won't you, miss?'

'I'll see he's not angry with you,' Beris assured him, wincing as the sharp stones of the path jabbed through her thin-soled shoes.

Two hundred yards farther down the bank Tommy pointed forward. 'There y'are, miss. See it now?'

At first Beris could see nothing. Then a tall, black silhouette, perhaps forty feet in height, appeared out of the darkness. She gave an exclamation of surprise. 'Why, it looks like a lighthouse.'

'That's what it is, miss. 'Course, it isn't used any more. Danny says it hasn't been used for nearly fifty years.'

No light shone from the tower as they approached it. Four walls, dilapidated, moss-covered, and no higher than Beris's waist, enclosed its base. A rusted metal gate hung ajar. They passed through it into a small enclosure that had once been a garden but was now a patch of tangled weeds and bushes. Above them the silent tower rose into the night sky, alone and derelict in the wilderness of river grass and mud.

Tommy led Beris to a door that was half hidden behind a sharp-thorned clump of bramble. 'He'll be upstairs, miss, so you'll have to bang on it hard or he won't hear you.'

Beris found herself whispering. 'Is he alone up there?'

'Yes. I told you – I'm th' only one who knows about it. Do y' mind if I get back now, miss? I told Ma Johnson I wouldn't be late.'

She had a twinge of apprehension, both for herself and the boy. 'Are you sure he's here? It looks very dark.'

'That's because he keeps the blinds drawn over the window. He'll be up there all right.'

'But isn't it a long way back for you? Hadn't you better wait for me?'

Tommy shook his head. 'I promised Ma Johnson I wouldn't be long. I'll tell you what, miss' – and he pointed to the rusted gate – 'I'll wait outside there while you knock on the door. If he comes, me and Minty will get along. If he doesn't come, we can go back together. How's that?'

She realized he was nervous of meeting Danny until she'd had a chance of conciliating him. She nodded. 'Very well. As long as you're sure you'll be quite safe on your own.'

'Me, safe?'– Tommy hastily changed a jeer into a cough – 'I'll be safe enough, miss. Minty and me'll be back in two shakes.' He moved towards the gate, then paused. 'Will you be comin' to see us again soon?'

Her eyes were on the tower. 'Yes, I'll come soon. We'll have another outing in the car.'

'Super. Thanks again for this!' Tommy pointed to the dark object under his arm, and for the first time since leaving the car Beris realized he was still carrying his precious football. 'I won't go until I hear him come down,' he promised. 'C'mon, Minty.'

The bushes and darkness hid him and the dog from sight, and Beris's loneliness returned. Something about the dark river bank, with its sighing reeds and lapping water, was almost unbearably melancholy. Its sombre atmosphere was not lightened by the dark and silent tower before her.

It took her a real effort of will to make her presence known. At first her knock on the heavy oaken door was timid. Then, receiving no reply, she took Tommy's advice and used the heel of her clenched fist. The noise reverberated inside the tower in a series of echoes; she found herself holding her breath as she waited. The wind, quiet for some time, chose this moment to rise again, booming around the tower in a series of gusts that hid all further noise within. It dropped as suddenly as it had come, and she thought she would have to knock again. Then she heard footsteps approaching the door. They had a hollow sound; she had to fight back a desire to turn and run. They stopped behind the door, followed by a voice she barely recognized as belonging to Danny.

'Who's that?'

'It's me – Beeda.'

A long pause followed. Then: 'What do you want?'

'I've got something for you. Please let me in.'

Another pause followed, then a bolt was drawn slowly back. In the distance Beris heard the receding bark of a dog: Tommy had taken his cue and was returning home. The door creaked open. Even in the darkness she could see his anger.

'Tommy brought you, didn't he? Where is he?'

'He's gone back home. Don't be angry with him. I asked him to tell me where you were.'

'What do you want? Why can't you leave me alone?'

She pointed to her parcel. 'I've got something for you. Please let me inside. It's cold out here.'

For a moment it seemed he might refuse. Then, reluctantly, he stood aside to let her pass through the dark doorway.

'Wait a moment,' he muttered, closing and bolting the door behind them.

Inside the tower there was the dank chill peculiar to stone buildings. The darkness was like a solid wall before her eyes. Then there was a click and a sudden brilliant ray of light revealed a spiral staircase directly ahead of her.

'You go first,' he muttered. 'I'll follow with the torch.'

She had a sense of unreality as she climbed. Their shadows, monstrously big and black, danced grotesquely on the stone walls ahead of them. Beads of moisture shone like eyes from dark corners and crevices. Their footsteps had a hollow, sepulchral sound. An alcove and door appeared alongside her. Danny motioned for her to keep climbing. 'Two more floors,' he said.

As she approached the third alcove she became aware of the smell of burning paraffin. Danny pushed ahead of her and opened the door. Yellow light flooded out on the stairs. He switched off his torch and motioned for her to enter.

She stepped into the room and gazed around her in astonishment. It was oddly shaped, all of it excepting the side containing the door following the rounded contours of the outer walls. The walls were of stone, the ceiling and floor of wood, the latter covered here and there with pieces of old coconut matting. For furniture there was a deal table and wicker chair, an old packing case, and a palliasse of straw and folded blankets. An artist's easel stood in the centre of the floor, directly under a paraffin lamp that hung on a cord from the ceiling. Near it was a small paraffin heater. There was one window, facing the river, but a black-out curtain hung over it.

The easel caught and held Beris's eye. An oil painting, obviously done from the viewpoint of the tower, was standing on it. Although not yet fully completed, it showed the river on a sunny autumn day. In the distance was the smoke of Darntown, its hundreds of cranes and derricks woven by distance into a fine and delicate tracery. Opposite, a trawler was heading out to sea and the far-off perilous Arctic, her bow-wave white and jaunty against the blue water. In the sky massive white barges of cloud were beating upriver for the safety of harbour and home. It was a picture that made Beris, even at that moment, realize how much there was in Lidsborough that was beautiful.

Her astonished eyes moved on around the room. Other work, sketches, oils, water-colours, lay on the packing case and on a piece of carpet at the foot of the palliasse. She turned to Danny in wonder.

'Have you done all this?'

His expression gave her the answer.

'But I never dreamed such a thing of you. I don't know what to say…'

'Never mind about that,' he said with sudden impatience. 'Tell me why you've come here. Why did Tommy tell you where I was? He promised to keep it a secret.'

'Don't blame Tommy,' she begged. 'He didn't want to tell me. It was my fault – I

174

had something to give you, and in any case I badly wanted a word with you tonight.' Timidly she offered him the parcel. 'Please take it, will you?'

He hesitated, then tore off the paper. He stared at the pullover, then up at her, a look of helpless anger in his eyes. 'Why did you buy this? You'd no right to do it.'

'I knew you might be angry, but as I was getting a present for Tommy and Mrs Johnson I felt I'd like to get you something as well. Don't wear it if you'd rather not. I shan't be offended.'

For a moment he seemed about to hand it back to her. Then his face twisted wryly. 'I'm not being very gracious, am I? Thanks. I'll not deny it's something I need badly.'

The tension ran out of her, leaving her weak. 'May I sit down for a moment?'

He drew up the wicker chair for her. 'You'd better have a cigarette too, now you're here. Where have you left your car?'

She told him as he gave her a match. The yellow light of the paraffin lamp was kind to him, washing out the bitter lines from his face. He looked more the Danny he might have been had the years been more charitable.

'Tell me about this work,' she begged, motioning to the easel and packing case. 'Tell me what started you, how long you've been doing it. Tell me everything.'

He was leaning against the table, back slightly bowed, staring moodily at the packing case. 'You wouldn't find it interesting.'

She was more than interested – she was fascinated. Until now she had known him only as a child or an adolescent delinquent – and so, lacking knowledge of the attributes that had developed in him since their separation, she had sometimes found her concept of him thin and shadowy. Now, like one of his pictures suddenly taking depth and movement, he sprang into life before her, a complex adult grown from the child who had been her playmate. It was one of the most exciting discoveries of her life.

'I can't wait to hear about it, Danny. Please tell me.'

He shrugged. 'It's quite simple. I've always wanted to be an artist, and I'm trying to be one. That's all there is to it.'

'That isn't even the beginning of it. When did you first want to paint? How long has it taken you to do all that work? How did you come to find this place? There are hundreds of things to tell me.'

He walked over to the packing case and stared down at it. 'This was sent on from London,' he muttered. 'Some of the work in it was done years ago.'

'What about this place? Why do you work here?' A strange urgent excitement was making her whole body tremble. 'Tell me the whole story, Danny.'

He turned slowly to face her. 'It starts a long way back … too far back. I don't think you'll like to hear it.'

His words and expression gave her fair warning, but she did not flinch. 'I want to hear everything – no matter what comes out.'

He stood silent for a long moment. Then he raised his eyes in sudden decision. 'All right – if you want to hear it.'

'I do, Danny. I'm ready.'

13

He inhaled on his cigarette and released the smoke slowly, obviously hesitant to begin. At last he said, 'Can't you remember how I used to like drawing and painting?'

'No,' she said, puzzled. 'I can't. At least, not any more than most children do. That's why all this is such a surprise to me.'

He was silent again. Then he nodded. 'Of course we were both away at boarding school in those days, and when we were home we didn't see much of one another. Not by that time.'

She winced at the bitterness in his voice. 'Did Daddy know about it?'

His smile was not pretty to watch. 'Oh,

yes; Daddy knew all right. I'd already asked him if I could attend art school. But don't forget I was in disgrace: I had to be punished. That was one reason for his refusal. There was another: his character. He was an honest wholesome Christian business man – to him it was positively indecent for a boy to want to be an artist. It offended his puritanical soul.'

Beris sat in silence, listening to the words that fell from his tongue like drops of acid. Suddenly his mood changed. He rose from the table and went to the window. Pulling aside one corner of the curtain he stared out for a moment, then went on in a low voice:

'As far back as I can remember, I was always fascinated by the river, and after I got the sack from school and was working here in Lidsborough, I often came this way for walks. One afternoon, while examining this place, I spotted a key in the lock. I turned it and entered. There was nothing inside but dust and mice and spiders – it had obviously been empty for years. When I left I locked the door and put the key in my pocket.

'All that night I lay awake thinking about it. You see, Father wouldn't allow me as much as a paintbrush in my room at home and I badly wanted a place where I could practise. But I think there was even more to it than that.' He ran a hand through his black hair, an abstracted gesture that caught her breath with its familiarity. 'I wanted somewhere where I could hide from people, hide from that look in their eyes. I suppose I was running away from myself but that wasn't clear at the time. All I knew was that I wanted a place of my own, and this seemed a gift from heaven.'

One sentence had caught her breath and driven the colour from her face. 'Did you say Daddy wouldn't allow you to paint in your room?'

He stared at her. 'Didn't you know that?'

'No,' she said slowly. 'I didn't.'

The brief silence that followed had a thick, nightmarish quality that gagged her voice.

His face had twisted mockingly. 'Do you want me to go on? I'll stop if you like.'

She made a gesture of protest. 'No. Tell me everything.'

'I made a few discreet enquiries from people in the district and they all told me it had been empty for years. One old man said it had been built in his grandfather's time and not used since the beginning of the century. No one knew who was responsible for it – it was just a ruin on the river bank and not worth the effort to pull it down.

'So I decided to make it my den. I begged an old oil stove, and bit by bit collected things to make it more comfortable. I was always very careful to keep the door locked, and did my best to make sure no one saw me coming or going. That was easy in the winter but not so easy on the light summer nights. I borrowed books on sketching and painting from the library, and spent every penny I got on pencils, brushes and paints.'

It was all very vivid. The lonely boy making his way along the melancholy river bank ... the gulls mewing around him ... the stone tower rising from the wet river grass. She closed her eyes, listening to the undertone of nostalgia that crept into his voice.

'It could be very beautiful here, with the lights of the town in the distance and the ships sailing by. Sometimes I'd forget all about time and work so late I dared not go home. I remember how Morrie used to go for me – heaven knows what she thought I'd been doing.'

She remembered the things they had said of him, and her shame became almost too much to bear.

'The summer nights could be very beautiful, too. But I was afraid of them: people sometimes came for walks this way. I was as careful as possible not to be seen, but one night in July I ran into trouble.'

Outside, the wind rose again. It moaned around the tower and made the paraffin lamp flicker. It had a lost and lonely sound that sent a shiver through her. Danny waited for it to die away before continuing. A harshness came into his voice now: his defence against memory.

'This particular night a gang of hooligans jumped me from behind the wall as I was unlocking the door. They were kids between fifteen and eighteen – I suppose they must have spotted me the night before and lain in wait for me. They pushed their way upstairs to this room, saw my things, and began jeering at my pictures. I lost my head, struck one of them, and that started them off... They smashed the lamp and the bits of furniture, tore up my sketches and books – destroyed everything. And they warned me not to come back or they'd do it again and give me a hiding in the bargain. So that was that.'

The thing was beyond tears. She saw it as if it were a film in her mind – the boy sobbing in the midst of his broken treasures. She bit her lips until the blood came.

He dropped the curtain back over the window and turned away. 'That was the end of it. I had to find money for the books, and I daren't tell your father what had happened. On top of that I wasn't feeling too friendly towards the world. So... Well, you know the rest as well as I do.'

'Was that the reason you–?'

'Was that the reason I robbed the office?' His face was a bitter, defiant mask. 'Let's not go looking for excuses this late in the day. Don't forget there had been four other little incidents before that one.'

181

'What about them, Danny?' The question came spontaneously: her eyes widened with shock when she realized its import.

For an unbelievable moment he seemed about to answer her. Then he turned abruptly away and began feeling his pockets for a cigarette.

'I'm sorry,' she said, rising and going to the window to hide her nervousness. 'I shouldn't have asked that. May I take a look from the window?'

He hesitated, then went over to the paraffin lamp and turned it low. 'Unhook the curtain at the top and pull it right away,' he muttered.

She did so, and gave a gasp of pleasure. The window frame was like a huge diorama. In its upper right corner the docks of Darntown sparkled like a patch of fairy dust on a midnight-blue carpet. Its neon lights were transformed into multi-coloured gems; its factories into dolls' houses strung with fairy lights. The broad river that ran diagonally across the frame was no longer the muddy highway for ships that she knew: it was a living mirror reflecting a thousand stars.

In that moment she felt she knew why he had returned to Lidsborough. This nostalgic old tower, with its magic view over the river, was the one place where he had been happy as a child. Probably it was the only place where he had been happy in his life and over the years homesickness had brought him back.

He was standing behind her, face pale in the gloom, watching the distant lights. She turned towards him. 'Coming back to this tower has helped your painting, hasn't it?'

He looked surprised at the question. 'How did you know that?'

She was convinced now that her guess was right. 'I've read somewhere that old associations often help an artist in his work. Have you had any art training?'

'Yes. I've attended night classes ever since I left Lidsborough.'

'Did you ever sell any of your work?'

'I've never tried to. I don't think it's good enough yet.'

'Then how do you manage for money? Have you got a job here?'

'I hadn't when I came, but last Monday I started with Jardine's, the commercial artists in Manor Street. I think I'm going to like it.'

The pathos of it made her eyes ache. His earlier secrecy, to which they had ascribed such dark motives, must have been born of fear. Fear of a repetition of that far-off July night when hooligans had desecrated his home, destroyed his treasures and left him sobbing among their ruins.

'You needn't be afraid that I'll tell anyone about this place, Danny. Not that my father would do anything: he isn't an ogre. But I'll promise not to tell him or anyone else.'

He nodded, and they stood together watching the coruscating lights on the broad river. Suddenly he gave an exclamation of pleasure. She followed his pointing finger and saw three crimson fountains, fully two miles away, rising up from the darkness on the opposite river bank.

'They're the blast furnaces over in Linthorpe,' he told her. 'They look like fireworks at this distance, don't they? I've often seen them and tried to think what they reminded me of. Do you remember – the things we liked that gave off a brilliant red glow?'

She watched the three blood-red fountains rising into the night sky. 'Yes; I know the things you mean – Daddy used to put them on the wall when he lit them.' She caught his arm in excitement. 'I've got it. Volcanoes!'

'That's it,' he said with pleasure. 'I've been trying to think of the name for days.'

Laughing, they turned to one another. As their eyes met his expression changed. His pale face blurred, his eyes became dark pools of great size. A hand seemed to push her forward into them.

'Danny. Oh, Danny...' Suddenly – she never knew how it happened – their arms were around one another.

'Danny! Can you ever forgive me? Will you try, Danny?'

14

He buried his face in her hair, sobbing without sound.

'Tell me everything, Danny. I'll understand now.'

His body was trembling like a faulty machine. As she held him his dry, racking sobs became more violent. Instinct told her she must make him talk.

'Get rid of it all, Danny. Talk to me the way you used to talk before it all started. Imagine we're children again, and we've just found this wonderful den to play in...' If only it were true, she thought. If only they were back in the time when there were no barriers of prejudice and pride between them... 'Talk to me, Danny. Tell me everything.'

The fierceness of his sobs was making him fight for breath. She grew frightened. 'Talk to me, Danny. Call me names, if you like... I shan't mind.' Her voice rose hysterically. 'Say anything, but please talk.'

His dry sobs were paroxysms of agony now. She had never believed anyone could suffer such torment. She dug her fingers fiercely into his shoulders. 'Danny! Call me a spoilt little bitch ... call my father names ... anything ... but for God's sake, talk.' Frantic, she said the one explosive thing that might shatter the floodgate inside him. 'Tell me why you stole from Daddy that first time.'

His body gave a convulsive jerk as if something had ruptured within it. He tried to pull away but she clung to him desperately. 'Tell me ... it'll help you. Hold on to me and tell me.'

The flood gate had collapsed at last: she felt the hot spurt of his tears on her face.

'Why ... couldn't you ... understand? He was holding back ... my pocket money for something I'd done ... and I wanted to buy a present... It was November...'

Her mind went reeling back in time, back to that day fifteen years ago when her father had caught him stealing money. He had never confessed his reason, but now he mentioned November and a present. *And her birthday was in November...*

The truth shivered her mind like the toll of a terrible bell. 'Oh, Danny. Why didn't you tell us?'

'I couldn't... Something always closed up inside me whenever he was angry. It all began the day he punished me by saying I wasn't your real brother... After that I always felt inferior to you... And he made it worse by treating you differently ... when your friends came to parties he always made it clear I wasn't one of you. I hated him ... hated him because he made me jealous of you when all the time I wanted to like you ... when I did like you. Oh; I can't explain. It's all so mixed up...'

'Go on,' she breathed. 'Just go on.'

'It was because I hated him that I stole from him to buy you a present... I can't explain why, but it seemed the right thing to do at the time. After that things got much worse. You stopped playing with me ... that was terrible. Now I felt certain I was inferior to you... I felt everyone was looking at me and calling me a thief...'

'Danny; I'm so sorry.'

'I began to hate everyone, even you. Not all the time, but whenever they found fault with me. Then I wanted to get my own back on them... That was why I stole from your father again, and why I stole at school...'

'What happened there, Danny? Tell me about it.'

'One of the teachers was always finding fault with me. I hated him... I suppose the real fault was mine – I imagined Father had warned all the teachers and that they were keeping a special watch on me. It made me sullen and suspicious ... touchy at the least thing said to me. I'm just the same now – I can't help it. One day we were out playing cricket and I saw this teacher's jacket lying near me on the grass. I took all the things from it … a cigarette case, a pen, and a silver pencil. I meant to punish him by throwing them away, but one of the boys had spotted me. They thought I intended selling them. The headmaster thrashed me and so did your father when he came… That only made things worse … I hated them more than ever, particularly this teacher. So a few months later I did the same thing again.' His voice cracked in agony. 'I just couldn't help doing it.'

Beris pressed his head with her hand, tried to soothe him. 'And then you came back home. Go on from there.'

'You know the rest. It was bad enough when you were away at school, but when you were on holiday it was hell. The way you kept your distance from me – as if I were a leper. It made me feel unclean – I went down fast after that… I didn't care about anything any more…'

'Except your painting, Danny. That still mattered, didn't it?'

'It did while it lasted. But they had to spoil even that, damn them.'

She held on to him tightly. 'Everyone isn't against you, Danny. They never were, no matter how it might have seemed.'

He shook his head passionately. 'Oh, yes, they were. I found that out after I left the approved school. No respectable employer would give me an interview, never mind a job.' His body shivered with hatred. 'God; how I loathe respectable people. They can't think of anything but their own virtues: they wouldn't stoop to help a dog over a stile. More and more I wanted to get my own back on them – that was how I landed in prison.'

The intensity of his bitterness terrified her, bringing back all MacTaggit's warning. 'It was our fault, Danny. We were the guilty ones... I see that now. But all people aren't like us. What about people like Mr MacTaggit and Mrs Johnson? What about little Tommy?... They'll put things right for you if you let them.' Her voice was frantic with pleading now. 'They will, won't they, Danny?'

He drew slowly away. Her body felt cold where he had stood against her. His silence was frightening.

'Danny, please believe all I've said to you. I see now we're to blame for what happened, and I'm desperately sorry. Believe that, or I don't think I'll ever be able to rest again.'

He remained turned away, but after a moment one of his hands opened and reached backwards towards her. The gesture broke her up completely.

'I was miserable too, Danny... Not as much as you, I know, but I missed all the games we had played together. And later on I often wanted to come to your room and talk to you, but by that time there was so much between us – all the respectable things I'd been taught were between us. Don't blame me for those things, Danny. I couldn't help them.'

He did not speak, but his hand closed tightly over her own. Hope came back to her, eager and uncurbed. 'It's all over now, Danny. If you'll forgive us, we can all make a new start together...' At that moment an image of her father, dour and unrelenting, entered her mind, and her words took on a hollow sound, like stones falling down a deep well. She tried desperately to bring conviction into them as his hand loosened and pulled away. 'Do you hear, Danny? We'll forget the past and start again.'

He turned towards her, his voice dull and bleak. 'What exactly does "start again" mean?'

She bit her lip. 'I know there's Father... But we could begin seeing one another again. And I could talk to him in the meantime...'

'What about your fiancé? Haven't you forgotten him too?'

There was a fierce triumph in giving him that news. 'I haven't a fiancé. I broke off the engagement the other week.'

His voice was hushed now, uncertain. 'You broke off your engagement? But why?'

'Never mind why. It's over – for good. So that isn't an obstacle any longer.'

There was a long silence before he spoke. 'There's still your father. If he found out you were seeing me, he might throw you out of the house. He hates me so much he probably would.'

Her sudden gust of rebellion startled her. 'Then let him. If he were as unfair as that I wouldn't care.'

'It's easy to talk like that. Where would you live? What would you do for money?'

'I could work as other people have to. It would probably do me good.' She drew nearer to him. 'I must see more of you, Danny. It's terribly important to me. Can't you believe that?'

His face was a white, shifting blur in the dimly lit room. 'Why? What's your reason?'

'I've already explained. I want to make up for all that's happened. I want to help you.'

Sooner or later it had to happen – the false step, the unintended emphasis that hurt his pride and freed his prejudice.

'And what if I don't need or want your help?'

'I didn't mean it that way, Danny. I want you for yourself, for your company.'

His reply to that made her wince. 'Are you sure you're just not feeling sorry for yourself?'

She knew what he meant and found the

honesty to admit it. 'Oh, I know I'm trying to ease my conscience too. Nothing in life is ever wholly black or white, Danny – that's one of the things I've found out recently. But there is much more to it than that. I want to talk and laugh with you as we did in the old days. Won't you try to believe me?'

His eyes probed hers in the darkness, trying to assess her sincerity. 'Can't you understand how impossible all this is?' he muttered. 'I'm a thief, an ex-jailbird. Sooner or later your friends would find out, and they'd make your life hell. That would change your views on me again fast enough.'

'People aren't as cruel as that, Danny.'

'Aren't they, by God.' The words swilled out of his lips like acid. 'If there's one thing they like better than lecturing sinners, it's throwing stones at them. And none of them are worse than the crowd you and your father mix with.'

Instinct told her she must now reduce the tension or reaction would drive him back to the intense bitterness that had frightened her a few minutes earlier. There would be other occasions for her to plead her case – somehow she would make them. Her task now was to consolidate the progress she had made.

'Have you ever thought of calling on Aunt Cecilia?' she asked as he was turning away.

'Aunt Cecilia? Why, no,' he muttered, pausing.

'Why don't you? I know she'd be delighted to see you. We were only talking about you a few days ago.'

'How is she?' he muttered.

'She hasn't changed a bit. Of course, she's been retired for quite a long time, ever since Mr Pearson died in 1950. Do you remember the time she took us to his offices, and he sent out for some of those lovely cream cakes Fowlers used to make?...'

As she had hoped, Aunt Cecilia proved a guide who led them gently back down the lanes of memory, picking with characteristic thoughtfulness the more sunlit ones. As they shared some of their many memories, so he gradually relaxed, and it took a particularly fierce gust of wind, finding a crack in the uncovered window and extinguishing the paraffin lamp, to bring both of them back to the present. He replaced the curtain and lit the lamp, glancing down at his watch as he did so. He gave a start.

'It's nearly nine o'clock. I'd no idea it was so late.'

'Does it matter?' Beris asked him. 'Have you anything else to do tonight?'

Ashamed of his breakdown, he was avoiding her eyes. 'I had promised to meet a friend at nine. That was one reason I came here early.'

She noticed with gladness that there was no enthusiasm in his voice. Nevertheless, she rose at once. 'I hope I haven't made you late.'

'It doesn't matter to a few minutes. But I had better be getting along.'

When she was ready he blew out the lamp and switched on his torch. As he opened the door to the stone steps she turned to him. 'Let me come here again, Danny. It's been wonderful talking about old times and there's so much more to talk about yet.'

'It's too dangerous for you,' he said, shifting uneasily.

She shook a finger at him. 'Now you can't use that as an excuse. Nobody but you and Tommy and I know of this place – you've said so yourself. And Father's away for the week, so it's easy for me to get away. Let me come, Danny, please.'

The news of her father gave him an excuse for his vacillation. 'All right. But only while he is away. Otherwise it's too risky.'

A whole week – much could happen in a week! 'When?' she asked eagerly. 'Tomorrow night? Could I meet you somewhere and come along with you? Then we'd have plenty of time – you could show me all your work.'

He nodded reluctantly. 'All right, if you really want to come. I'll meet you at the street corner at six-thirty.'

Jubilant at her first victory, she descended the glistening stone steps with him and went out on the wind-swept river bank.

15

The following morning, although off duty, MacTaggit took Beris to a tea-room in town – his reaction to the news she had given him on the telephone an hour earlier. Over buttered scones and cups of hot coffee his gnome-like face grinned at her.

'You've done well, lassie. A fine job.'

She was anxious to know the extent of her progress. 'Shouldn't things be easier now he's told me his reasons for stealing?'

MacTaggit's quick movements were never so noticeable as when he was enthusiastic. His head jerked up and down briskly. 'Definitely. Until he broke down the lad had an enormous plug of bitterness jamming up his works, and every time he had a tiff with someone the pressure grew worse. That plug had grown so tight over the years I couldn't see anyone but yourself loosening it. You had all his childhood associations, his old-time affection for you, to help lever it out. If you couldn't do it, I didn't feel anyone else could. But you had to have the chance – the right time and place – and that old lighthouse provided it.' MacTaggit's expression grew thoughtful. 'I thought I'd got everything out of him, but he never told me about that any more than he told me about your birthday present.'

'I'm certain the lighthouse has something to do with his coming back. For one thing, it's all mixed up with his ambition to become an artist.'

'I'm sure you're right. As a sanctuary where he was free to paint, it must have meant an enormous amount to him as a child and he's never shaken off the desire to return to it. It's become intrinsically mixed-up with his ambitions, his desire to rehabilitate himself, his confidence, a hundred things he couldn't define even if you asked him to.' MacTaggit gave her a quizzical smile. 'You can see now the effect childhood impressions have on us, can't you?'

She nodded, a little intoxicated to learn that her success was as real as she had hoped. 'Then he should be more friendly to me now this plug of bitterness, as you call it, has gone?'

His reply was characteristically cautious. 'Relatively more friendly, yes. But don't expect too much at once. Remember the complexity of human nature. At this very moment he'll be feeling two emotions towards you. One will be gratitude for helping him get rid of something that's been choking him. But the second Danny will bear you a resentment for breaking the tough front he's been presenting so long to the world.'

'What do you mean – the second Danny?'

'The part of him his defence mechanism has created – the defiant, suspicious Danny who doesn't want to come to terms with a society he believes unjust. It was created to protect him against further hurt – it couldn't live if he learned to trust society again. So you're it's deadly enemy and it'll fight you all the way. At this moment it'll be telling Danny he was a fool to trust you and that he mustn't make such a mistake again.'

'Will I win?' she asked quietly.

'Of course you'll win. You've got all those childhood associations on your side. Use them – they're your weapons.'

Listening to him she realized how much she had grown to like and admire this peppery, intensely human man. Her *tête-à-tête* with him took on a new significance, a thing of value for its own sake as well as for the advice it gave her. She brought her mind back to Danny again. 'So each time we meet it should be a little easier to make contact with him?'

MacTaggit nodded. 'By bringing him back this far into the family from which he was rejected, you're undermining the foundations on which that second Danny was built. You see, so much of his trouble later on was due to his losing contact with you.'

She knew he was right and gave a slight

shiver. 'It's a big responsibility. What mistakes could I make?'

'Only one you're not likely to make – deceive or betray him in some way. That would give the second Danny something substantial to bite on and we mustn't underestimate him – he's still quite formidable. Otherwise just go on as you are. In fact,' and MacTaggit's bushy eyebrows drew comically together, 'my advice would be for you just to follow your natural instincts. They've served you very well so far.'

Something in his expression puzzled her. 'I don't quite understand what you mean.'

He gave a wry shrug and reached for a scone. 'Never mind. You soon will.'

Beris was early that evening for her rendezvous with Danny, drawing up on the main road near the corner of Lambert Street at six-twenty. As she sat waiting, traffic swished by her on the wet road. It was a bleak night with more than a suspicion of rain in the east wind. The few pedestrians who passed the car were huddled up in raincoats and hidden under umbrellas.

Fifteen minutes passed before Danny rounded the street corner, hands thrust into his mackintosh pockets, collar turned up around his ears. As always he was bare-headed, his black hair slightly awry in the wind. His lateness and appearance told her

MacTaggit had correctly forecast his behaviour. He saw her car, hesitated, then moved slowly towards it. She reached out and threw open the door.

'Hello, Danny,' she smiled. 'Jump in.'

He did not move. The shadow from a street lamp lay across his face, giving it a sullen, forbidding aspect.

'You shouldn't have come,' he muttered. 'Someone might recognize you.'

She laughed reassuringly. 'What if they do? I'm not breaking the law. Come on, jump in.'

He shook his head abruptly. 'I don't want the car to go out there. The police have kept an eye on me ever since that affair in the Erebus, and if they're around tonight and trail the car it might spoil everything for me.'

'Then we'll leave it,' she said immediately. 'I'll park it down a side street and we'll walk there.'

'It's too far for you to walk. And it's too muddy.'

She lifted a foot for his inspection. 'Don't worry about the mud. I've come in low heels this time. Jump in and we'll find a hiding place for the car.'

His voice rose sullenly. 'If you must have the truth, I don't want you to come tonight. I've thought about it a good deal and decided we mustn't see one another again.

Otherwise something's sure to go wrong.'

She was left with no alternative but to make a direct appeal. 'Danny; you promised I could come tonight to look at your work. All day I've been looking forward to it. I'll take any precaution you like; I'll leave the car anywhere you choose; I'll even crawl through the grass to the lighthouse if you think it necessary. But please don't break your promise to me.'

She waited tensed, not caring to think what a refusal would mean to her plans. To her intense relief he let out a sullen exclamation and jumped into the car, slamming the door behind him. 'I can't understand what you want to come for: it's all so pointless. But if you must come you'd better drive there. Only don't use your headlights.'

'I'd much rather walk than take the slightest chance of our being seen–'

He made a gesture of irritation. 'Stop arguing about it, for heaven's sake.'

Without another word she drove down Lambert Street and took the uneven road through the darkness to the old jetty. There she collected a large handgrip from the back seat, switched off her parking lights, and locked up the car. The fine rain, sweeping up river, stung her face as she followed Danny up the bank to the towpath.

He spoke no more than half a dozen words to her during the walk to the tower. He kept a few paces ahead of her, his watchful eyes peering into the darkness. The crunch of the wet stones under their feet seemed to disturb him: twice he made her pause to listen, but she could hear nothing but the soughing of the grass and the lapping of the river. As the tower came into sight he motioned for her to wait, going forward alone into the enclosure. After a minute he reappeared and waved her to follow him.

He locked the lighthouse door behind them, switched on his torch, and they climbed the stone steps to the third-floor room. After checking the black-out curtain was in position over the window, he lit the paraffin lamp and the oil stove. He then turned to her sullenly.

'Well, here we are. What do you want now?'

'I want to see your work. But first I think we should make ourselves comfortable. What about a cup of tea to warm us up?'

He stared at her. 'I've no tea to give you.'

'Don't you ever make a drink for yourself when you're here?'

'I have, once or twice, but it's too much trouble. It means bringing water, and in any case it's difficult to boil it on the stove.'

'I guessed as much,' she said. 'Well, we're going to have tea tonight.' Going over to her grip she pulled out a small primus stove and a kettle. Standing them on the table she

201

placed alongside them a large bottle of water, a packet of tea, sugar, and a bottle of milk. She turned to Danny with a smile: 'We can have a cup each now and another one later, with some rolls I've brought. There'll be plenty of water.'

He moved slowly across to the table, staring down at the primus stove.

'Do you know how to work it?' When he nodded she went on: 'I wish you'd see to it, then. I'm always afraid of blowing myself up.'

As he pumped the stove she chatted to him, ignoring his silence. 'How is Tommy getting on with his football? You know, the way he plays with that dog of his reminds me of us and Jack. Do you remember Jack, Danny – how we used to use him as a fielder when we played cricket? He was as good as any of us, wasn't he?'

His back was turned to her, but she noticed he had stopped pumping the stove.

'Do you remember that time we were playing with that awful Marsden boy on the waste land behind the house?' she went on. 'I stumped him when he was out of his crease and when I said he was out he went all peevish and slapped me.' While speaking she moved to the other side of the table, facing him. 'Do you remember what happened then, Danny?'

His head lifted slowly. As their eyes met his

expression blurred. It was as if one image, once perfectly superimposed on the other, were now drifting out of focus. He nodded. 'Jack took a bite at him, didn't he?'

'Jack took more than a bite at him. He took a piece from the seat of his trousers. And as if that wasn't enough, you punched him on the nose. I can see him now, one hand holding the back of his trousers, the other holding his nose, running hell-for-leather across the field home. The fuss his mother made... Father was away at the time, I remember, and Morrie told me that as punishment we wouldn't be allowed to go to Uncle David's farm for our holidays. I didn't really believe her, of course, but just the same I didn't sleep very well that night.'

Danny put the kettle on the hissing blue flame of the primus. 'Was that the year we had the fortnight on the farm?'

'Yes,' she said eagerly. 'Wasn't it fun? Do you remember Timothy, Uncle David's old dray horse? He was so broad across the back we had to sit sidewards on him. And there was Susie, the old sow. Do you remember her chasing Jack into the house? She'd just had a litter and he must have gone among them. I'd never seen him so frightened before; I think he believed her some kind of dog.'

The lines of his face were changing as she watched, a smile pulling at his mouth. 'Yes;

that was very funny. He wouldn't go near the pig-sty after that, would he?'

'Not on your life he wouldn't. He developed an allergy for pigs of all shapes and sizes. I think he was the only one of us glad to get back to town.'

It was difficult for her to conceal her delight as every passing minute found him more and more responsive. After tea she asked him to show her his work. She knew little about art, but after viewing the contents of the packing case she needed little knowledge to realize he had considerable talent. Realizing the extent of his enthusiasm she encouraged him to talk about art and this subject alone provided conversational material for most of the evening. Nine-thirty came before either of them realized it, and she still had much to hear.

They had their second cup of tea, he seated on the packing case, she in the wicker chair, sitting opposite one another with a pile of ham rolls on the table between them. The room, fully warmed by the oil stove, gave Beris a strange sense of cosiness and security.

'This is a nice old place,' she told Danny, wriggling down comfortably in her chair. 'It gives me the same feeling I used to get as a child on finding a snug den where I imagined no one could find me. You know, the kind of place you smuggled food into to have a feast. I wonder what gives it such an atmosphere? You feel it too, don't you?'

His reply drew her eyes. The sullen mask had completely gone from his face now: in the yellow lamplight his features were young and sensitive and grave. 'Perhaps it has that atmosphere because it's near and yet so far from life. Darntown is only a few miles away – when the wind is in the right direction you can hear the rumble of cranes and machinery. And large ships often pass close by. Yet you can go out on the river bank at this time of the year and never see anyone. There's nothing but grass and seagulls and the river.'

She leaned forward in her chair, voice soft. 'Danny, when you talk like that you're an entirely different person from the man I met on the road tonight. Do you know that?'

He flushed and turned his eyes away. 'I know I was rude to you. I'm sorry.'

'I didn't want an apology, Danny. That wasn't why I said it.'

His gaze fell on the primus stove and the other equipment she had brought. 'I haven't thanked you yet for bringing me these things. They'll be very useful.'

'The only thanks I want is permission to come again. We've so much more to talk about. When can I come, Danny?'

'When do you want to come?'

She laughed gaily. 'Oh, tomorrow night

and the next night and the night after that. I've had such a wonderful evening I want as many more as I can get.'

'When does your father get back?'

'As far as I know at the moment, on Thursday.'

There was real regret in his voice. 'I promised to meet Jack Clinton, a friend of mine, tomorrow night, and as other people are involved, it's rather short notice to call it off. But Monday would be all right.' Then quickly afraid of appearing too eager: 'Perhaps that's too soon. Better make it Tuesday.'

She laughed, eyes bright. 'That's not soon enough, Danny. I'd much prefer Monday.'

16

In all Beris went to the tower three times during the following week. On Monday evening Danny's behaviour followed much the same pattern as on Saturday. Although this time not actually trying to dissuade her from accompanying him, he showed little enthusiasm until the second Danny, as MacTaggit called his defence mechanism, gave ground before her. Then, as before, he became a different person and the rest of the evening was as successful as on Saturday.

On Tuesday evening she knew her battle to gain his confidence was going well. This time he showed little more than diffidence on meeting her, and even that mood vanished once they were in the tower. Smiles came readily to his lips now, often he laughed with her at amusing recollections of their childhood, and before the evening was over she found the courage to try yet again the next step in his rehabilitation.

It was not an easy one for her to take, for she knew at least some of the risks to her father. Yet to withdraw her influence from Danny until after the New Year might well allow his bitterness to dominate him again, and there was no telling what dangers it might lead him into during the next few weeks. At the same time she had the uneasy feeling her decision represented a choice in sorts between Danny's security and her father's. This thought she tried to allay, telling herself the risks of exposure to her father were negligible alongside the dangers of loneliness to Danny.

He had been doing a sketch of her and had been engrossed in the task for the last hour. Now, cigarettes in hand, they were sitting before the oil stove with the kettle simmering on the primus near by.

'Danny,' she said suddenly after there had been a brief silence between them. 'I don't want to stop seeing you after this week. I want to keep on coming here. And I'd like you to take me out somewhere one night. Anywhere – I don't mind where we go – but I would enjoy it very much.'

His face grew serious. To gain time he leaned forward and inspected the primus stove. Then he looked up at her.

'I can't take you anywhere, Beeda. You know that as well as I do. And it'll be too dangerous for you to keep on coming here once your father's home. Sooner or later he'd find out.'

'But why should he? I'm grown up – I don't have to tell him where I'm going in the evenings. And I'll be careful.'

He shook his head. 'You couldn't deceive him for long. You're too close to him.'

She could not help wondering what proportion of his concern was for her and what proportion for the safety of his tower. 'I don't want to do anything that would jeopardize your coming here – I know what this tower means to you. But if that's worrying you, couldn't we meet somewhere else? Why shouldn't we? We're free people.'

Until now no mention of his recent court case had passed between them. Now he reminded her of it. 'Have you forgotten what happened the other week? Can't you realize the police believe I robbed that shop and are keeping an eye on me? If you go out in public with me they'll spot you straight away. And how long do you think it'll be then before your father hears about it?'

His words made her suddenly realize how deeply she was committing her father, and sent a qualm of fear through her. It was no longer possible to deceive herself that his danger was slight.

Danny was watching her closely. 'You see now the trouble you'd get yourself into, don't you?'

She wanted to take this long-awaited opportunity of asking him about the affair in the Erebus. At the same time, realizing he had noticed her alarm and misunderstood its origin, she wanted to explain it to him. The struggle between question and explanation lost her the opportunity for either as a film of bitterness, like oil on blue water, spread over his eyes.

'Free people,' he muttered, turning away. 'You'd soon learn how free we are.'

Seeing he was slipping away from her, she dropped alongside him on the packing case, gripped his arm tightly. 'Stop feeling the world's against you, Danny. It isn't! Everything will come right if only you'll give it a chance. You'll see it will...'

For a moment it seemed he would pull away. Then his expression softened. One of his hands moved up as though to touch her face. When he hesitated she bent forward impulsively and brushed her cheek against it. A pause, and then his fingers, gentle for a man, touched her eyes and followed the contours of her cheeks. His voice was low, husky.

'You've been good to me, Beeda. I don't know why, but you have.'

She gripped his other arm. Her face was very near his own, so near she could see a tiny scar under his left eye. She remembered the scar – the result of his falling from a tree she had dared him to climb… 'You've got to lift your head up again, Danny, and stop feeling you aren't as good as the rest of us. Do you hear me?'

His face was very pale. 'It's hard to get back, Beeda. Much harder than you think.'

She reached out and touched the tiny scar. 'You can do it, Danny. You can do it if you try.'

'You don't understand, Beeda. You can slip so far you don't care… That's how I am.'

That frightened her. She dug her fingers fiercely into his arms. 'Don't talk like a fool. Of course you care.' Hardly knowing what she was doing, she bent forward and kissed him hard on the mouth. 'Don't talk such rubbish,' she whispered, kissing him again.

His body jerked with shock. For a moment he clung to her thirstily, then he pulled away, eyes wide with protest.

Her voice seemed to come from a

stranger, came with a high singing note. 'It's not the first time, Danny.'

'We were children then,' he muttered. 'It's different now.'

It was different now. Her mind was in a ferment, trying to make sense of what had happened to her... With an effort she pushed the confusion aside. Later she would try to understand herself: her task now was to hold on to what she had fought for. Afraid of having gone too far she tried to reduce the emotional tension between them. Giving his shoulders a last friendly squeeze, smiling into his face without shame, she turned to pick up her cigarettes.

'How can you talk that way?' she asked. 'You've got a job you like and there's no earthly reason why you shouldn't do well at it. As for the police, they'll soon get tired of watching you when they discover you're doing nothing wrong.'

His eyes, still dazed from his contact with her, fell away as she held out her cigarettes. Noticing how his fingers were trembling she offered him a light. When he did not answer her she went on:

'You've got to face the world again, Danny. Not just the people in pubs, or the people at work, but the kind of people you were brought up among. I'll help you if you'll only let me.'

He stared down at his cigarette, avoiding

her gaze. 'You make it sound so easy – as if it just depended on you and me. You keep forgetting the police and you keep forgetting your father. Remember – he comes home the day after tomorrow.'

It was strange how she did keep forgetting her father, particularly as he represented a seemingly insurmountable obstacle between them. But failure was something she could not contemplate: her words were like running footsteps trying to escape from it. 'We'll get round it, Danny. We'll think hard and by tomorrow night we'll have found a way. You see if we haven't.'

He shook his head despondently. After a long pause he looked up at her.

'I've been thinking about tomorrow night. I don't think I'll be able to come.'

Her voice faltered in dismay. 'But I thought we'd already agreed on it.'

'I know we did, but I'd a phone call today from a girl I know here. Some time ago I promised to collect an old aunt of hers who lives in Merriby and bring her in to town. Apparently the old woman gets lonely every now and then and comes in to stay with the girl's family. She's nervous at travelling alone on the buses at night and can't get away before seven-thirty because she gives piano lessons on Wednesdays.'

Beris wondered if the excuse was genuine or the result of what had just happened between them. If it was genuine, who was the girl? The one Mrs Johnson had mentioned – Madge?

'Couldn't your friend fetch her herself?' she asked.

'Normally she does, but she's working overtime at the moment – that's why she asked me. I don't see how I can get out of it – the old woman won't be able to come if I let her down.'

The kettle was boiling itself dry. As Beris made tea she had an idea and her face brightened.

'I'll tell you what we can do. You meet me a little earlier than usual – at six-fifteen – and then about seven o'clock go off in my car and fetch her. Merriby's only ten miles away – you can be there and back by car in less than an hour. It'll be more comfortable for the old woman than travelling by bus, and will still give us most of the evening together. What do you say to that?'

'It's risky,' he muttered. 'If I had an accident everything would come out...' He paused, then went on thoughtfully: 'But I might be able to borrow Jack's car.'

'Who's Jack?'

'Jack Clinton – a friend of mine.'

She would have liked to ask him more about Clinton but her immediate problem was too pressing. 'Why borrow a car when mine is here? – you'd only have to return it to

213

your friend and that would waste more time. And why should you have an accident – you can drive, can't you?' As he nodded she went on: 'Take mine, Danny. I don't want to lose tomorrow evening.'

A last hesitation and then he nodded. 'All right. It certainly would be quicker that way.'

'Then that's settled,' she said with relief. 'I'll meet you at six-fifteen in the usual place.' She glanced down at her watch and gave a start. 'I'll have to go after tea. Morrie always sits up for me when Daddy's away. I get furious with her but it's no use.'

A quarter of an hour later they left the tower. The night was clear with a crescent moon hanging over the river. The lights of Darntown shivered ahead, a thousand gems scattered over a velvet cloak. Behind them rose the tower, dark and silent against the sky. As they left the enclosure and started down the path she took his arm, squeezing it tightly.

'This is the first time the night has been clear since I started coming here. It's a good omen, Danny. Everything's going to turn out right. I'm sure of it.'

And in the conspiracy of the night it did seem there was no problem that could not be solved. Life appeared as simple as the river, the grass, and the stars.

17

Mrs Johnson buttered her last slice of bread, frowned at the clock, and marched purposefully to the foot of the stairs. With arms akimbo on her ample hips she let out a shout that started Minty barking in the back garden.

'For the last time you two, get up! It's gone half past seven. If you aren't down in two minutes I'm throwing your breakfasts into the back yard.'

Upstairs Tommy, who had been waiting for this ultimate threat, leapt out of bed and went into action. Like some animated cartoon, vest, shirt, trousers, socks, and shoes appeared to jump like magic from their resting places to clothe him. In a climax of breathless speed he tossed his pyjamas on the bed, threw the coverlet over them, and flew out on to the landing. Pushing open Danny's bedroom door he thrust a tousled head inside.

'Better get a move on, Danny. She's gettin' steam up. What's the matter? Have you lost something?'

Danny was on his knees, searching the floor. His wardrobe door was open and his

215

only suit lying on the bed. As Tommy entered he stood up and began searching the pockets of his suit again.

'I've lost my duplicate key to the light-house,' he said. 'I thought it was in this suit.'

Tommy had a look under the bed himself. 'Maybe you lost it outside somewhere.'

Danny nodded. 'I'm trying to remember when I last wore the suit.'

'Sunday night,' Tommy announced. 'The night Mr Clinton called for you. I remember seein' you come down in it.'

'I could have lost it then, I suppose. Or perhaps it wasn't in the suit. I can't remember.'

'It doesn't matter much, does it? Nobody'd know what it was if they found it, and you can get another one made, can't you?'

Danny reached out and ruffled the boy's hair. It was obvious he was in a happy mood. 'No; it doesn't really matter, I suppose. Tell me, young 'un – do you like watching good swimming?'

'Swimming! Yes, 'course I do. Why?'

'They're holding the North of England swimming trials in Lidsborough this year – a week on Friday – and a chap at work has told me he can get me two tickets. How would you like to go with me?'

Tommy's eyes grew very bright. 'Do you mean it, Danny? Really?'

'Of course I mean it.'

'Gee, thanks, Danny. That'll be super. You can have the bathroom first, if you like.'

Danny laughed. 'I've already been in. You go ahead.'

The wind, never long absent from Lidsborough in the winter, returned during the day and was blowing lustily when Beris left home that evening. Mrs Morrison saw her to the door.

'I've never known you do so much gadding about,' she grumbled. 'You've only had one night at home since your father left for London. Mind you're home earlier tonight. I have to get up in the mornings even if you don't.'

'You don't have to sit up,' Beris reminded her. 'I've got a key.'

'You know I can't sleep until you're safely in.' As Mrs Morrison opened the door a violent gust of wind invaded the house. 'Goodness,' she gasped. 'It's blowing a gale. You never should be going out alone on such a night.'

The sodium lights of Markham Road were swinging wildly overhead, throwing shadows in all directions as Beris drove to her appointment. The wind was even fiercer on the river bank, growling out of the darkness and doing its best to bluster her and Danny off the towpath. Windswept and breathless, she gave a laugh of relief as Danny closed the lighthouse door, shutting out the wind.

'What a night! It's a good thing you're going to use the car or the poor old woman would be blown off her feet.'

Upstairs, after he had lit the lamp, he turned to her. 'I'm still not happy about using your car. If anything should go wrong the police would soon know you'd been seeing me. And your father would know half an hour later.'

'I don't care who knows,' she said, not over-truthfully. 'But why should anything happen? You can drive all right, can't you? If not I'll come along with you.'

She could tell from his expression that he did not want her to meet Madge. 'I can drive all right. But I wish I'd borrowed Jack's car instead.'

'Stop worrying about it.' As he knelt down to light the oil stove she took the opportunity of asking him more about Clinton. 'Who is Jack? Someone you used to know before you went away?'

For a moment his face twisted. 'Good lord, no. None of those people would speak to me now. No; he's someone I met the day I came back.' He went on to tell her the favour Clinton had done him. 'One way and another he's been very decent to me. I usually see him once or twice a week.'

She felt gratitude towards Clinton for

befriending him in this way. 'What is he?'

'He runs a garage in Darntown. He gave me a couple of days' work there when I was looking for a job. He's a bit of a rough diamond, mind you – likes dog-racing, cards, and that kind of thing – but underneath he's a decent chap.'

She reproached herself for prejudice as her mental picture of Clinton grew less prepossessing. 'Do you ever go dog-racing with him?'

'Yes; I've been once or twice. I'm not too keen – but I don't like to offend him.'

'Does he know your other friend – the girl you're doing the favour for tonight?'

His embarrassment at her mention of Madge pleased her with its implication. 'No. He met her once for a couple of minutes; but that's all.' He changed the conversation abruptly. 'Are you certain you're going to be all right?'

'Of course. You shouldn't be away much more than an hour, should you?'

He shook his head. 'If the old woman is on time I should be back by eight-fifteen.'

'Good,' she said, reaching out and opening the handgrip she had brought with her. From it she pulled out a bottle of sherry and two glasses. She laughed at his look of surprise. 'I thought a drink would warm you before you went out.'

He drank a glass with her, then buttoned

up his mackintosh. 'I'd better be going. I'm meeting her at the bus stop and mustn't keep her waiting in the cold.'

Beris went down the stone steps with him to the lighthouse door, the rough grey stones glistening in the torchlight. At the door she gave a laugh and caught hold of his arm. The sherry made her feel light-headed, a trifle irresponsible.

'I feel like a wife seeing her husband off to work. What do they always say – don't be late home, darling?'

His face was a white blur behind the torch. 'Are you quite sure you're not going to be frightened?'

'Of course I'm not. This home's built like a fort. Nobody could break in here.'

'I shan't be able to let myself in,' he told her. 'I lost my duplicate key the other day. So I'll bang hard on the door when I get back. But don't open it until you hear my voice.'

'I won't,' she promised.

He made as if to open the door, paused, and then unexpectedly reached out and touched her face. Instantly she found herself moving towards him. For a moment he hesitated, then, with an exclamation of self-reproach, he switched off the torch and released the door. The wind, cold and disruptive, leapt in between them.

'Don't forget to lock yourself in,' were his last words before he vanished among the threshing bushes in the enclosure.

Beris had to push the door hard to beat back the wind. Turning the key and switching on the torch, she started back up the stairs. An illogical happiness that refused to speculate on the future was bubbling up inside her, preventing her settling down to the book she had brought. Instead she roamed around the room, touching things that were his, looking again through the collection of his work that lay in the packing case.

She discovered two pictures he had not shown her: one a sketch of herself as a child, the other a painting of herself as a teenage schoolgirl. From their appearance they had been done for some time – certainly before he returned to Lidsborough. Probably they had been copied from photographs. Great care had obviously gone into the composition and the preservation of them – both were mounted behind glass.

She stared at them a long time before returning them to the packing case. Turning the lamp low, she went over to the window and drew aside the curtain. Far up river the lights of Darntown sparkled and glowed. A squall of rain, sending raindrops lashing against the window, refracted the coloured gems and made them swirl and mingle like a shifting kaleidoscope. Beneath her feet the lighthouse shuddered under the fierce buffeting of the wind.

The tower, high above the melancholy river, surrounded by desolate, wind-swept grass, gave her a sense of detachment in time as well as space. Watching the distant city was like watching a jungle from a near, yet isolated, mountain peak. Thinking of all the thousands who fought in it to survive, her mind turned to those who failed as well as those who succeeded, and for the first time in her life she realized how fine and perilous was the distinction between sinner and saint.

At length she replaced the curtain, turned up the lamp, and went to the chair with her book. Finding herself unable to concentrate she laid it aside and sat listening to the wind. In the warm, friendly light, thinking of Danny, she lost all track of time and it came as a pleasant surprise to discover it was already eight o'clock. Afraid she would not hear Danny for the blustering wind, she opened the door that led to the stairs.

Twice in the next five minutes she was brought to her feet by noises she eventually attributed to the wind. Finally, she picked up the torch and made her way downstairs, where she waited by the door.

Not wishing to exhaust the battery she switched off the torch and stood in darkness. Cold draughts played around her legs, making her shiver. A minute passed and then suddenly something brushed against her foot. Startled, she jumped back and switched on the torch. Two tiny brilliant eyes shone at her before vanishing from sight.

The incident frightened her and completely changed her mood. Resisting the temptation to run back to the warm room upstairs she retreated to the third step of the stairs, where she swung the torch in a wide arc to keep any further rats at bay.

The bluster of the wind outside had other noises intermingled with it: the threshing of bushes, the distant swish of waves, and other sounds she could not determine. After a few more minutes, during a lull in the wind, she heard a tap, tap, tap on the door. Relieved, she ran forward and was about to unlock the door when she remembered Danny's instructions.

Her voice echoed hollowly around her. 'Hello. Is that you, Danny?'

There was no reply. She called again, louder this time, but with no more success. Intensely frightened now she switched off the torch to prevent light seeping through the door. Instantly, like a black cylinder, darkness closed around her. For a moment the rush of wind outside filled her ears. Then, as it dropped, the tapping sound came again ... very distinct, very deliberate.

Badly needing an explanation to ease her fear, she seized one. The bush outside – one of its branches was tapping against the door! But she could not find the courage to open it. Instead she waited for the next gust of wind to prove her correct.

But, although the wind came again and again, the tapping ceased. Afraid to think what it could mean, she crept back in the darkness to the room above.

Chilled by both fear and cold, she held her hands over the oil stove. With her nerves badly shaken she no longer found the yellow light of the paraffin lamp restful – too many shadows lay on the walls around her. Outside, the wind, tearing and scrabbling at the window, was a fierce animal trying to gain ingress.

A strong draught that blew up the stairs was killing the warmth of the room but she dared not close the door in case she missed hearing Danny. Time and again she imagined hearing his knock, only to realize her mistake before reaching the foot of the stairs.

This new mood gave her a deeper insight into the condition of Danny's mind as a child. Nights such as this must have been common to him, and it was frightening to imagine the mental suffering he must have undergone at home to have found comfort in such loneliness as this.

Soon a fear that he had been involved in a an accident added itself to her nervousness. To occupy her mind she busied herself making tea, almost welcoming the difficulty she found in managing the primus stove.

Two strong cups and a cigarette did a little to raise her spirits, but reaction soon followed as the minutes dragged slowly on.

It was after nine-thirty when he returned. At first she was afraid the distant knocking was yet another false alarm, but this time it sounded again as she reached the foot of the stairs. He answered her call, there were a few seconds of wind and cold as she flung back the door, and then he was standing beside her and for the moment all her fears were driven back.

She caught hold of him. 'It's good to have you back, Danny. I thought you were never coming.'

His voice was sharp, anxious. 'Were you very frightened? You're trembling!'

'I thought something had happened to you. Has anything gone wrong?'

'Nothing serious, except that I've wasted the whole evening. I haven't seen the old woman.'

'You haven't seen her? Why?'

A certain brittleness about his manner made her feel he was suffering from something more than irritation as he led her up the stairs. 'I was supposed to meet her at the bus stop – and I was there five minutes before time. I waited twenty minutes for her, and then went off to find a phone box. I called Madge and she said she hadn't heard anything new from her aunt, so I took the old woman's address and went round to her house. It took me some time to find it and when I got there all was in darkness. I couldn't make anyone hear, so went back to the bus stop. I waited another fifteen minutes, then phoned Madge again. And what do you think?'

She laughed. 'She had arrived at Madge's house.'

'That's right. Apparently she'd got the wrong time and gone to the bus stop fifteen minutes too early. When she'd found no one there she'd taken the first bus that came along... And that's how I've spent my evening.'

'Never mind,' she told him as they entered the room. 'Take your coat off and have a sherry. You've earned one.'

He went over to the oil stove and stared down at it. 'Why is the room so cold?'

'I had to leave the door open so I wouldn't miss hearing you.'

'You must be half frozen,' he muttered. 'I'll make some tea. It'll warm us better than sherry.'

'I had some half an hour ago, but I wouldn't mind another cup. There's plenty of water left.'

She watched him closely as he worked on the primus stove. There was a tight, wary expression about his eyes and mouth, and more than once he paused as though listening for something. She wanted to ask him what was wrong, but did not know how to commence. Then she remembered the tapping on the downstairs door. His eyes gave a flare of alarm as she mentioned it. He stared up at her, voice overpitched.

'What was it?'

She attempted a laugh. 'It must have been the bush outside blowing in the wind. But it gave me a fright for a minute or two.'

'Did you hear it again afterwards?'

His anxiety had communicated itself to her. 'No; but that doesn't mean anything. Perhaps the branch blew away from the door... What's the matter, Danny? You're worried, aren't you? What's happened tonight?'

He filled the kettle, placed it on the primus. 'I had the feeling I was being watched tonight when I went for your car,' he muttered. 'I couldn't see or hear anyone but when I reached Lambert Street I looked back and saw two lights moving behind me in the darkness. They looked like the parking lights of a car.'

'A car!'

'Yes. I pulled up but the lights went out immediately and nobody passed me. If it was a car it must have gone out by one of the other tracks – there are others leading to the main road. Or else it went back to the jetty.'

'But who could it have been?'

'I don't know. Anyway, I went on to Merriby as I've told you and on my return parked the car at the usual place by the jetty. I couldn't see any lights this time, but kept looking back over my shoulder all the way to the tower. And just before I reached the enclosure I saw two lights again. They were moving back from the jetty to the main road.'

She felt the blood leave her face. 'Who do you think it was? The police?'

He nodded despondently. 'It seems like it now.'

'And you're thinking that after you left for Merriby they came here and knocked on the door? But why should they do that?'

'To confirm that you had stayed here, I suppose,' he muttered.

'Then why didn't they answer when I called out?'

'Perhaps they didn't want to give themselves away. They wanted to wait until I got back.'

'But why should they do all this? You aren't doing anything wrong here.'

'Of course I am. I'm occupying a place that isn't mine.'

'But it's a ruin. Nobody uses it.'

'That's no excuse. It's just the kind of offence they'd love to pin on me.' He shook his head moodily, turned away. 'I've been afraid this would happen. That car of yours

– it made it too easy for them to trace me.'

The thought she might be the cause of his losing the tower made her feel sick. She could not help but protest. 'You don't know it was the police, Danny. The tapping on the door could have been the bush. And the car might have belonged to a courting couple. If it belonged to the police why should they drive off when you came back?' Her voice gained a little confidence as she developed her idea. 'Surely it would have been much more likely they'd have followed you here.'

He refused to be comforted. 'They've probably got some reason for it. Perhaps there was only one policeman and he wanted help before arresting me.' He turned restlessly towards her. 'I think we ought to go. I don't want them to catch you here.'

Somehow she had to resist this disruptive wedge that was splitting them apart. If they left now, in these circumstances, she did not know when she would see him again. 'Let's be sensible, Danny. If it was the police they'd be certain to take my car number, so whatever happens they'll know I've been here. So what's the point in running? Let's make ourselves comfortable instead, and have tea.'

For the moment she forgot her father's danger in the thought that, if the police did come, he might fare better if she were with him.

'Come on,' she urged, seeing her argument was carrying some weight. 'I'm sure it wasn't the police. But if it was I'm not going to miss my cup of tea for all the policemen in Lidsborough.'

His hesitation, his obvious unwillingness to go, warmed her with its implications. 'I suppose you're right' he muttered at last. 'All right. We'll stay another half hour and see what happens.'

After that he made an effort to conceal his anxiety, but his restless eyes and the fidgeting of his hands betrayed him. She had never seen him so nervous before. Once he went out on the landing, stood there a full minute listening. On his return he gave her a tight, ashamed smile. 'Sorry. I thought I heard something.'

She rose from the basket chair, took his hand and led him to it. 'Sit there for a while. That packing case is enough to make anyone restless. And have a drink. It'll help to relax you.'

She poured him a large glass of sherry and put it on the table before him. 'Stop worrying, Danny. If it was the police they'd have been back here long before this. Is there anything else that's worrying you?'

He gave a sharp, startled glance before staring moodily down at the floor. 'No,' he muttered. 'Except I don't want to lose this place.'

She put an arm around his shoulders. 'You're not going to lose it, Danny. Your nerves are bad tonight: you're looking on the black side of everything. It'll seem different tomorrow...'

He suddenly stiffened in his chair. His eyes were wide, the tiny scar livid against his white cheeks.

'What is it?' she whispered, frightened again. 'What's the matter?'

She listened but could hear nothing for a squall of wind that shuddered the tower to its foundations. Then she heard the sound too, a hollow thudding from below like the distant beating of a bass drum.

Danny jumped to his feet, jarring the table. His glass fell to the floor, shattering to fragments and sending a red stream glistening over the bare boards. His eyes, bright and hunted, searched the room as though looking for a hiding place. For a moment Beris was equally panic-stricken as nightmare visions of police courts, with their disastrous consequences to her father, flashed in her mind. Then she pulled herself together and caught hold of Danny's arm.

'We must let them in. Otherwise it'll look much worse.'

His face was a white parchment mask as he went down the stairs with her. She wanted to comfort him but could think of nothing to say. As he stood alongside her in front of the door she felt the violent trembling of his body. His voice was cracked, unrecognizable.

'Who's there?'

The answering voice was torn away in the wind. 'Unlock it,' Beris urged. 'There's no point in arguing with them.'

With infinite reluctance he turned the lock. The wind flung the door back with rude violence. For a moment the threshing bush outside hid the waiting figure from their sight. Then the bush blew aside and Beris gave a gasp of shock.

18

It was Tommy, a small, dishevelled figure in pullover and jeans, who stood in the doorway. Beris, the first to recover from her surprise, pulled him inside and slammed the door against the wind.

'Tommy! What on earth are you doing here?'

In the torchlight the boy's face was pinched and cold. He turned to Danny, teeth chattering, shrill voice urgent. 'It's the cops, Danny. They're round at our house waitin' for you.'

Beris caught hold of the boy's shoulder,

swung him towards her. 'The police – at your house! But what are they doing there?'

For once in his life Tommy was very near to tears. 'They've come for Danny, miss. They asked Ma Johnson where he was, and she said she didn't know. Then they came to my bedroom to ask me, an' I said I didn't know either. But as soon as they went downstairs again I ran 'ere to tip Danny off.'

She noticed how violently the boy was shivering and for the moment concern for him drove all other thoughts from her head. 'Why didn't you put a coat on, Tommy? It's terribly cold and wet outside.'

'I couldn't, miss. They were waitin' for Danny downstairs and my coat was on the hallstand. I 'ad to get out through the bedroom window.'

His knees were badly grazed and his pullover torn. She pulled him towards her, a lump in her throat. 'You might have killed yourself.'

'It wasn't too bad,' he muttered. 'I jumped on the wash-house roof and slid down to the yard.'

She turned to Danny. 'It doesn't sound as if the police can know about this place after all. But what else do they want you for?'

It was Tommy who answered her. 'It's about a burglary, miss.'

'A burglary!'

'Yes, miss. Some house that's been broken

into. They think Danny's got somethin' to do with it.'

'But when was this?'

'Tonight. I heard one of 'em say some time between eight and nine o'clock.'

She could not suppress a gasp of dismay. In the torchlight tears were rolling down Tommy's cheeks like glistening gems. 'I knew you'd been 'ere during that time, Danny, but I couldn't tell 'em without breaking my promise. But Miss Carnes can tell 'em, can't she?' He turned his pleading eyes to her. 'You won't let him go to prison, will you, miss?'

Beris felt as if some nerve in her mind had received a blow, paralysing her voice. She could only shake her head mutely.

The boy brushed a sleeve across his eyes to clear them. 'Then it'll be all right, won't it? They can't do anything then.'

Danny's voice made her start with its harshness: 'You're staying away from the house. You're not getting involved in this.'

'But I'm already involved, Danny.'

'I don't want your help, I tell you,' he almost shouted at her. 'I'll handle this alone.'

Tommy's fearful eyes were darting from one of them to the other. She squeezed his arm. 'Run upstairs and warm yourself over the stove. We'll join you in a minute.'

The boy hesitated, then did as he was told. She waited until he had vanished up the circular staircase before turning to Danny, her voice quiet.

'I must witness for you, otherwise they'll never believe you've been here the whole evening.'

His face was a twisted mask. 'I haven't been here the whole evening. I was away from six-fifty until after half past nine.'

'Did you meet anyone while you were in Merriby – anyone who could give you an alibi?'

He shook his head.

'Then you've no proof to give them that you went there.'

'Not a scrap,' he taunted.

'Then we mustn't tell them you went,' she said, ignoring his tone. 'We'll say we've been together since six-thirty.'

All his bitterness was back in full measure. 'How do you know I didn't do it? I'd plenty of time while I was out.'

'Don't be ridiculous. I know you didn't.'

'That's not true. I noticed your expression when Tommy mentioned the time it had been committed. You're not certain at all.'

'Danny,' she pleaded. 'Don't let's start quarrelling. There's too much at stake. I'm trying to help you.'

'I don't want your help. Can't you understand plain English?'

'But if I don't witness for you, you won't have an alibi. And without one you might find yourself in serious trouble. You needn't worry about anything happening to me. They'll have to believe my story.'

His mood seemed to change, to lose some of its defiance. 'It means your father will hear we've been meeting,' he muttered. 'And I don't want that to happen.'

Things had gone too far for that to worry her.

'I intend telling them whether you agree to it or not,' she told Danny. 'If I can't do it at the house, then I'll go to the police station. You can't stop me, so it's far better you let me do it now. It'll look much better for us both.'

She checked him as he began sullenly protesting again. 'There's no time to argue, Danny. The longer we're away the worse it'll look. Let's turn the lamp out and go.'

For the moment he did not argue further. He put his mackintosh around Tommy and covered his own shoulders with a blanket from his palliasse. Then turned out the lamp, locked the door, and started down the towpath. The rain had ceased, but a fine spray from the river kept sweeping into their faces. Danny did not speak a word until they were descending the bank that led to the jetty. Then he turned to Beris.

'Don't come with me all the way. Drop me off at the bottom of the road. I'd much rather do it that way.'

'But I must come, Danny. It's the only way to make them believe you.'

His words blew into her face like torn leaves as the wind swooped out of the darkness. 'It's not only that... If we tell them everything I'm going to lose the tower–'

She waited until all three of them were in the car, Danny at her side, Tommy in the rear seat. Then she turned to Danny.

'I know how you feel about the tower, and the last thing I want is to tell them about it. But what alternative is there? If we can't prove where we've been they'll become suspicious.'

He said nothing, staring out into the darkness with bitter, unseeing eyes. She wanted to comfort him, but there was nothing more to say. Starting the engine, she turned the car and drove slowly back to Lambert Street, her headlights picking out the tangled grass that lay in windswept ridges around them.

The car jolted over the old railway track. The wartime pillbox stood out in the lights, ghostly and derelict. As they turned a slight bend in the road the figure of a man suddenly appeared. He was leaning against the wind, one hand holding on to his hat. As they drew nearer to him Tommy let out an excited shout. 'Look, miss. It's Mr Mac-Taggit.'

Her surprise was exceeded by her relief.

There was no one in the world she would sooner have encountered at that moment. Drawing level with him she pulled up and threw open the rear door. MacTaggit peered in, recognized them, and gave a sharp bark of relief.

'Just what I've been hoping for.' He climbed into the car and thrust his gnome-like face at Tommy.

'I guessed this was where you'd gone. How did you get out – from your bedroom window?'

Tommy nodded.

'You imp of Satan. Do you realize you might have killed yourself? Ma Johnson's nearly throwing a fit back there. She thinks you've run away from home.'

Beris had twisted round in her seat. 'Is it true the police are blaming Danny for a burglary that was committed tonight?'

'Not blaming him, lassie. But they're waiting to question him.'

'How do you come to be out here?' she asked curiously.

'A friend at court tipped me off and I came straight round. When I found Tommy had done a bunk I took a guess where he had gone. I didn't say anything to the police – just slipped out to warn Danny not to run away or do anything foolish.'

'We're just going to tell them what fools they're making of themselves. We've spent the evening together in the lighthouse.'

'All the evening?' MacTaggit asked, turning his sharp eyes on the silent Danny.

Beris answered for him, voice defiant. 'Yes. I picked him up at six-fifteen; we went straight round to the lighthouse, and we've been there ever since. That should be good enough for them, shouldn't it?'

MacTaggit grinned wryly. 'If you say it like that, it should be good enough for anybody.' He turned to Danny again. 'I hadn't dared to hope your sister would be with you tonight. It's a great stroke of luck for you, laddie.'

Danny stared morosely out into the darkness without answering. MacTaggit's voice grew testy. 'What's the matter with you? Lost your tongue?'

Beris broke in hastily. 'He's worrying about my getting involved with the police. I've told him it can't be helped.'

MacTaggit frowned heavily. 'I don't see how it can be, although it's a great pity. If the two of you were alone all evening, he has no alibi at all without your testimony.'

At that Danny swung round sullenly. 'They have to prove me guilty – they can't do that just because I haven't an alibi. Thousands of people in Lidsborough wouldn't have alibis tonight – doesn't prove they're all burglars.'

'I know that well enough, laddie. But remember – you're a suspect already. Even if they couldn't pin anything on you – and don't be too sure of that – they'd be more certain than ever you're the man they're looking for. And that won't make things any easier for you in the future.'

'In other words you admit that once you're down they go on kicking you,' Danny sneered.

MacTaggit's temper, never renowned for its stability, had been badly ruffled by his walk in the blustering wind. Anxiety for both Danny and Beris did nothing to compose it. 'Don't talk like a fool, man,' he snapped. 'They can't be blamed for suspecting you – all the facts they've got seem to point your way.' He turned to Beris, his voice softening. 'I wish there was some way of keeping you out of this, lassie. But if you want to clear him I can't see it.'

'What about the tower?' she asked. 'Danny doesn't want to lose it. Couldn't I say we'd been for a drive instead? Or that we'd been sitting in the car down at the waterfront?'

MacTaggit shook his head firmly. 'Never. They'd ask you where you went, what you did, who you saw – they'd trip you up in no time. And then you'd both be in trouble. And you can't say you've been sitting in the car down there since six-fifteen – it's nearly eleven o'clock. No, lassie; tell 'em the truth or you'll both end up in a mess.'

She turned to Danny appealingly. 'I'm

sorry, Danny, but what else can I do?'

He neither looked at her nor spoke. Biting her lip she put the car in gear and drove slowly on. They entered Lambert Street by the lower end. Under a street lamp near number 57 they could see a stationary police car and a policeman on the pavement outside the house. As she started up the street Danny put a sudden hand on her arm, forcing her to pull up. His voice was urgent, frantic.

'I don't want your help – can't you understand that? I'm getting out here and you drive straight past. Go on – leave me to do things my own way.'

MacTaggit's bushy, uplifted eyebrows were right behind Beris's shoulder. He answered for her. 'Stop talking like a damned fool. This is your one chance to be proven innocent.'

Danny threw open the door. 'For God's sake leave me alone, both of you.' With that he slammed the door closed and started up the street. Beris jumped out after him, the wind striking her face like a blow.

'Danny… Danny, wait for me.'

He did not pause or look back. She ran after him, catching him a few yards from the gate. The constable, young and irresolute, stared at them curiously.

'Danny; try to understand … it's for your sake. Don't look at me like that, Danny.'

She tried to catch hold of him but he pushed her roughly aside and walked on towards the house. The constable, sure of himself now, came forward to meet them.

19

Late the following afternoon, as the winter twilight was closing in, Beris went to the station to meet her father's train. He had wired her that morning giving his time of arrival. *Arrive 4.15,* the telegram had read, *Love, Father.*

Lidsborough was not at its best that day. The wind, although not as boisterous as it had been earlier, had switched to the east and was carrying now on its gaunt wings a mixture of sleet and rain. In winter Lidsborough seemed to possess the power of absorbing colour and resolving it into a drab uniform grey, and on this afternoon it had excelled itself. Everything was grey, the buildings, the wet streets, the lowering sky. People walked about the city like automatons, going through the motions of living as if it were an unpleasant duty.

The railway station was a bare, ugly building, its glass roof blackened by the smoke of a century. It appeared to have been designed to give maximum discomfort to all who waited there, for with each of its three sides containing a wide, open entrance, unlimited hospitality was offered to the wind, no matter from which quarter it blew. A half-hour wait in Lidsborough station on a winter day was an experience strangers long remembered.

As usual the London train was late, and Beris sought shelter behind the tobacconist kiosk that stood before Platform 6. For the first time in her life she was not looking forward to greeting her father home. Knowing it was only a matter of time before he heard of the previous night's happenings, she had decided to tell him everything herself, and was dreading the ordeal. On her most optimistic assumption – that he might show some tolerance regarding her relations with Danny – the fact remained that she had been deliberately deceiving him, and it seemed inevitable that his trust in her would suffer as a consequence.

As she stirred restlessly behind the kiosk, activity broke out on Platform 6. A ticket collector walked ponderously towards the barrier, unlocked it, and pulled one gate aside. Three porters rose reluctantly from their trolleys and pulled them through the gate on to the platform. Three minutes later, with a hiss of steam and clanking of pistons, the 11.30 from London drew into Platform 6.

Shivering as much from nervousness as from the cold, Beris joined the small group of people crowded before the barrier. The train was half empty, and she soon saw her father, a chunky, aggressive figure in his black overcoat and Homburg, striding a few paces ahead of a porter. He caught sight of her a few seconds later. Thrusting his ticket at the collector he pushed his way eagerly forward through the crowd.

'Hello, darling.' He put an arm around her and kissed her cheek. 'It's good to be back.'

She felt oddly shy with him. 'It's good to have you back. What sort of a trip have you had? Was it successful?'

He winked at her and squeezed her hand. 'Couldn't have been better. How's everything at home?'

It was difficult keeping her voice steady. 'Much the same as usual.'

His keen, pale-blue eyes were suddenly attentive. 'You're looking a bit pale. You aren't off-colour, are you?'

'Of course not. I'm as fit as a fiddle.' Hastily she diverted attention from herself. 'Hadn't we better be moving? Your porter's waiting for you. The car is round at the side entrance.'

They walked the breadth of the station, coming to a small and draughty car park. Here he hesitated, drawing her back out of the rain. His voice and expression were apologetic. 'I've got an important business telegram this morning that ought to be attended to right away. Would you mind very much going home by taxi and lending me your car? I'm sorry but it really is important.'

'Will it take long?' she asked, afraid of what he might hear while in town.

'Not more than an hour. Probably less. I'll come straight home afterwards.'

She wondered why he did not suggest she go with him to the factory. 'It's all right, of course. Only don't be too long, will you?'

He squeezed her hand again. 'Not likely. I'm too keen to be with my girl again...' Fumbling in his overcoat pocket he pulled out a small parcel which he handed to her. 'A little thing I saw in a shop down there,' he said gruffly. 'I thought it would go nicely with your new evening frock. Go on – open it.'

It was a heavy silver bracelet, beautifully chased. She stared down at it with some emotion.

'Well, do you like it?'

'It's beautiful. But you shouldn't have bought it.'

'Why not?' His shrewd eyes searched her face again. 'There is something the matter with you. What is it?'

The story had to be told in the right surroundings, at home. She made herself laugh. 'Nonsense. You're imagining things.'

Leaning forward she kissed his cheek. 'Thank you very much. Now go and get your business done and then hurry home. Here are the car keys.'

'I'll see you to your taxi first.'

She stopped him. 'No; don't bother. I may call in one or two shops before going back.'

'All right, but don't be too long. I want you home when I get there.'

With that he led the porter to the car. She gave him a last wave and then turned back into the station. Braced as she had been for the ordeal, she now felt let down and badly in need of moral support. MacTaggit came at once to her mind – she had phoned him early that morning only to learn that an important case would keep him occupied until four o'clock. She wondered if there was a chance of seeing him now. The desire to find out became irresistible as she drew nearer a telephone kiosk.

His peppery voice was a comfort in itself. 'Of course, lassie. I'm only sorry I couldn't see you earlier. When is your father due home?'

'He's here now: I've just met him in.' She went on to explain what had happened, finishing somewhat plaintively: 'I've got an hour to pass before I tell him, and I'd love a few words with you first, if you can manage it.'

His voice became astonishingly gentle.

'Come right away, lassie. No, wait; give me just ten minutes and I'll be clear. As a matter of fact a little point regarding Danny has just cropped up and I wanted to discuss it with you. I was going to phone you tonight.'

Hypersensitive as she was at that moment, it took little to alarm her. 'Something about Danny? What's happened now?'

'Now don't start worrying. We'll sort it all out between us. See you in ten minutes' time.'

After leaving the station Carnes drove through the city centre and to the southern limits of the old town. Here he drew up outside a telephone kiosk and made a call. He then turned the car and backed well down a narrow side street. Georgian houses rose stiffly on either side, typists dimly visible in the yellow light that seeped through their grilled basement windows. Rain beat steadily down on the cobblestones and ran in rivulets along the narrow gutters. Lifting his overcoat collar to conceal his face Carnes lit a cigar, his eyes fixed on the end of the street.

After five minutes he looked down impatiently at his watch. A few minutes more and then Clinton turned the street corner, his hands thrust deep into his belted mackintosh, his trilby hat slanted down to shield his face. Carnes threw open the car door, motioning him to enter.

'Well,' he grunted, 'I got your wire this morning. What did it mean – important developments?'

Clinton removed his dripping hat and brushed his smooth hair with a handkerchief.

'Sorry I had to send it, sir, but you told me to let you know if anything happened.'

The smell of brilliantine was filling the car. Carnes waved an impatient hand. 'Never mind the apologies. I was coming home today in any case. Tell me what's happened.'

Clinton wiped his face, dabbed at his moustache, and returned the handkerchief to his pocket. 'Have you heard about the burglary we had last night, sir?'

Carnes stiffened. 'Another one?'

'Yes – a private house in Trinbury Park. Done by the same character who pulled the first job – or so the police think.'

In the brief hush the patter of rain on the car roof sounded loud and urgent. Carnes's voice was hoarse. 'Danny's involved, isn't he? Come on – out with it.'

'I'm afraid so.'

'Have the police got him?'

'No; that's the queer thing about it. They've had to let him go again.'

Carnes gave an audible grunt of relief. 'Suppose you tell me the whole story instead of giving it to me in bits. Just what has happened?'

The enquiry agent pulled out a packet of cigarettes. 'Have you seen your daughter yet, sir?'

Carnes scowled his displeasure at this mention of Beris. 'Yes; she met me in. Why?'

'I wondered if she said anything to you.'

'What could my daughter say? What the hell are you getting at?'

Clinton eyed him warily. The old fool had a devil of a temper … he didn't want a smack across the face for his pains… He tried to sound sympathetic. 'I'm afraid your daughter has become friendly with Meadows. She's been seeing a good deal of him recently, and it's ended up by her getting mixed up with the police.'

For a moment Carnes looked as if he had been hit with a bludgeon. Then he turned on Clinton like a savage bull. 'You must be mad. My daughter can't bear the sight of him. What the hell's your game, giving me a cock-and-bull story like this?'

'You're paying me to get you the truth,' Clinton said sullenly. 'Don't blame me if you don't like it.'

The industrialist's eyes were inflamed and his breathing heavy. After a long moment he drew back. 'All right – tell me all you know. But, by God, it had better be the truth.'

'Why should I lie to you?' Clinton protested. 'I tell you your daughter has been seeing Meadows. I've been keeping an eye on him at nights, as you told me to, and I've learned a good deal more about his movements. On Sundays he usually sees me, and once or twice a week he takes a girl called Madge out, but the rest of the week he goes out on his own, leaving home just after six and not getting back until after eleven. He doesn't tell anyone where he goes, but last week I solved the mystery. He goes to an old lighthouse by the river, and that's where he's been seeing your daughter while you've been away.'

Carnes had the expression of a man expecting the whole world to come tumbling down around his ears at any moment. 'Meeting Beris – in an old lighthouse?'

'Yes. You know the one – a mile or so past the timber yards. Stands on its own on the river bank. As long as I remember it hasn't been used.'

'But it's impossible, man. I tell you she can't bear the sight of him. When I told her he was back in town, she was more upset than I was.'

Clinton shrugged. 'Maybe she was. But I tell you she's been with him nearly every night this week. That's how she got herself mixed up with the police last night.'

Carnes was as alert and vigilant now as a threatened animal. 'Go on. What happened?'

'The police went round to pick him up about ten-thirty last night. The housebreak had been between eight and nine, and the *modus operandi* pointed straight at Meadows. About eleven he arrived home in company with your daughter. She must have witnessed that she'd been with him all the evening because they left without him.'

In spite of his deep concern for Beris, there was relief in Carnes's voice. 'But that means he can't have done it.'

Clinton blew smoke out slowly through his nostrils. 'That's what it should mean. But I'm afraid that isn't all the story. You see, I know she wasn't with him all the evening.'

It was some seconds before Carnes understood. 'You mean she gave false evidence?'

'That's all it could be, or they'd have fetched him in.'

Sweat had broken out on Carnes's forehead. 'Good God. I didn't want him involved in a scandal, but not on terms like that. She must have gone out of her senses.'

Clinton coughed, hiding his expression with his hand. 'Sorry, sir, but I think she had another reason for doing it. I think she's grown pretty fond of him.'

Carnes was now a man wandering in a nightmare world where everything familiar changed substance under his hands. 'How do you know she gave false evidence?' he muttered after a pause.

'I know because he wasn't with her for

most of the evening. He left her alone in the lighthouse and drove off in her car.'

Carne's face turned a sickly grey. 'In her car? You don't mean–'

Clinton did not spare him. 'You've got it – that's when he did the housebreak. Listen, and I'll tell you how I know…'

When he finished there was a hushed silence in the car, broken only by the swill of rain and Carnes's heavy breathing.

'Good God,' he muttered at last. 'It's incredible. She could land herself in dock as an accessory.' Another pause and then his powerful hands clenched. 'You say you think MacTaggit's behind all this?'

The enquiry agent nodded. 'That's my guess. From what I can gather he's got a soft spot for Meadows, and without any thought for your daughter's safety, has used her to help straighten Meadows out. From what I've seen of him now, neither of 'em has a cat-in-hell's chance. Meadows doesn't look the type he is, and doesn't act the type either – particularly in front of girls – but I've found out that underneath he's as twisted as any crook I've come across. If she's not careful your daughter's going to find that out one of these days.'

Carne's face was as grim and minatory as a piece of frozen granite. 'All right. You get along now and keep your mouth shut on what you know. I'm going to see MacTaggit.'

20

As always MacTaggit showed pleasure at seeing Beris, meeting her at the door and leading her into his office. Evidence of his industry was everywhere, particularly on his desk where reference books, papers, and files were scattered in great disarray. It was obvious that he was not a tidy worker.

Beris took the chair he offered her, waving an amused arm at the desk. 'You look as if you've had an earthquake in here.'

MacTaggit sat down at his desk, shoving aside a pile of files to give himself a clear view of her. 'Aye; I'm a messy devil and it's been a brute of a day. It's a good job I've got a secretary to clear up after me.' He leaned forward on his elbows, a contented motion, and gave her a roguish grin. 'After seeing nothing but sullen faces all day, you're a pretty picture sitting there. I like that coat you're wearing. It suits your colouring.'

Sensing his need to relax for a moment she tried to enter his mood and to chat light-heartedly with him. In spite of everything she found it surprisingly easy. MacTaggit had a way of taking a moment out of its chronological context and making it a thing of pleasure in its own right. After a few minutes he tapped the telephone alongside him.

'I had a call from Mrs Johnson not half an hour before you phoned me. She had a bit of news about Danny.'

At once Beris felt her body stiffen. 'Not the police again, surely?'

'No. Something else that I've been afraid might happen. Danny arrived home just after two o'clock with a week's pay in lieu of notice in his pocket.'

She gave a gasp of protest. 'You mean Jardine's have discharged him? But why?'

He shrugged. 'You know what people are like – they always argue there's no smoke without fire. And they'll have heard this was his second affair with the police since he returned to Lidsborough.'

'But he wasn't charged this time – he was cleared. How have they even found out about it?'

'Some mischief-maker has tipped them off,' MacTaggit growled. 'I'd like to know who it was.'

She was frightened. 'But it's the worst thing that could have happened, coming on top of his losing the tower.' She paused. 'I suppose he has lost it?'

'Oh, aye,' MacTaggit said gloomily. 'They'll never let him use it in the future.'

'He's going to become terribly bitter

254

again. Can't you do something for him?'

MacTaggit scowled, rubbed his chin. 'The difficulty is getting him the right kind of work. The lad's educated – work as a labourer would only frustrate him more than ever.'

'But surely there's plenty of office work these days?'

MacTaggit's scowl deepened. 'They're pretty finicky in those jobs – that's where his record goes against him.' A sudden wicked grin superimposed itself upon his scowl. 'Do you know what I was going to suggest when I phoned you about it?'

She shook her head.

'I was going to suggest your father gave him work. He must have plenty of jobs in that factory of his.'

She did not know whether to take him seriously or not. 'Surely you don't mean it?'

His voice became disturbingly serious. 'I couldn't mean anything more. Until last night, thanks to you, the lad was coming along very nicely. Now, because of that damned robbery, he's had two very nasty set-backs. He's lost his job and his old tower, and something has to be done for him quickly. It isn't going to be easy for me to find him suitable work, but your father could do it in five minutes. And why not? After all, one good thing came out of last night's affair. Whatever the police go on thinking, we know now the lad's innocent of these thefts. And that's something really big.'

Until now she had been able to rely on his advice and support on the road she was taking. Now, because of her previous night's deception, she realized that in the future she would have to journey on alone... It was a cold, lonely thought and made her voice falter. 'Things are bad for him, aren't they?'

'They aren't too good, lassie, I'm afraid. That's why I wanted to speak to your father.'

'But he wouldn't consider it for a moment.'

'Maybe not... But I'd still like a meeting with him. Try to arrange one for me, will you?'

'Yes, I'll try. The trouble is, he's certain to ask me why you want to see him. And if I tell him he'll never agree.'

'Then tell a fib and say you don't know. Do you mind doing that?'

She smiled ruefully. 'I've told so many these last few weeks I don't suppose another will make much difference. But I think I'll have to wait a day or two before asking him. Don't forget I still have to tell him what happened last night. He might take a poor view of me for a time – he has a pretty healthy temper.'

In spite of her tone, almost light-hearted, her apprehension was obvious enough, and

MacTaggit showed instant concern.

'I keep forgetting the risks you've run for that lad. You're quite right – it is too dangerous to ask him yet. Leave it a while and see how things go.'

She shook her head, deeply troubled. 'For Danny's sake we can't wait very long, can we?'

MacTaggit shifted, scowled, then let out an impatient grunt. 'Forget Danny for a while. You're just as important as he is. Leave it until things straighten themselves out. I'll see what I can do in other directions.'

Amused at this switch in his concern, she was about to comment on it when she heard a man's voice coming from the adjoining room. Muffled though it was, it sounded familiar and she listened more closely. Her eyes were rounded with alarm when she lifted them to MacTaggit.

'That's my father next door.'

He started. 'Are you sure?'

'Quite sure. What is he doing here?'

MacTaggit shook his head. They both faced the closed door, Beris feeling as if a strap were tightening over her temples. A few seconds later MacTaggit's secretary knocked and entered the office. 'There's a Mr Carnes to see you, Mr MacTaggit. Shall I ask him to wait?'

MacTaggit motioned the girl to close the

door behind her, then turned to Beris. Even at that moment his appearance, with his bright excited eyes, made her think of a mischievous squirrel.

'Well, lassie,' he chuckled. 'It looks as if the mountain has come to Mahomet, and without an invitation at that. What would you like to do?' He pointed at the second door that led out into the corridor. 'He shouldn't see you if you go out that way. Or would you rather stay and hear what it's all about?'

Her first inclination had been to escape. Now she hesitated. 'What can he want?'

'I haven't the slightest idea. But if you want to find out you're welcome to stay.'

A last second of hesitation and she made up her mind. 'It's possible he's heard about last night. If you'll risk having a scene in your office I'll stay.'

MacTaggit gave her a congratulatory wink. 'Then sit down and try to look unconcerned.' He returned behind his desk, then grinned at the puzzled secretary. 'All right, June, show Mr Carnes in, will you?'

Beris waited, heart pounding heavily. Her father appeared in the doorway. On seeing her he gave a start, then his face set in grim lines. She knew what it meant and felt slightly sick.

He nodded to her, then turned his attention to MacTaggit, his heavy jaw jutting forward. They faced one another across the desk, an aggressive bulldog facing a defiant terrier.

'You're the fellow who used to come round to my house seven years ago, aren't you?' Carnes growled.

MacTaggit nodded cheerfully. 'Aye; that's me. I'm glad to see you, Mr Carnes – I've been wanting a word with you. How are you these days?'

Carnes ignored his outstretched hand. 'I haven't come on a courtesy call, MacTaggit. I want to know what your game is – why you've been influencing my daughter into seeing these damned delinquents of yours.'

MacTaggit lifted a bushy eyebrow comically. 'My game? I don't think I'm quite following you.'

Carnes took a step forward, his voice threatening. 'Don't play the innocent with me, MacTaggit. I've just heard what happened last night, and, by God, I feel like wringing your neck for being the cause of it.'

At this threat MacTaggit forgot his control and began bristling. Beris hastily intervened, tugging at her father's arm.

'Mr MacTaggit isn't to blame for anything I've done. If you've any complaints to make, please wait until we get home.'

He turned his inflamed eyes on her. 'A month ago you were as sorry as I was to hear Danny had returned to Lidsborough. Now you spend your evenings alone with him in an abandoned lighthouse and even witness for him in front of the police. You change as much as that and then expect me to believe no one's been influencing you?'

'It hasn't anything to do with influence,' she said unsteadily. 'I'm just seeing things in a different light, that's all.'

'And who's shown you that different light?' He swung back on the probation officer. 'What kind of sentimental trash have you been giving her, MacTaggit?'

MacTaggit's eyes were wickedly bright. 'Do you really want to hear it, Mr Carnes? It's pretty strong medicine.'

Carnes's eyes were slits of ice-blue glass. 'Go on,' he growled. 'I'll give you a chance to state your case.'

MacTaggit motioned to a chair. 'Why not make yourself comfortable while you listen?'

'I'll stand. Now get on with it.'

MacTaggit shrugged and leaned back in his chair. 'All right. Here are my views on your adoption of the lad. You never wanted the boy for his own sake: you wanted him as a plaything for your daughter. Do you deny it?'

Carnes's voice was as ominous as overhead thunder. 'Don't try to cross-examine me, MacTaggit.'

MacTaggit grinned. 'All right; that's my allegation. It wouldn't have been so bad in itself – plenty of folks adopt children out of selfish motives – provided you'd given the little chap a chance to win your affections later. But you never did. You never saw him as anything else but a toy for your daughter – a plaything to be on hand when he was wanted, or put aside when he wasn't.'

'Are you saying I didn't give him a good home?'

MacTaggit's expression became quizzical. 'What do you call a good home? I'd like to know.'

'You know what I mean well enough, MacTaggit. A place where a child gets good food, good clothes, and good education.'

'Is that all? Is that all you gave your daughter?'

'What the devil do you mean? What else can you give a child?'

MacTaggit let his chair fall forward with a bump, making Beris start. He thrust his sharp, condemnatory face forward. 'And they let people like you adopt children! Don't you know that none of those things matter a damn without affection – that without it a child's better off in an orphanage. If I had to choose between a wealthy home without affection and a hovel with it, I'd choose the hovel every time. I do – I choose 'em every day.'

There was a brief silence, followed by Carnes's growl. 'Who told you I never gave him affection – Danny?'

MacTaggit shook his head. 'No one had to tell me – I saw it. I watched the way you treated him when I was there. Little things – but they all added up. And what I didn't see I gathered from the things I heard. It was one of the reasons I recommended he was sent to an approved school. I could only see him getting worse while he was with you.'

Carnes's voice was incredulous. 'Are you saying it was *my* fault he turned out the way he did?'

MacTaggit met his challenge head on. 'Aye; if you want the truth, I am. Foster parents like you make me think of bad shepherds. You offer to look after another man's sheep, but when they're entrusted in your care you don't give 'em a tenth of the attention you give your own flock. Your indifference turned that lad bitter, Carnes, and a bitter child becomes a bad child and often a bad adult as well.'

The storm broke. Carnes's clenched fist crashed down on the desk. 'You're a damned liar, MacTaggit. You'd rather believe in your delinquent mongrels than in the people they rob. And listening to you I'm not surprised – you've the same kind of rotten, twisted mind. You'll take a decent girl like my daughter, play on her feelings, and then use her as a handkerchief to wipe the filthy nose of one of your Teddy boys. By God; I've a good mind to lay my hands on you.'

Beris had run back to his side and was struggling to restrain him. He pushed her away and swung back on MacTaggit. 'That boy got the same treatment as my own daughter, but those muck-raking eyes of yours were only looking for dirt. You had to find an excuse for him somehow.'

MacTaggit, not giving an inch before this onslaught, gave a snort of disgust. 'You never gave the lad a scrap of affection, and you know it.'

'What the hell was I supposed to do – kiss him on both cheeks every time I entered the room? He was a boy – I didn't want a sissie for a son.'

'You don't get sissies by giving children affection, whether they're girls or boys. Your duty was to give the lad the same treatment as your own daughter, and you didn't do it.'

'I tell you you're a damned liar. Until he began stealing that little mongrel got everything my daughter got. Ask her – she'll tell you.' In his anger, his outraged rectitude, Carnes did the thing Beris feared – turned to her for confirmation. She hesitated as long as she could, her mouth dry.

'No, Daddy,' she faltered. 'You didn't mean to hurt him – I know that – but you did make more of a fuss of me. I'm sorry, but it's true.'

Shock at her rebellion took much of the

fire from him. 'So you're against me too, are you?' he said slowly.

'I'm not against you at all' she protested. 'Nothing has changed between us. It's just that I want to make things up to Danny, to let him know that we're sorry...'

'Sorry?' he repeated in amazement. 'What in heaven's name have we to be sorry about? It wasn't our fault he had a bad streak in him.'

'He hadn't a bad streak in him, Daddy. No child has.'

Carnes's fist came down again. 'Rubbish. Absolute bunkum. It's in some of 'em when they're born and nothing can change it. You'll find that out when you've seen a bit more of life, m' girl.'

'Carnes,' MacTaggit interrupted dryly. 'Am I right in believing you're a bit of a churchman?'

Carnes swung round aggressively. 'What's that got to do with it?'

'Quite a bit, I think. If you, as a churchman, believe some people are born bad, how do you square that up with your faith in a just God? The Sins of the Fathers, I suppose?'

'Well?' Carnes growled. 'What's wrong with that?'

MacTaggit wrinkled his face in distaste. 'I've never seen the justice of it, and I don't think you would – not if you'd been punished all your life because thirty years before you were born your grandfather lifted his firm's petty cash. But let's assume for the moment that you are right, and that some children are born sinful. Then what are your feelings about the law and punishment?'

'What are you getting at?' Carnes growled suspiciously.

'Do you believe it's right to punish people for wrongdoing?'

Carnes gave a contemptuous laugh. 'It'd be a damned queer world if they weren't punished. Of course I do.'

MacTaggit scratched his ear. 'But aren't you being inconsistent then? If some children are born bad, then they can't help being bad, can they? They can't help stealing money from their father, for example, or from their teacher at school.'

'Don't be such a fool, man. Of course they can help it.'

'Not on your argument they can't. They can't help it any more than a boy born with a squint can help squinting. You're saying they're predestined to sin, just as the other boy is predestined to squint. Then surely – still using your argument – it must be quite unfair to punish them for it.'

Carnes stared at him resentfully. 'If there was no law and no punishment, there would be anarchy. Society would collapse and you know it.'

MacTaggit shrugged. 'Whether society would collapse or not isn't the point. As a churchman you shouldn't want to perpetuate it on an injustice, and if you believe all you've said, it's clearly unjust to punish people for doing what God made them do. In fact, it all sounds a little presumptuous to me.'

Carnes flushed resentfully at his sarcasm. 'You're an atheist, of course,' he grunted.

MacTaggit gave a twisted smile. 'If it was the only way I could become charitable, then I'd become one. But I don't believe it is. I think some of you chaps have got your religion all mixed up. You aren't charitable to your fellow men: you aren't even charitable to your God.' One of MacTaggit's eyebrows lifted, a comical gesture in spite of his words. 'Do you realize what your argument does? – it passes the baby for Danny's delinquency from yourself to God, which is surely rather irreverent of you.'

'You're nothing but a sarcastic fool,' Carnes growled angrily. 'You know as well as I do that all children aren't born equal.'

MacTaggit leaned forward sharply. 'If you mean they aren't born with equal brains or bodies, then I'll go with you. I'll go even further – I'll say that some have mental weaknesses that could make them more prone to delinquency if brought up in the wrong environment.'

'Isn't that saying exactly what I said, only using different words?' Carnes asked triumphantly.

'Not in a hundred years it isn't. Morality has no direct connection with intelligence, however the more clever of us would like to think it has. The wrong environment is still necessary to turn a child sour, and that environment is man-made. We shouldn't blame God or the child for it.'

'And you're trying to tell me Danny had the kind of environment that turns children into thieves?'

'Yes, I am,' MacTaggit snapped. 'You gave all your affection to your daughter and none to him. And lack of affection does to a child's mind what lack of food does to its body – it weakens and twists it.'

Watching them both Beris felt the tug of divided loyalties. She saw contempt grow on her father's face.

'You're a typical broken-down idealist, MacTaggit. It hurts you to believe sin exists in the world, doesn't it? But now you're old enough to know it does exist you try to excuse it away by blaming the innocent people instead of the guilty. You're like all your kind – you'll do anything to avoid facing the truth. But I've listened to enough of your wishy-washy piffle. Tell me what your game is and why you've dragged my daughter into it.'

'I'd have thought that clear enough by this

time,' MacTaggit said dryly. 'I believe it was no fault of his own that Danny became a child delinquent. Now that he's back in Lidsborough and in more trouble – again, as it seems, through sheer bad luck – I felt I'd like to help him. Your daughter, bless her, decided she felt the same way. So we've been doing what we could.'

'And it's ended up by her giving testimony to the police to keep him out of jail.'

MacTaggit nodded regretfully. 'Aye; and there's no one more sorry about that than I. But surely that's better than an innocent lad getting into further trouble with the police.'

Beris, never more conscious of the deception she had practised on MacTaggit and the police and with her perceptions razor-edged as a result, thought she saw a momentary look of triumph leap into her father's eyes. With sudden apprehension she listened intently to him.

'You've a good deal of faith in him, haven't you, MacTaggit? You're quite certain of his innocence, aren't you?'

MacTaggit shrugged. 'It's never been a case of having faith in him. It's been simply a matter of giving a helping hand to a lad who badly needed it. But if it's proof of his innocence regarding last night's affair that you want, you of all people should be satisfied of that. You couldn't ask for a more reliable witness.'

The quick glance her father threw at her confirmed Beris's suspicions. Somehow he had learned of her deception... She sat as cold and stiff as marble, waiting for his next move.

All his confidence, which had shown signs of wear a few moments earlier, was back as he turned again to MacTaggit.

'Those burglaries aren't the reason I won't have my daughter associating with him. I know he didn't do them: he wouldn't have the guts... My reason is that he's a thoroughly bad character: a nasty, seedy specimen that no decent girl should mix with.'

Of course, she remembered... He could not give Danny away by destroying her testimony – to do that would be to destroy them all... With her fear relieved, a numbness came over her, a remoteness that made her feel she was watching a play.

Aggressive again, Carnes stared at Mac-Taggit. 'When I came in just now you said you wanted to see me about something. What was it? Danny?'

'Aye.' MacTaggit leaned back in his chair, gnome-like face expressionless. 'I was going to ask you to give him a job.'

Carnes's heavy jaw tightened again. 'I've taken a good deal from you this afternoon, MacTaggit. Don't go too far.'

'I'm not joking. I'm serious. The lad had a good job at Jardine's, one he liked. But someone has tipped them off about last night. They must have mentioned the previous case too, because the lad was paid off this morning.'

Watching with her odd feeling of detachment, Beris imagined her father's eyes shifted at this news. She remembered Danny's suspicions, then felt shame at her disloyalty.

Carnes gave a loud laugh. 'And now you expect me to run to his help. You're crazy, man. Completely crazy.'

'He's your adopted son, Mr Carnes.'

'Not any longer. I washed my hands of him seven years ago. He's not coming within a mile of my house or my factory.'

MacTaggit shook his head stubbornly. 'He lived under your care and under your influence for nearly thirteen years. Whether you like it or not that gives you a moral responsibility in his welfare. You can't throw it away just because you don't like it.'

'Can't I? Wait for him to apply for a job at my factory and see what happens.'

MacTaggit picked up a ruler from his desk, squinted down at it. 'There's something you should know. This lad has never recovered from his childhood experiences – he's stayed bitter. And that kind of bitterness is explosive stuff. It drove him to theft in his home, at his school, and later in London. You don't know what it might drive him to here.'

'What are you trying to say?'

'Just this. The police here have got the idea that Danny is behind these recent robberies. Your daughter and I gave him the benefit of the doubt and last night's affair proves we're right. But that's no guarantee of the future. The lad's had some bad breaks since he returned to Lidsborough, and the loss of his job might prove the last straw. With his record he's certain to find difficulty in getting suitable employment, and nothing embitters a man more than that.' MacTaggit lifted his eyes from the ruler and looked Carnes straight in the face. 'If you take my advice you'll give him work. If you don't, and there is trouble – well, don't say you haven't been warned.'

His words sent a chill through Beris. She watch the conflict on her father's face, understanding its origin. A pause, and then he shook his head violently.

'No. No matter what happens. That's out.'

'Not even if it might save a lad's future, and save a bit of scandal as well?' MacTaggit asked softly.

Put to the challenge, all Carnes's tough, dour northcountry stubbornness came to the surface. Caution, ambition: everything was forgotten at that moment. He growled his challenge like a great bull.

'You can't frighten me, MacTaggit. I've never had dealings with crooks in my life, and I'm not starting now. That's final. And in the future you'll keep out of my affairs and stop seeing my daughter. If you don't I'll make this town too hot for you. Do you understand?'

MacTaggit was also on his feet now, a battle-scarred terrier with every hair pointing stiffly upwards. 'If your daughter wants to see me, my office door will be open. At any time. Do *you* understand?'

For a moment the tension was at breaking point. Then Carnes swung round on Beris. 'Come on,' he ordered. 'We're going home.'

One half of her longed to resolve her inner conflict by simple obedience. But the child in her was no longer the master. She heard her voice answering him. 'I still have something to say to Mr MacTaggit. I'll be down in a few minutes.'

He halted as though a spear had been flung at him. Then he came growling forward again. 'I still have something to say to you. I'm taking you home now.'

'Not yet, Daddy. You go on ahead. I'll take the bus back.'

She tried not to see the stricken look that showed through his anger. He tried to speak but his voice choked away. He wrenched the door open and started down the stone corridor. His footsteps, although heavy and determined, echoed back to her with an oddly hollow ring.

21

Beris stood very still, eyes hot and painful. The footsteps died away before she closed the door and turned slowly and a little resentfully back to MacTaggit. He had picked up the ruler and was digging one end of it into his palm with short, angry jabs.

His voice was harsh with self-reproach as she dew near his desk. 'I'm sorry, lassie. I went too far. It's this damned temper of mine.'

'It wasn't your fault,' she muttered. 'He had to be told – just as I had to be told. It's just that...' She bit her lip and turned away.

The sight of her distress heightened MacTaggit's self-annoyance and paradoxically triggered off the temper that had caused them both.

'It's just that he happens to be your father, and if it wasn't for me this would never have happened. Why don't you say it?' Stiff-legged, like an angry cockerel, he walked a few sharp paces towards the window, then swung round on her again. 'You don't think I enjoy being the cause of trouble between a father and his daughter, do you? But when you're cursed with a temper like mine, what can you do when people won't try to be more charitable?'

At first she did not understand this resurgence of temper and was startled by it. He flung the ruler down on the desk with a clatter. 'Every day of my life I'm up against this sort of intolerance. What's the matter with people? Why can't they try to see sinners as human beings instead of cracksmen, liars, cheats, adulterers…? Why must they think the sinner is only composed of his sin? He isn't – very often it's only a small part of his make-up. There's a great deal more in him, and if you bother to cultivate it, you often find it crowds the sin right out of the garden. There aren't any blacks and whites in life – if there were it would be too easy. And life isn't meant to be easy.'

Beris stood watching him while the white flame of his temper burned down to red. 'It's the smugness I can't bear,' he said bitterly. 'The holier-than-thou attitude. Can't people realize we all have vice in us – perhaps an equal amount? But some are luckier than others, their vices don't clash with society. A man's vice may be for food, he may be a glutton, but nobody calls him a sinner because all the world loves a fat man. A man's vice might be for wealth, or power, or glory, and as long as he's clever enough he'll be respected by the very society he plunders. But if he's unlucky enough to have one of the anti-social appetites, then God help him. If he likes wine, he's a drunkard; if he likes women, he's a lecher; if he likes freedom, he's a tramp.' The skin around his eyes was drawn as if he were in pain. 'But there's one type of sinner who puts 'em all to shame – the type who's sorry for the down-and-outs. All the respectable people hate him – he's so damned anti-social. In fact, ever since Calvary society has been hanging 'em up on crosses.'

With this final explosion of bitterness the flame in him lost its heat, became lambent. He stared down at a pile of folders at the end of his desk.

'If only people would try to be kind,' he said slowly. 'That's all they have to do – to think the best of others instead of the worst. It's not as if it were difficult – if it's practised long enough it becomes a habit. Why don't they do it?'

He lifted his eyes up to her. 'I've said it to you before, lassie, and I'll say it again. The only virtue in the world worth a damn is kindness. Tolerance, loyalty, charity, integrity – every other virtue stems from it. And do you know something, lassie – and this is the most hopeful thing I know – people can learn kindness.'

'Learn it,' she said doubtfully. 'Are you sure of that?'

His voice was very positive. 'Oh, yes. Quite

sure. A hundred years ago, in this country, children could be thrown into prison for stealing a loaf of bread. They could starve to death. Things like that couldn't happen today because over the years good and imaginative men have taught us the injustice of it. But such teaching has all been left to chance, and in many other things we remain as prejudiced and unfair as people were in the Dark Ages. It may take centuries to develop our consciences fully ... in fact it may never happen – we may destroy ourselves first. But if we were given a comprehensive course of ethics in childhood, things would be very different.'

'But where would we be taught?' she asked, puzzled.

'Where we are taught mathematics, history, and geography.'

His answer surprised her. 'In schools? But surely the Church is far more fitted for that kind of instruction?'

He gave a slow, regretful shrug. 'I've two answers to that. Both are based on hard, practical facts. A comparatively small proportion of young children go to church today – and I want to get ethics in 'em all. The second point is this: In the last century, when children could and did starve to death and their parents often lost all faith in Divine Justice as a result, the Church had had the sole mandate on teaching morality for nearly a thousand years. And they couldn't complain of their attendances in those days, because it was almost obligatory for everyone to attend on Sundays.'

'You're saying it has failed in its duty,' she interrupted.

MacTaggit frowned. 'That's not my purpose, but I suppose in a sense it's true. I can't help feeling the Church spends far too much of its time on dogma and the cult of self-interest, and that's why so much social reform has come from sources outside it. To be frank, I've never seen anything particularly noble about the man who spends so much of his life taking care of his own soul that he's no time to bother about other people's – I feel the man who switches things around, who pays more attention to other people's troubles and forgets all about himself, has a far better chance of that seat in heaven that the Church promises, if only because he's not consciously working for it. If the Church had taught more of that kind of unselfishness instead of chanting hymns, marching in processions, and generally luxuriating in its own magnificence, we might have had a different morality today.' Then MacTaggit's tone changed. 'But my idea isn't to start something in competition with it but something that would be complementary. One would help the other.'

Beris nodded. 'I think I see what you

mean. But how on earth would you go about teaching kindness in schools? Surely it's something one feels – not something that can be taught?'

MacTaggit smiled at her. 'Why can't it be taught? What about its converse – cruelty? We believe that can be taught. We say the Nazis taught their children to be callous and destructive, and I believe it was true. Then why can't we teach children the opposite – to be understanding and creative? Of course we can teach it. It would be as easy as teaching science and mathematics.'

'But how? How would you go about it?'

'I've just told you – by giving children a comprehensive course in ethics. From these lessons they would learn their duties – Christian duties, if you like – towards their fellow men. They would learn tolerance, understanding, and their ethical responsibility in a world of H-bombs and ballistic missiles. They would also lose the worst of their prejudices, both inborn and acquired. For example, take a child's aversion to an infirm person. That's an inborn aversion: all animals have it. But it's an unpleasant one, and in any case we're not animals – we possess the God-given factor to rise above our worse instincts and we should use it.'

'But how?' she insisted. 'How would you teach a child to stop ... to stop poking fun at a deaf-mute, for example?'

A wicked grin signified the return of the old MacTaggit. 'Stuff cotton wool into the little devil's ears, gag him so he couldn't yell out when he was hungry, and he'd soon learn the score. Seriously, the development of imagination would be an important part of the training. I believe most of the gossips and scandalmongers of the world aren't really cruel by nature; they just lack the imagination to realize the suffering they cause. One of the best practical ways to develop a sympathetic imagination in children would be to introduce into schools plays specially written around the lives of less fortunate people, and let each child in turn act the primary part. They'd soon get the hang of it: children have imaginations just waiting to be developed. Of course, one wouldn't keep only to the problem of infirmity – senior classes would be introduced to adversity and problems of all types to broaden their minds. Couple such plays to regular lessons on ethics, and then watch out for results. Remember that in only a decade or two these children would be having children of their own, and so adding their influence to the lessons being taught at school. I believe that in two generations, perhaps even in one, a new world could be born.'

His enthusiasm was infectious. Beris's eyes were bright with interest. 'I understand now. Those plays sound a wonderful idea. But I can see one or two practical problems. To put these lectures over really well, wouldn't you need a very superior kind of teacher? And, in the beginning at least, wouldn't it be difficult to find enough of them to staff all the schools?'

MacTaggit nodded. 'You're quite right, but I think I've got a way round that. I'd use television. It would have two advantages: firstly, it would mean the very best man available could be used, and secondly it would assure the same code of ethics were taught to all classes. That's very important; we don't want a gradual mutation until those at the top are taught a different code to those at the bottom, as we've had in the past.' He grinned at her. 'Any more snags?'

'I can think of another,' she admitted. 'Wouldn't parents tend to resent schools taking away from them a responsibility they might feel was peculiarly their own?'

MacTaggit rubbed his nose. 'I'll have to answer that in two parts, lassie. First take the parents who genuinely feel they have a responsibility to teach ethics to their children. I think that the more sincere they were the more they'd agree that a qualified teacher could do a more thorough job, and they'd be only too glad to have him supplement their own efforts. After all, even qualified men don't object to other qualified men teaching their children their own subject at school.'

'That's true,' she admitted.

'Now let's take the other type of parent, the irresponsible ones with whom I'm really concerned. Often the only lessons their poor kids get from them are language lessons when Ma and Pa have a drunken quarrel on pay night. You find mothers sending their little boy of three off on an errand that means crossing a busy main road on his own … that sort of thing is going on all the time, ask any van driver who goes around Darntown. Can you imagine a mother who does things like that finding time to teach her children the right way to live? Can you imagine what they'd be told if she did?'

He noticed her expression and gave a wry grimace. 'I know, you think I'm exaggerating. That's one of my problems – getting intelligent people to believe just how simple and irresponsible the class of people I mix with can be. That's why we get so many clever solutions on delinquency that fail and never simple ones that would work. People just can't *think down* enough. There's a widespread illusion today that because we've got a welfare state and better wages, this kind of parent has become magically enlightened and more responsible. In some cases all the extra money means is that Ma and Pa can spend longer in the pub, leaving little twelve-year-old Fanny the job of putting her five brothers and sisters to bed. And wonderful little girl though Fanny often is, you can hardly expect her to throw a lesson of ethics in with her bedtime story.'

'You've converted me,' Beris smiled at him. 'If there are many homes like that, the sooner those lessons start the better.'

'There are thousands and thousands of homes like that, lassie, here and all over the industrial world. Children brought up in them don't get a chance. They grow up in a moral vacuum; it's a miracle to me the courts aren't twice as full as they are. But it isn't only the delinquents who would benefit – the rest of us aren't paragons without sin, either, or the world wouldn't be in the mess it's in today. Think how crazy things are at the moment. We all live in a world that every day is making us more and more dependent on the other man's conscientiousness and morality. In dozens of countries, hundreds of thousands of youths are being introduced to new discoveries that, if missed, can blow the world to bits under our feet. Yet as far as I know hardly a word is said to any of them about the ethical responsibility that should go with that knowledge. It's all physics, dynamics, chemistry, mathematics … as if anything was a hoot as important as learning to live with one's fellow men. It's terrifying, lassie. In fact, sometimes I've the feeling we're almost taught the reverse – that our primary task is to look after ourselves. That was certainly the undertone at school in my day. Can you wonder we have bad managements, strikes, delinquency, and, ultimately, wars?'

'And you really think that in time the teaching of ethics might prevent those things too?'

'Why not? They're all born of selfishness in some guise or another. Of course, care would have to be taken that no political bias was slipped into the lessons – you'd have to watch your politicians there – but provided that was done I can't see how it could do anything else but good.'

'It's an exciting idea,' she laughed. 'It's so exciting I shall have to think more about it. But right away I can see how it could help to solve the juvenile delinquency problem.'

MacTaggit grinned. 'It would do much more than that, lassie – remember all the delinquents aren't roaming the streets or in jail. Some are in power.' Having converted her to his idea, he now became the cynic again. 'That's one very good reason why we'll never get it in schools. Where would we get all our nice ruthless shop stewards, business men, soldiers and politicians from? They'd all be so busy helping one another we wouldn't have any more strikes, cartels or wars. And that would never do, would it?' His grin twisted. 'No, lassie, kindness, ethics, or whatever you care to call it, is too anti-social. Did I ever tell you about old Adams?'

She shook her head.

'He was a farmer, the only man I've ever met I'd call a real Christian. A five-year man called Hodges broke out of jail and Adams found him hiding in his barn, weak from exposure. Instead of being a good citizen and calling the police, Adams took him into his house and made his wife nurse him. But one of the labourers found out, tipped off the police, and poor old Adams ended up in court. His defence was that his Christian principles wouldn't allow him to give up a fellow creature, but of course that didn't save him. He got two months' hard, and dirty looks from everybody when he came out. People called him a fool, but they didn't know what I knew.'

'What was that?'

'I'd had a good deal to do with Hodges, and he was a really tough baby – the kind you think will never go straight. But we never had a scrap of trouble with him after that, and when his term was over he went straight to Adams and got a job with him as a labourer. And as far as I know he's there yet. So maybe old Adams had the last laugh, after all.'

She had only one thought at that moment. 'My father called you an atheist,' she said.

His eyes were bleak. 'Well, I couldn't hold that against him. It's a long time since I was in church.'

'No,' she protested. 'No one who loves his fellow men like you do could ever be an atheist.'

He laughed, then gave her a comical scowl. 'Love 'em – with my temper! I hate 'em most of the time. Think of the things I've been saying about them. Think of the things I said to your father.'

'He was ruder to you than you to him. But don't get a wrong opinion of him, Mac.' The friendly nickname came spontaneously and she saw his eyes wrinkle with pleasure. 'He can be very kind and good. I know he's wrong about Danny, but it's only that he doesn't understand – just like all the other people you've spoken about.'

At once he came round his desk and took one of her hands between his own. 'Beris, girl; it was just that I'd had a hard day – in fact I've had a hard week – and our little quarrel started me off. Those things I raved about weren't directed at him – they were against all the intolerant people I've been meeting for years. I know he's not an unkind man – he couldn't be your father if he was. It's just that we both have tempers and couldn't help using them.'

There were so many lovable things about this man, she thought, a lump coming into her throat. 'I know. You were just letting off steam at mankind generally. I knew it was that.'

The grip of his hands tightened. 'Good girl. There was nothing personal in it. Your father was bound to be a tougher nut than you to crack – for one thing he's got thirty years' more prejudice behind him. But don't worry – we'll crack him yet.'

She gripped his hand in turn as he was drawing back. 'I enjoyed listening to you, Mac. I liked your ideas. And there was something else I liked too – the way you spoke to me as if I were nearer your own age. You haven't done that before.'

He grimaced at her. 'Did I do that? How unchivalrous of me.'

'How old are you?' she asked.

'Not too old yet to enjoy the company of a pretty girl,' he grinned. 'I'm forty-nine.'

'Are you married? Have you any children? I've often wondered.'

He shook his head slowly. 'No. At least, not now. My wife and son were killed in the raids during the war.' He turned away, one finger aimlessly tracing a pattern on the desk. 'The boy resembled Danny as a child – in fact he'd have been the same age today if he'd lived. It's difficult to believe.'

'I'm sorry,' she said quietly.

A distant look had come into his eyes. 'Believing what I've always believed – that within limits you can make almost anything you like out of a child – I had all kinds of strange thoughts when I watched him crawling about the floor and taking his first few steps. In spite of all I've just said to you I couldn't help wondering whether, for his own sake, I shouldn't let him grow up tough, self-interested, and not over-concerned about the feelings of others.'

She stared at him in surprise. 'You wondered that – about your own child? I don't understand.'

Memories had brought back something of his earlier bitter mood. 'It's simple enough. A rose among roses gets its chance to bloom. So does a thorn among thorns. But mix 'em up and watch the rose gets its petals torn off.'

She understood him now. 'You believe thoughtful, sensitive people suffer too much in this world: that's one reason you wish to change it. But even as things are, you'd still have wanted your son to have been one of them. What about yourself? You wouldn't change your own nature, would you?'

His answer to that was curt. 'It's easy to take punishment yourself – anyone can do that. But to inflict it deliberately on those you love – that takes courage.'

'I'd never thought of it that way before,' she said slowly.

'You will one day – when you have

children of your own. It's a problem a good number of thinking parents must have.' His voice filled with disgust as he went on: 'What an indictment of our world it is – that people should fear the consequences of bringing up their children decent and kind and sensitive.'

'You're in a black mood today, Mac,' she laughed, her eyes moist and bright with affection for him. 'Surely things can't be quite as bad as that.' Then her tone changed. 'So it was really your son who gave you these ideas on education. I think that's wonderful, Mac. Doesn't it seem to make everything terribly worthwhile to you?'

At her words a curious expression crossed his face. His mask of bitterness seemed to fall away, leaving his face oddly luminous. 'That's a sweet thought of yours, lassie,' he said, a catch in his voice. 'Bless you for it.'

She found herself moving nearer to him. 'Mac, while we're talking this way, there's something I want to say to you. I owe you so much ... more than any other person in the world, including my father ... and I want you to know how much I appreciate it. I'll never forget it, Mac. Never.'

A look that startled her came into his eyes. He fought it back until only the slight pallor of his seamed cheeks was left to betray him.

'You'd better be getting along, lassie,' he said gruffly. 'I've got you into enough trouble with your father already.'

She did not miss his deliberate effort to make his seniority obvious. 'What about Danny?' she asked. 'Should I go to see him as soon as I can?'

'I wish you would. I can't think of anyone more likely to pull him together. But I'm afraid you'll have to handle him like a crate of eggs.'

'Is he so bitter?'

'From what I hear I'm afraid he is. So watch your step.' At the door he said quietly: 'And be careful what you say to your father. I'm very worried about you.'

She nodded, trying to laugh. 'I've always looked forward to going home, but I can't say I feel that way tonight.'

His face was very pale now. 'Don't spoil things for yourself, lassie. You're just as important as Danny, you know. Don't forget it.'

The rain was still falling when she walked out into the street, and after the warmth of MacTaggit's office it felt cold on her face.

22

The front of the house in Crescent Avenue was in darkness when Beris arrived home. As she walked up the path the porch light was switched on and Mrs Morrison appeared, framed in the yellow rectangle of the door. Her very silhouette, grim and disapproving, announced she had been given a working knowledge of Beris's offence.

She stood stiffly back as Beris entered the house as though afraid of catching some contagious disease. 'Where's Daddy?' Beris asked, removing her hat and coat.

'He's in his study, where he's been waitin' for you for the last half hour.' At this juncture Mrs Morrison gave a great sniff of disgust. 'I don't know what things are comin' to. To think that you, of all people, could want to spend your time with that young scoundrel... I could hardly believe it when your father told me. And the shameful way you've deceived me – sayin' you were going round to a friend's house...'

Her strictures were somewhat wasted on Beris whose mind was occupied with the ordeal ahead. Leaving Mrs Morrison statuesque with indignation, she went to her father's study, knocked, and entered.

His appearance suggested he had heard her arrival and prepared himself for her entry. He was standing before the fire, facing the door, his heavy face set and resolute. She could see he was going to be true to his assertions: his stubborn nature would not let him be anything else. Yet, in spite of his grim appearance, a certain pallor about his cheeks suggested his own dread of the ordeal, and she could feel nothing but compassion for him as she closed the door.

There was a tight, awkward pause as he searched for words to growl at her. 'Well! Have you finished your business with Mac-Taggit?'

She nodded. 'You said you'd something to say to me about Danny. What was it?'

He gave a short, hard laugh. 'I've got plenty to say to you about him. What exactly did you tell the police last night?'

'I told them the truth,' she said, forcing her voice to be steady. 'That he was with me from six-fifteen until the time we reached his house – which was nearly eleven. Why?'

'Did he ask you to say that?'

She nearly fell into the trap. 'Why should he ask me?' she countered instead.

He leaned forward, one hand on either arm of the hide chair, his swollen eyes staring straight into her face. 'Let me have the truth now. Not the pack of lies you've told

MacTaggit and the police. What exactly did happen last night?'

Her heart was hammering so fast now she felt sick. 'I don't understand. I picked him up at six-fifteen, we went to the old lighthouse, which he has been using as a studio, and we stayed there until nearly eleven. On our way back we met Mr MacTaggit who told us the police were waiting to question Danny about a burglary that had been committed that night. So I went back with him and–'

'And told them you'd been with him all evening. But it was a lie, wasn't it? He hadn't been with you for more than an hour. The rest of the time he'd been out driving around town in your car.'

Her legs were trembling so much she found it difficult to stand. She moved across to his desk, supported herself against it. His challenging eyes followed her, giving her no time to recover.

'Come on – out with it,' he growled. 'I know everything that happened. He went off about seven, and you stayed alone in the tower until he came back two and a half hours later. Then you went to his lodgings with him and told a deliberate lie to the police.'

She saw the hopelessness of denial. 'How do you know this? Who have you been talking to?'

There was triumph in his voice now. 'I'll

tell you how I know in a minute. First you tell me something. Why did you lie to the police?'

Her bewildered mind was still trying to work out how he knew the duration of Danny's absence. Not even Tommy knew that…

'I told them because I knew he was innocent,' she told him.

'What proof have you of that? The police say the robbery was committed between eight and nine o'clock.'

'I don't need any proof. He had gone to do an old woman a favour.' As he told him Danny's story and saw his expression, she realized with distress how ineffectual it sounded. 'Through missing the old woman he didn't have an alibi. That's why I was forced to go with him to the police.'

There was genuine astonishment in his voice. 'You witnessed for him on the strength of a yarn like that? Good God; it's the thinnest thing I've heard in years.'

Hastily she threw up a palisade to protect herself against doubts of Danny. 'How many of us have an alibi at any given moment? I believed his story because it was the kind of thing that could happen to anybody.'

He shook his head resentfully. 'That wasn't your reason at all. You've let him get round you; you've grown fond of him, and ended up by giving false witness for a common thief. Because that's what he is.' He paused for effect, then went on deliberately: 'I *know* he robbed that house the other night. And that almost certainly means he robbed the shop in Mason Street as well. Shall I tell you what really happened?'

She waited tensed, afraid of what she might hear.

'There's a widowed woman in Trinbury Park who lives alone in a large, old-fashioned house,' he told her. 'She owns a fair-sized grocery business, left her by her husband, and she carries her takings home every night and banks them the next morning. Every Wednesday evening she plays whist at the social club across the road, the game starting at eight o'clock. Last night she went over as usual but found she'd left her handkerchief behind. So when tea was served at nine o'clock she ran home to get one. She found the back door ajar and her takings stolen – that was how the police established the house had been broken into between eight and nine o'clock.'

'But all this was in the newspaper this afternoon,' she interrupted. 'It doesn't prove anything against Danny.'

Carnes lifted a grim hand. 'I'm coming to him now. When he left you last night he didn't go to Merriby. He drove to Trinbury Park instead, hid the car in a dark lane, and watched the house. Obviously he must have checked on this woman for weeks, because he had all her movements worked out. He waited until she had gone over to the whist drive, then broke in and took the money. He then drove back to Darntown, parked the car in a side street, and disappeared into a house in a nearby alley. Half an hour later he came out without the money and returned to you.'

She was remembering the lights near the jetty that Danny had seen, the tap on the lighthouse door that had frightened her, and she was white to the lips.

'How could you know all this? – you only came back this afternoon. I don't believe you.'

His confidence was terrifying. He went over to the fire, turned with deliberation, and faced her. 'I'll tell you how I know. I've had a man watching his every move since the day he returned to Lidsborough. A private detective. Now do you believe me?'

'A private detective!' A sound came into her ears like the tumbling of heavy waves on a beach. Through it she heard his slow, deliberate voice.

'Yes. He followed him by car last night from the river bank to Trinbury Park. Of course, he didn't know at the time what his game was, and wasn't able to shadow him closely enough to watch him break into the house, but if you add on to it what he saw afterwards – his leaving his handgrip at an accomplice's house in Darntown – you can't help two and two making four.'

She was dazed with shock. 'Who is he? Someone Danny knows?'

'Of course not,' he lied. 'Danny doesn't know he exists.'

Her mind was a frantic searcher, scrabbling in the soil for a lost faith. One thought kept working to the surface. It offered no hope, but when hope is lost bitterness is a tempting palliative.

'Apart from spying on Danny, what else have you paid this man to do?'

He stared at her. 'I don't follow you.'

Her voice took on an hysterical ring. 'When I first met him he told me someone had spoken to his landlord and been the cause of his losing his room. He said you were behind it, and I told him you would never do such an underhand trick. This morning he lost his job at Jardine's because someone told them about last night. Was that your man's work too?'

His slight start was enough for her who knew his every expression. In her anger she gave him no opportunity of contradiction.

'What right had you to set spies and informers on him the moment he came back? It was none of your business. How can you go preaching in church and yet do such things to people?'

Her reference to his church activities goaded him into a temper that scorned refuge in denial. 'As someone who knew his record, it was my duty to keep him under observation. There were the innocent people to think about. And haven't events proved me right?'

'Did your duty include dirty tricks like losing him his lodgings and his work?'

'I never lost him his lodgings. My enquiry agent did that on his own. But anyway, the less comfortable he finds it here, the sooner he'll get out. And that's the best thing that can happen for every decent person in Lidsborough.'

'Stop being such a hypocrite,' she cried. 'If you were a Christian you'd try to help him, not push him back into the dirt. You aren't thinking of other people at all – if you were you'd denounce him to the police. You're thinking of yourself. I know all about this knighthood – I've heard about it from Aunt Cecilia. Why don't you admit that's your reason instead of talking as though you were the self-appointed saviour of the city?'

Her words, double-barbed by his affection for her, struck deep through the hide of his temper, halting him for a moment. Then, a bull mad with wounds, he came growling back into the fray.

'You'd be in a fine mess if I denounced him, wouldn't you, my girl? And don't pretend to me that you've known all along he was the thief the police wanted. You thought him innocent, a victim of police suspicion. You wouldn't believe me when I told you he was a wrong 'un through and through. Why can't you admit you've been let down by him?'

She tried to steady her voice, to bring some usefulness into the quarrel. 'You don't know him as I do now, Daddy. I've seen the rest of him – the Danny that loves painting beautiful things, the Danny who seems so shy and timid. Perhaps he is a thief – I don't know now – but even if he is, there's so much of him that's good and decent.' She remembered MacTaggit's words. 'If that part of him is given a chance, it might drive the other part right away.'

'Don't be such a sentimental little fool. He's not a child any longer: he's a fully grown man, a hardened criminal. You haven't a hope of changing him. All that can happen is that he'll drag you down with him.' Carnes's tone suddenly altered. 'You haven't told him anything about my prospects of the knighthood, have you? Or mentioned the exhibition I'm giving?'

She tried to remember. 'I think so…' Her voice faltered at his expression. 'Does it matter very much?'

He almost choked at her folly. 'Does it matter!… This collection is valuable – gold that could be broken up and sold. And if he knows the damage he can do me by stealing it... Do you realize I'm showing it the week after next?'

She was suddenly intensely frightened. Her eyes widened in protest. 'No... He'd never do a thing like that out of spite. He's not vicious.'

'Not vicious! Oh, no; he only steals from middle-aged widows and old men. You young fool, you've let him get round you until you can't see through his game. He's used you as a tool ... you've lent him your car to make a housebreak easier for him, you've acted as an influential witness when he wanted an alibi...' Anxiety for her, fury against Danny, brought the veins out on Carnes's forehead. 'The young swine will be laughing his head off – using my good name to keep himself in the clear. But this is the end of it. You won't see him again, you won't phone him, you won't write him. If you make any contact whatever with him in the future, by God, you'll wish you'd never been born.'

His threats brought out his own nature in her. 'I'm a woman of twenty-four and I shall do as I wish. You may as well know that now as later.'

For a moment her defiance stunned him. 'But, girl, he's a thief. We've proved it now. Can't you understand that?'

'I can't help what he is,' she said quietly. 'If

I feel I ought to go to him I shall go. And that's the end of it.'

The storm broke in earnest as he lost all semblance of control. Resentful of his threats, of the wild things he said, she answered him back in kind. As the quarrel grew more and more bitter an odd schism divided her mind. Part of her moved outside it, listening aghast at the things each of them was saying, agonizingly aware that every new dagger-thrust was destroying their old relationship for ever. Yet with him she went on saying them, wondering all the time at the perversity of the human mind that can attack so viciously the things it loves most.

When it was over they were both white-faced and exhausted. As she moved blindly for the door she heard his voice again. It was low and with a tremor – it came from a different man.

'What are you going to do now?'

She turned to face him. 'I've already told you. I can't live with anyone who is so unforgiving. I'm moving my things to Aunt Cecilia's.'

'How long are you going to stay with her?'

'I don't know… A few weeks perhaps until I've found a job. Then I'll get myself a room somewhere.'

His breathing was laboured. 'Don't carry things too far. You don't have to go, you know.'

She was only too ready to meet him half-way. 'If you'll promise to stop this man, whoever he is, from spying and informing on Danny, then I'll stay. But I must make that my condition.'

He stood silent a good fifteen seconds before slowly nodding his head. 'All right. If you in turn will promise to stop seeing Danny I'll do it. You must, Beeda, or you'll end up in serious trouble.'

She faced him squarely. 'I can't make that promise, Daddy. I'm sorry, but I can't.'

All his vigour had gone: he spoke like an old man, not fully understanding the nature of this problem. 'But you must. He'll get you into trouble if you don't. He's a thief.'

'I can't help what he is, Daddy. I don't know yet what I'm going to do, but I can't tie myself not to see him.'

'If you go on seeing him it may mean ruin for us both. Do you realize that?'

'I know the risk, Daddy. But I can't make you that promise.'

'Then we've nothing further to say to one another,' he said slowly.

She could not bear to look at him as she turned and left the room.

23

In the firelight Aunt Cecilia's face was grave. 'This has come as rather a shock, dear. If what your father tells you is true, then it's clearly impossible for you to go on seeing him.'

In the pause that followed the hiss of rain-drops finding their way down the chimney could be heard. It was nine o'clock that same evening. Beris, who had arrived with her car and suitcase fifteen minutes earlier, was sitting in an armchair opposite her aunt. She was still wearing her raincoat.

'I feel I ought to go,' she muttered. 'He'll be terribly bitter at having lost both the tower and his job – someone ought to keep faith with him.'

'But surely that bitterness can't be genu-ine, dear. He can hardly expect to keep honest employment if he persists in stealing from people.'

'But it *is* genuine. If you'd seen him … heard some of the things he's said…' She went on to tell her aunt about some of the things she and Danny had discussed in the tower, and Aunt Cecilia's face grew more and more puzzled.

'I don't know what to make of it, dear. He sounds just the same boy I knew seven years ago. Yet surely your father wouldn't lie to you?'

Beris shook her head. 'He hates Danny, but he wasn't lying. I'm certain of that.'

'Well, there you are – you can't associate with him any more. Why, you could end up in prison as an accomplice. The best thing you can do is tell Mr MacTaggit everything.'

'Oh, no. He'd be forced to tell the police; it would be his duty. I couldn't give Danny away.'

Aunt Cecilia sighed. 'I suppose not. But you mustn't think of seeing him again. That's quite out of the question.'

'But surely you understand. Mr Mac-Taggit has made me realize I'm responsible for what he's become. I deserve everything that he gets.' Her voice rose accusingly. 'You always thought we treated Danny unfairly; I know you did. That was why you were so kind to him.'

Aunt Cecilia nodded. 'I admit I thought it would have been better if the boy had been left in the orphanage. But you can't be blamed for what happened, dear. Goodness me, you were only a child copying your father, as all children do. You have no responsibility whatever towards Danny.'

'I wasn't such a child when I turned away so my dress wouldn't brush against him,'

Beris said bitterly. 'I knew what I was doing well enough. But that isn't my only reason. It's difficult to explain but somehow I feel involved with him.' Unconsciously a note of pride entered her voice. 'I've helped to take the sullen look from his face: I've helped to make him laugh again. He's become a friend, and I can't abandon him now that he's in trouble...' She paused, suddenly embarrassed by the strange intentness of her aunt's gaze. 'What's the matter? Why are you looking at me like that?'

Aunt Cecilia gave a gentle nod. 'I think I'm suddenly beginning to understand, my dear.'

'You are?' Beris was puzzled.

'Yes.' Aunt Cecilia leaned forward, her voice soft. 'Have you fallen in love with him, my dear? Is that what it is?'

At first the significance of her words did not register on Beris. 'What did you say?'

'I asked if you had fallen in love with him. People often do fall in love with those they help, you know. Didn't you know that?'

This time the reaction was immediate. A hundred scattered pieces that until now had lain in disorder in her mind suddenly leapt together, making a picture that stunned her with its radiance. Her aunt's voice suddenly sounded far away. 'Poor child. Hadn't you known this before?'

There was no time to luxuriate in the

bright picture, not if she wanted to keep it safe. With an effort she locked it away and turned to her aunt. 'If you're right and I am in love with him, doesn't that change things? What would you do now if you were me?'

A sudden hush settled in the room. Her aunt sat motionless.

'Tell me,' Beris persisted. 'What would you do if you were young and the man you loved was in trouble?'

A coal tumbled in the fire and the shaft of light seemed to blur and alter her aunt's appearance. For a moment, as she turned to Beris, her face was that of a young, ardent girl. 'What would I do? You know very well what I would do...' Then her tone changed. 'Oh; you wicked girl to ask me such a question. Come over here.'

Stumbling a little Beris went across to her chair. Aunt Cecilia took her hand and gripped it firmly. 'We must both stop being sentimental, dear. If you are certain Danny is a thief, your duty as a good citizen is to report him to the authorities. If you feel unable to do that, then the least you should do is stop associating with him. There's no question about that.'

'But that isn't what you would do, is it, Aunt Cecilia? Why won't you admit it?'

A long pause, and then her aunt gave a deep, resigned sigh. 'No; I suppose you're right. That's always been the trouble with me

– every now and then my conscience clashes with the things a good citizen is supposed to do. I suppose, in a way, it's to be expected occasionally when they try to give a common denominator of morality to fifty million of us.' She lifted her moist, wrinkled eyes up to Beris's. 'I've always had the feeling that one should obey his own conscience, and mine tells me that the person who doesn't stand by those he loves when they are in trouble isn't worthy of being called a human being. But it's probably just sentimental nonsense. Victor once told me I wasn't a very good citizen and I think he was right. I'm sure I wouldn't last very long in one of the totalitarian countries.'

Beris, eyes bright, bent down and kissed her. 'I think you're a wonderful citizen, Aunt Cecilia. Thank you.'

Rain was swilling down the deserted Lambert Street when Beris pulled up outside number 57 forty minutes later. Mrs Johnson answered her knock: surprise showing on her plump, good-natured face.

'I'm sorry to bother you so late at night,' Beris told her. 'But is Danny in?'

'Yes, miss. He got back about ten minutes ago.'

'May I see him? I won't stay long – just a few minutes.'

Mrs Johnson's row of chins wobbled as

she gave a doubtful nod. 'I suppose it'll be all right. But I ought to warn you, miss, that he's been in a wicked mood since gettin' his notice this morning.'

'Where is he? In his room?'

'Aye. Usually he joins me in a cup o' tea when he gets back as early as this, but tonight he brushed by as if he'd never seen me. By the look of him, he's had a drop too much to drink. If you don't mind that, then go right ahead, miss.'

'Thank you. I won't be long.'

Beris went upstairs and tapped on his door. There was a long pause before he appeared. He showed no surprise on seeing her; the house was tiny and he had heard her voice in the hall below.

His black hair was awry, his collar missing, and his eyes heavy-lidded. A sour smell of beer hung around him. He stared at her sullenly. 'What do you want?'

'I felt I had to come and see you. May I come in?'

He stood back reluctantly and she entered the room. From the rumpled condition of the eiderdown she guessed he had thrown himself straight on the bed on his arrival home. He closed the door and faced her, voice slightly slurred.

'What've you come at this time of the night for?'

'I couldn't get earlier, and for one thing I

wanted to hear what had happened about the tower.'

'What's the matter – are you beginning to feel sorry you told them about it?' Then dejection took the place of sullenness as he dropped on the bed. 'They haven't taken any legal action,' he muttered. 'I think Mac-Taggit helped there. But I've had to get my things out today and to give my keys up to them.'

'How did you manage? Where have you stored everything?'

'Jack Clinton helped me with his car. We've dumped most of the stuff in his garage – he has a bit of spare room. It'll all rot in the damp, of course, but that doesn't matter now.'

Beris bit her lips, 'I also wanted to say how terribly sorry I am to hear about your job. I think it's disgraceful.'

He laughed sourly. 'If you've only come to offer me sympathy, you can save your breath. I don't want any of it.'

There was an explosive quality about his bitterness – standing alongside him was like standing alongside a stick of fused dynamite. A wrong move, a slip, could be fatal. When she remembered what she had to tell him, her nerve almost failed her.

'That isn't all, Danny,' she said, dry-mouthed. 'I've had a long talk with my father. He got back this afternoon, you know.'

Alcohol had dulled his memory. Now he looked up at her sharply. 'Has he heard about last night yet?'

She nodded. 'Yes. He heard very quickly.'

'I told you he would. What happened?'

'We had rather a quarrel,' she admitted. 'Don't worry about that – it'll all blow over. I've come to see you about something he told me.' She hesitated, then went on with a rush: 'Danny, Father has found out that we weren't together all yesterday evening. He knows you borrowed my car and went in it to town.'

The news appeared to stun him. 'But how could he know?' he muttered. 'Nobody knew but you and I.'

Telling him was like putting a match to the fuse of the dynamite. 'He's had a private detective watching you ever since you came back to Lidsborough. That's how he knows.'

He gave a violent start. Before her eyes his face turned chalk white. The silence hurt her ears.

'This man followed you in another car, Danny. He says you never went to Merriby, but to Trinbury Park instead. Don't you see what it would mean if he gave evidence?'

He sounded dazed. 'Who is he?'

'Daddy wouldn't tell me, but he says it's nobody you know – he keeps well out of sight. But he knows everything you've been doing.'

His dazed voice ran on: 'Then I was right... That would be the man who told the innkeeper about me. And the one who tipped off Jardine's this morning...'

She shook his arm. 'Never mind about that now. Think of your danger. Father won't tell anyone yet – for his own sake as well as mine – but what if this man talks? What if the police hear what you really did last night?'

At her last sentence he went as rigid as a statue, staring at her as if she had changed her very shape.

'Daddy knows everything you've been doing,' she went on frantically. 'And now he's afraid you'll go for this collection of gold antiques that he's exhibiting next week. He's afraid you'll do it out of spite, to ruin him. If that were to happen he'd go crazy and destroy everything and everybody around him. I know he would.'

Her words had been like some Jekyll-and-Hyde drug, distorting every line of his face as he drank them in. The sudden aversion in his voice made it unrecognizable. 'What exactly have you come here for – to ask me not to do it?'

'I know you won't do it, Danny. Not for my sake. I came to warn you about the detective and to ask you to leave town before something serious happens to you. If you don't go, the police must catch you sooner or later, and I couldn't bear that...'

The fuse reached the detonator and the dynamite exploded. With a violent exclamation he jumped to his feet, throwing her heavily against the wall. 'So that's been your game,' he gritted. 'You wanted me out of the way as much as your father did, but were a damn sight more subtle in the way you set about it. I see it all now.'

She couldn't understand what she was hearing. 'You're ill, Danny. Can't you remember – I witnessed for you only last night.'

'You witnessed all right, but not for me. You did it to save your father's skin. I wondered why you were so keen to tell them about the lighthouse...'

She shook her head, trying to clear the nightmare from it. 'You're like Daddy – you've let all this hate poison your mind. I meant all I said and all I did. I couldn't help telling them about the tower – it was the only way of saving you...'

'Don't lie. You were softening me up with those visits – eventually you'd have talked me round into leaving town so the two of you could have slept peacefully in those soft beds of yours again. So you'd be safe from scandal and hear people kow-towing to your father when he got his knighthood. People don't change ... I should have remembered that.'

In her desperation she lost all her control, and found herself hammering his chest with her fists. 'What are you talking about? I was trying to help you... I'm still trying to help you. I want you to leave town for your sake, not for ours...'

He caught hold of her wrists, bent her backwards. His white, distorted face stared down at her savagely. 'Well; I'm not leaving, do you hear? And nothing you or your father do can ever make me... So he's worrying about his gold antiques, is he? That's funny ... really funny. If I were you I should go straight back and tell him to keep them well guarded because, of all the things in the world, there's nothing I'd sooner do than ruin him...'

Somehow she found herself outside in her car, staring blindly out into the rainswept street, alone in her nightmare.

24

On Monday Clinton sent a message through to Carnes asking for an appointment. As usual Carnes met him in his car and drove into a quiet side street before turning to him.

'Well; what's happened now?'

'I had Meadows round at my flat last

night,' Clinton told him. 'And after a drink or two he began talking about you and your daughter. It's the first time he's mentioned either of you to me, but you should have heard the stuff that came out.' He gave a wide grin. 'Apparently the night before he'd heard about the private detective you've been employing to trail him.'

A heaviness came into Carnes's voice. 'Then he is still seeing my daughter?'

Clinton shook his head. 'Not any longer. He's had a quarrel with her – he's got the idea from somewhere that she's only been seeing him for your sake, to get him out of town. He's turned completely against her now – he says he never wants to see her again.'

'Are you certain of this?' Carnes grunted.

'No doubt about it. He must have been pretty gone on her before and is taking it badly. I think that's why he opened up last night.'

'How do you stand in all this? Is he likely to suspect you?'

'No, I told you before – I've had it all covered from the beginning. He thinks the garage is my only job. I even gave him a couple of days' work there once to ram the point home. Don't worry about that.'

'What exactly did he say to you last night?' Carnes asked uneasily.

'Oh; he was breathing fire and brimstone.

Said you'd been down on him ever since he got back, blamed you for getting him the sack from Jardine's, told me what he'd like to do to you if he got the chance. I should watch yourself if I were you, sir.'

Carnes's jaw set aggressively. 'You mean he might try to assault me?'

Clinton shook his head. 'His type seldom go in for the rough stuff – he's more likely to try to get you in a different way,. I'm getting more and more worried about this collection you're showing next week. Last night he mentioned it more than once, and then started sneering about a knighthood you're hoping to get soon. 'Course, he didn't say too much, but I got the impression he's seeing the collection as a way of doin' you harm. Is that possible?'

Carnes's florid cheeks went suddenly pale. 'Very possible,' he muttered.

'But surely the stuff's insured?'

'Of course it's insured. But money can't replace antiques. No; I'd be in a real mess if any of it were stolen.'

'Then you'd better watch out,' Clinton warned him. 'I'll tell you what convinced me it was in his mind – that article about the collection they put in the newspaper last night. I'd just finished serving up the grub and called for him to come and get it. When he didn't answer I went into the other room and found him sittin' on the bed reading the paper. I had to speak to him twice before he heard me. After he'd gone through into the kitchen I took a look at the paper and saw it was open at the article. An' when he went home he took the paper with him. That was more than enough for me.'

Carnes nodded, face grim. 'You're probably right.'

'What are the security arrangements like?' Clinton asked. 'I read last night that you've arranged for the stuff to go on exhibition at Merriby at the end of the week. That's where you want to watch out. Country cops aren't used to dealin' with smart kids like Danny. He'll need close watching.'

Carnes nodded again, shifted restlessly. 'I know. I'm worried about Merriby.' He paused, then gave a start. 'What about you helping me out there? Can you get two or three men to help you? I want a proper guard around the place.'

Clinton shrugged. 'Sure; that's easy enough to arrange if you want it. You're only there on Friday night, aren't you?'

'That's right. We take the stuff out early Friday morning, exhibit it until eight that night and until six on Saturday. After that we shall bring it straight back.'

'O.K., sir. I'll see to it. When can I see you to fix up the details?'

Carnes looked down at his watch. 'I can't stay now – I have a conference in half an hour. What about next Monday at the exhibition? – that'll give you a chance to see the collection. That won't be too late for you, will it, if you engage your men in the meantime?'

'That'll be all right, sir. What time shall I come?'

'Make it two-thirty,' Carnes told him, staring up his engine. 'We'll get down to all the details then.'

With that the enquiry agent left the car and Carnes drove back to his town office.

To Beris, afraid what the following week might bring, the days passed at lightning speed. During them she made three unsuccessful attempts to see Danny. On her third visit Mrs Johnson told her that he appeared to be making no effort to find employment and seemed to have lost all interest in painting. He was spending his days in billiard saloons and public houses, and from his general abandoned behaviour – twice that week he had arrived home drunk – he appeared to have gone completely to pieces.

Monday, the opening day of the Delmont exhibition, arrived all too quickly. After an uneasy night Beris drove in to town on Tuesday morning. As she had expected the exhibition was organized with her father's customary thoroughness and vigour. Posters were everywhere – a visiting circus could not have received more publicity. Loyalty tried to convince her that her father, in his relative ignorance of cultural exhibitions, was unaware they could have only a minority appeal, but in her heart she knew the publicity was aimed at a wider audience than the stolid citizens of Lidsborough.

In an effort to reassure herself of the safety of the collection she drove round to the Town Hall. A small permanent museum was normally resident in the basement – it was these rooms Carnes had succeeded in borrowing. Afraid her father might be inside, Beris did not enter the building. Instead she sat gazing at the massive stonework, trying to convince herself that no one in his right senses would attempt to break into it.

On her arrival home she learned from Aunt Cecilia that her father had called round on his way to town, and left only a few minutes earlier. It was not his first attempt at a reconciliation with her – he had phoned her twice over the weekend. Although as eager as he for this reconciliation, she had nevertheless told him it was better they live apart until their differences on Danny were resolved one way or the other. It had not been easy for her to take this stand, particularly after his statement that her monthly allowance would be paid into the bank as usual. This however she had no intention of drawing, having decided to find work as soon as possible.

'Did he say how the exhibition went last night?' she asked, removing her coat and patting the fussing Roger. 'I nearly had a look at it this morning, then thought better of it. It would have been embarrassing for us both if he'd been there.'

'I think it went fairly well, dear, although he won't get his money back on what he's spending on publicity alone.' Tolerant on most things, Aunt Cecilia had no tolerance for self-aggrandizement. 'It's a shameful waste of money just to impress one or two pompous politicians. Really, I do wish he would grow up.'

Beris kept her eyes down on Roger. 'Did he mention Danny at all?'

'Oh, goodness, yes; I had to go through all that again. He's not so worried about the wretched antiques while they're here in Lidsborough, but he's terrified of what might happen when they go out to Merriby on Friday. I said if he is so scared he should cancel the exhibition there, but he says he can't do that in case he offends the local dignitaries. The complications his ambition gets him into...'

'Why is he so worried?' Beris asked.

'Oh, he doesn't think the building there is any too safe, and because the collection is to be shown on Saturday morning there won't be time for it to go into a strong room for the night – it's a very large collection, you know. So he seems almost convinced Danny will make an attempt on it on Friday night. And he is doubly frustrated because he can't warn the police of his suspicions.'

Beris started. 'Does that mean the collection will be unguarded?'

'Goodness me, no. As things are he might get into trouble from the insurance company if they found out the antiques weren't going into a strong room. No; apart from hiring a Merriby policeman, he's also sending a private detective and his men there. How he expects Danny or anyone else to get through such a cordon I really don't know.' Noticing Beris's distress, Aunt Cecilia grew more patient. 'You haven't managed to see him yet, dear?'

'No. I tried again yesterday and Mrs Johnson said he'd left a message that I had to stop going round, that he never wanted to see me again.' Her voice suddenly cracked. 'I'm frightened, Aunt Cecilia. They hate each other so much I'm frightened they'll destroy one another.'

Aunt Cecilia put a solicitous arm around her shoulders. 'You mustn't worry so much, my dear. I still don't believe the boy will do anything.'

Had her aunt been in possession of all the facts, Beris might have found some comfort in her assurance. But, although she had told her aunt everything else that had been said between her and Danny at their recent meeting, she had omitted one single item – Danny's threats to her father.

25

Until Friday the week proved uneventful. Late on Wednesday afternoon Beris tried again to see Danny. Mrs Johnson was over at a neighbour's house and it was Tommy, not long home from school, who greeted her at the door. From him she learned that all the week Danny had been going out before four o'clock and not returning until after midnight. The boy's doleful expression told her how much he was missing his newly found companion: to cheer him up Beris took him for a ride in her car and later that evening returned to Lambert Street to take him to the cinema. There was no sign of Danny on their return, nor did he appear later although Beris dwelt as long as possible over the cup of tea Mrs Johnson provided for her. On her way home through the dreary, deserted streets she was nearer defeat than at any time since her campaign to save Danny commenced. All her instincts warned her a crisis was imminent, yet now there seemed nothing she could do to avert it.

Friday arrived, an icy day with a tenuous fog that froze on everything it touched. Phantom ships, grey and shapeless, nosed cautiously down the river, while in the city cars crept as gingerly as cats over the pebble-sprayed roads. The small grass plot outside Mrs Johnson's house was white with rime, and the television aerials on the houses opposite vanished upwards into an opaque grey void. The cold and fog had an extraordinary power of penetration; seeping not only through brick and mortar, but also through flesh and blood, bringing to the mind a sense of gloom and adversity.

In his room at the rear of the house Danny lay on his bed. The time was four o'clock and the fog lay against the window like murky sea water. Although the light was not switched on, his occasional nervous movements showed he was not sleeping. Once he rose sharply up on his elbows as though an alien sound had startled him. Another time he rolled sharply sideways, a movement of protest as if he were turning his back on a temptation.

A few minutes passed during which he lay motionless, then a sharp rap on the front door brought him upright with a jerk. Body rigid he sat listening intently. There was an enquiring bark from Minty, the pad of Mrs Johnson's slippers, then the minor pandemonium of joyous barking and shrill laughter that signified Tommy's return home from school. Slowly the man relaxed.

Reaching out he switched on the light. It showed his face to be tightly drawn with a shadow of beard on his cheeks. With eyes half closed against the light, he sat a moment as though uncertain of his next movements. Then, swinging his feet to the floor, he reached for his jacket which lay across the back of the chair. As he shrugged it on his eyes moved furtively to the wardrobe and paused there, only to be dragged away as he lit himself a cigarette. Restlessly he walked over to the window and tried to peer out through its frost-stained glass. Seeing nothing but his own image he turned away, only for his image to face him again in the mirror of the wardrobe. The sight seemed to offend him; with an exclamation he jerked open the door to destroy it. As he did so, his eyes fell on a newspaper that lay on the floor of the wardrobe. Twice he tried to turn away from it, twice he turned back with an odd fascination. At last he pulled it out and laid it on the bed.

His attention was devoted entirely to a single article which he read three times before folding the paper and thrusting it in his jacket pocket. At once his movements became more decisive. Throwing his cigarette into the empty grate he reached for his mackintosh, which hung behind the door, and threw it on. Stepping out on to the landing, where he paused a moment to listen, he moved quietly down the stairs until he could see the living-room door from over the handrail. Seeing it was closed he continued down the stairs to the front door. As he carefully drew back the catch it gave a sharp click, making him wince. The sound brought a warning bark from Minty, and a second later Tommy opened the living-room door. The boy's face lightened, only to cloud over as quickly when he saw Danny's intentions.

'Hello,' he muttered. 'Y' goin' out?' As Danny nodded he went on dejectedly: 'Are you goin' to be out very long?'

Danny's voice was sharp. 'Yes. Why?'

Tommy looked crestfallen. 'I thought you an' me were goin' to the swimming trials tonight. Don't you remember – you said you were gettin' two tickets.'

Danny gave a start at the reminder. He hesitated, then turned reluctantly back. 'Wait a minute,' he muttered, running up to his room. He returned with two tickets which he thrust at the boy. 'Here you are. I can't come but you can take a friend with you.'

There was no enthusiasm in the boy as he took the tickets. 'But it isn't th' same, Danny. You said you were comin' with me.'

The reproach in his voice brought shame and sullenness to Danny's face. He threw open the door abruptly, letting in the icy fog. 'I can't help it – there's something else I've got to do.' He hesitated, then turned back to the disconsolate boy. 'It's a job for Mr Clinton. He came round this afternoon – one of his men at his garage has fallen sick and he wants me to help out for the night. I can't let him down.'

Tommy did not speak, but his disappointment was palpably evident as he stood with hanging head. Danny stared at him for a long moment. Then, with a sharp exclamation, he stepped out from the porch and vanished into the thickening fog.

As yet the fog was not as thick in the northern suburbs as it was by the river, but it was no less severe in its effect on the spirit. Beris had her full share of dejection as she stood gazing from her room window early that evening. Obsessed all day with the fear that the night might bring ruin to both Danny and her father, she was strongly tempted to find Danny at all costs and warn him about the detectives her father was employing. Had she been certain such knowledge would have prevented his making an attempt on the collection she would have gone. But the danger was too great that such a warning would only help him to evade the guards and reach the collection unmolested. Clearly she could not let loyalty to him be the cause of her father's ruin.

Now, in any case, it was probably too late. By this time Danny would probably have gone out, and she could do nothing to alter his subsequent actions. Unable in her anxiety to face her aunt, restless, yet with no course of action open to her, she stood gazing through the frosted window into the quiet street where patches of fog clung like bright cobwebs around the shining street lamps.

At last, with draughts from the window chilling her, she turned to the gas-fire that burned on the hearth. At that moment a car pulled up outside. She turned back to the window in time to see the figure of a man vanish into the porch below her. A second later the door-bell rang.

Crossing the bedroom swiftly she stood listening at the door. She heard her aunt shuffle into the hall and pull back the latch. The familiar voice that addressed her aunt a moment later brought her running down the stairs.

MacTaggit, hatless, looking more like a gnome than ever in a thick overcoat, was standing in the porch. From his expression she knew at once something serious had happened.

'What is it?' she panted. 'Danny? Is he in more trouble?'

MacTaggit's voice was dry. 'That depends.' He turned to Aunt Cecilia. 'I wonder if I may talk to your niece in private for a few minutes?'

Aunt Cecilia led them into the living-room, threw an anxious glance at Beris, and withdrew. MacTaggit waited until the door had closed before turning his sharp eyes on Beris. 'Lassie; I've heard something today that's given me a shock. I haven't time to go into the whys and wherefores, but I've heard that someone saw Danny alone in a car about nine o'clock on the night that second burglary was committed. In other words, that he wasn't with you all the evening as you told me and the police. Now, is it true?'

She tried to speak but her throat seemed to have closed up.

'I must have the truth,' he warned her. 'You know my feelings towards the lad, and you know I've done my best to help him. But if he really is doing these robberies, then I'm duty-bound to tell the police. If he's done two, he's likely to do more, and we have innocent people to think about.'

She had never known her brain could work so fast. While her body stood paralysed, it was inventing excuses and discarding them at fantastic speed. Suddenly it seized one, dressed it up in words, and threw it at her. She clutched it thankfully.

MacTaggit had lowered a sharp forefinger and was pointing it at her like a pistol. 'Now, come on, lassie – out with it. Did you tell a lie that night to cover him? I want to know.'

She took a deep breath. 'Yes, I did. But I can explain why.'

His voice was grim. 'You mean you weren't together all the evening in the lighthouse, as you told me?'

'No, but it was such a short time it didn't matter – he couldn't possibly have done a robbery so quickly. You see just before nine o'clock he ran out of cigarettes. I didn't mind, but you know how edgy he is – how he has to keep smoking all the time. I knew the rest of the evening would be spoiled if he didn't get a packet, so I told him to take my car... He wasn't gone half an hour, and as it took ten minutes to walk to the car he couldn't possibly have done anything in that time.'

'Why didn't you tell this to the police? They're not fools; they would have known that. I told you to keep nothing back from them.'

She had an answer ready for this. 'I was afraid that if I said he'd been away from me even for a few minutes they might suspect him. You know how it is when you're upset

– you can't think clearly.'

His eyes, as keen as a squirrel's, watched her intently. He was silent a moment, then turned sharply for the door.

Her voice was shrill, anxious. 'Where are you going?'

'I'm going round to check up with Danny. You aren't both likely to think up the same excuse, particularly one as thin as that.'

She followed him out into the bleak December night, watched him enter his car. 'You won't find him at home. He hasn't had a single evening there since he was dismissed from work.'

He lowered his side window. 'Then I'll have to look around Lidsborough for him, won't I?'

For the moment she was all woman, fighting with every weapon at her disposal to save Danny. 'I don't see why you can't believe me,' she said sullenly. 'I thought we trusted one another.'

He leaned his head from the window, and in the lamp light she saw something hurt and disappointed lying behind his eyes. 'Do you know something, lassie?' he said slowly. 'I thought the same thing once.'

With that he turned the car, and without a backward glance drove off up the street.

She ran back into the hall where her aunt was waiting anxiously for her.

'Whatever is the matter, dear? What did he want?'

Beris snatched her coat from the hallstand and threw it on. 'I haven't time to tell you now. Don't wait up for me if I'm late home.'

'But where are you going, dear?'

She flung the words back over her shoulder as she ran through the house to the back door. 'I'm going to see Danny. I'll explain everything when I get back.'

Her car was in a small garage at the bottom of the garden. She backed it into the lane, straightened out and headed for the main road, leaving the garage doors gaping open. The lane was pitted and broken, she drove along it recklessly and was on Markham Road in under a minute. The emerald eyes of traffic lights gleamed out of the fog, changing to amber as she approached. Gritting her teeth she accelerated, swinging sharply to the left as a shadowy car emerged from a side street. The road was frozen, reflecting the misted sodium lights above. A lorry, heavily loaded with wooden crates, appeared in front of her. The driver, not expecting anyone to try to pass him on such a night, was hugging the centre of the road. In desperation Beris put her thumb on the hooter and kept it there. The startled driver swung over to the kerb, leaning out of his cab to stare at her as she accelerated by.

She drove recklessly, eyes straining to

pierce the fog ahead. In parts it was thin, allowing her to make better time. Feeling certain MacTaggit would follow Markham Road to the city centre and take the old town route to Lambert Street, and afraid he might recognize her car if she passed him, she swung right, down one of the side streets that ran through to Darntown.

As soon as she reached the industrial suburb and turned left down Barferry Road, she realized her mistake. Being nearer the river the fog was denser in Darntown. But there was no time to turn back. Switching on her headlights she drove into it.

Lighted shops, shapeless orange blurs, fell slowly behind her. For minutes she was forced to drive almost at a walking pace. Then suddenly the fog thinned and reaction drove her foot down on the accelerator. The frozen road flowed under her headlights, dipped under a bridge, took her past two slow-moving cars and a trolley bus. A long wall appeared on her left, frost sparkling as the fringe of her headlights skimmed it. A railway track ran along the opposite side of the road; an engine, glowing like a fiery dragon in the mist, ran alongside her for a few seconds before thundering off towards the river. Then the fog closed in again. Two minutes, three minutes ... the shadowy outline of houses again ... the glow of shops ... then she swung recklessly across the road and thirty seconds later pulled up with a jerk outside Mrs Johnson's house. There was no sign of MacTaggit's car.

She flung open the gate and hammered on the front door. Mrs Johnson appeared, looking alarmed at the urgency of the summons.

'Whatever is it, miss? What's happened?'

'Danny,' she panted, 'I must see him. Have you any idea where he is?'

'He went out just after half past four, miss. He said he was goin' to help out for the night in a garage.'

For a moment her mind blazed with hope until she realized he might have been preparing an alibi. Yet, whatever its worth, it was news of him – something more than she had expected...

'Whose garage? Mr Clinton's?'

'That's right, miss. Mr Clinton called round to see 'im early this afternoon and I heard 'em talking about it. Apparently he's a man short tonight.'

This time she could not stifle her hope. 'Do you know where this garage is?'

'I'm afraid I don't, miss.'

'Does Tommy know?'

As Mrs Johnson hesitated Beris threw a glance up the fog-choked street. Mac-Taggit's car must appear at any moment... She swung back on Mrs Johnson. 'Please call Tommy. It's terribly important.'

'He's gone to a friend's house, miss, to ask

'im to go to the swimming trials tonight. It's up the street – number 23. I'll go and fetch him if you like…'

Before she finished speaking Beris was running back to her car. Without wasting time in turning, she threw the gear into reverse and backed up the street. She had to guess the locality of the house, the numbers were invisible from the car. Pulling up she jumped out and ran to a gate. Number 15. Four houses farther down… As she turned to run the muffled sound of a car entering the street made her stiffen.

A street lamp made her feel naked. She stood motionless before the gate, her back to the road, willing MacTaggit not to notice her or her car. His car drew nearer, reached her … for a second she believed it had passed by. Then the engine note changed, dropped, and she knew it was hopeless. Slowly she turned to face him.

She felt no personal resentment. Since her last meeting with Danny the inevitability of defeat had grown on her – now it was a fact. Things were as simple as that. Dull-eyed she watched him jump from his car and approach her.

His voice was grim, pained. 'So it's true, is it? We got at him too late to save him.'

Her shoulders sagged. 'I'm afraid so.'

'How long was he away in your car that night?'

'Two and a half hours. From seven until after nine-thirty...' Jerkily she told him everything except Danny's threats regarding her father's exhibition. On mention of her father's private detective MacTaggit's bushy eyebrows lifted in surprise. His slow, resigned headshake when she finished seemed to throw the last dust and ashes on her hopes. He motioned down the street. 'Let's go to Mrs Johnson's. There are one or two things I want to ask her.'

Neither thought of the cars; each walked silent with his thoughts down the quiet, foggy street. At the gate of number 57 she suddenly turned on him.

'If you believe everything you've told me, that environment made him what he is, then how can you betray him to the police? How can it be right to punish people for what they can't help? You asked my father that when you were quarrelling with him.'

When he did not answer her voice turned bitter, jeered at him. 'Where's all your sympathy and kindness now? You're doing exactly the same thing that I would have done two months ago. Was I right, then, after all?'

For once there was no peppery flare of spirit from him, nor was there any acrimony. He looked pinched and cold and oddly tired. 'You're sorry for a person with an infectious disease, but you have to isolate them in hospital until they're cured. There should be institutions for people like Danny where they can get humane corrective treatment to straighten out their knots and kinks. Is it my fault society only provides jails?'

The desire to hurt him was strong in her at that moment, but she could think of nothing more to say. Her resentful eyes scourged him, then she pushed through the gate and knocked on the front door. Mrs Johnson, surprised to see MacTaggit with her, led them both into the living-room. After questioning her about Danny's recent movements, MacTaggit asked if she would go and fetch Tommy. As she bustled out he moved across to the fire to warm his hands. After a moment's hesitation Beris followed him.

'I'm sorry,' she muttered. 'I didn't mean those things I said. It's just that ... oh, what's the use?'

He turned towards her immediately. 'I know the reason,' he said quietly. 'I've known it some time.'

'You know ... how I feel towards him? But how could you know? I only realized it myself last week.'

He shrugged. 'Little things you said: the way you looked when you said them. It all added up.'

She nodded, face puzzled. 'It's so strange.

Two months ago I couldn't stand the sound of his name. And now–' She paused, watching him drop into an armchair. 'Aunt Cecilia says you grow to like the people you help. I suppose that's what it must be.'

He picked up the poker and prodded the fire. 'Your Aunt Cecilia sounds like a very wise woman,' he said slowly.

At that moment she was certain of the thing she had suspected in his office, and could not bear to look at him as she drew nearer.

'If you know how I feel towards him, then you can't feel hurt because I lied to you. What else could I do? But I hated doing it like hell. Won't you believe me, Mac?'

He stared down at the poker a moment, then raised his eyes and gave a wry smile. 'Aye; you're right. With the way your mind was working I suppose you didn't have much choice, poor lassie.'

She dropped on her knees alongside him and pressed her face against his shoulder. 'You're the finest person I've ever known, Mac. I couldn't bear to think I'd hurt you.' Suddenly afraid of what she was doing she tried to lighten the moment, only for her tearful voice to make matters worse. 'I think so much about you that if it wasn't for Danny I'd chase you all over Lidsborough. I would – really I would.'

His hand lifted and touched her cheek

gently, his only concession to the moment. Then, equally gently, he rose from the chair. His face was pale but the pain behind his eyes had gone. He helped her to her feet.

'It's not like you to cry, lassie. Dry your tears.'

She brushed at her eyes. 'I seem to have plenty to cry about just now, Mac.' Inevitably her thoughts returned to Danny. 'What do you think Tommy can tell you about him?'

He frowned moodily. 'I'm not certain myself – perhaps I'm just hoping for the impossible. I'm not exactly looking forward to the questions the police are going to ask you when they discover you sheltered him.' He paused, then shot an enquiring glance at her under his bushy eyebrows. 'Lassie, are you sure you've told me everything? I can't do the right thing unless I'm in possession of all the facts.'

She realized the absurdity of keeping anything back now. 'There is something else, although it's just the opposite of what you're hoping for.' She went on to tell him about Danny's threats to her father's exhibition. 'I'm terrified he might try to do it, Mac. If he does he'll destroy both himself and Father.'

MacTaggit's sharp face had turned very grave at her news. She eyed him anxiously. 'What do you think? Do you think it's likely he'd try to do such a thing out of revenge?'

Her heart sank as he gave a reluctant nod. 'I hate saying it, but it's quite possible,' he muttered. 'It was your father's unfair treatment that caused Danny to steal from him the first time; it established a complex that has remained with him ever since. And as your father, in Danny's mind at least, has done something equally unfair, the danger's very real he may retaliate again.'

The very logic of his argument made her fight against it. 'But equally it might be true about the garage. We can't be certain he hasn't gone.'

'Was it Tommy you were looking for when I found you?' he interrupted.

'Yes. I thought he might know where this garage is.' She caught hold of his arm pleadingly. 'Can't we go and look for it, Mac? At least give him a chance to explain before you give him away to the police.'

'But that might be nothing but a yarn. There's your father to think about. His collection would be much safer if we told the police about Danny immediately.'

'That's the last thing Daddy would want,' she said with conviction. 'Can't you understand – he wants to keep his name free of scandal. I'm not even certain he would let his detective hand Danny over to the police if he caught him.' A thought came in support of her plea, tightening her grip on his arm. 'What if you tell the police and then Father's detective refuses to confirm your statement? He might, if Father pays him enough... Give Danny a chance to confess himself, Mac. We've been his friends – we don't want to be the ones to give him away. That'll make him more bitter than ever.'

Her last words made his frown deepen. Seeing his hesitation she went on pleadingly: 'I'm not worried about Father's collection – I know he has got it well guarded. I'm thinking about Danny – he's going to need faith in someone in the months ahead. Even if he has none left in me, he still has it in you... Don't take that away from him, Mac. It's all he has left.'

With a sharp exclamation he swung away to hide his distress. For a moment he stood rigid, hands clenched at his sides. Then he turned back, his voice gentle. 'All right, you poor lassie. If it'll make you feel better we'll have a look for the lad first.'

At that moment she realized a fundamental truth – that in spite of what society in its expediency has ordained, in reality the human heart is capable of many loves and each love may be as sincere and loyal as the rest.

'Oh; you're good, Mac,' she breathed. 'So very, very good to me. Thank you.'

Shortly afterwards Mrs Johnson returned, followed into the room by Tommy, an order of precedence that even without his doleful expression would have told Beris something had upset the boy. MacTaggit turned to him.

'You've seen Mr Clinton – the chap Danny is friendly with. Do you know where his garage is?'

Tommy shook a dejected head. 'Only that it's somewhere in Darntown,' he muttered.

Mrs Johnson felt obliged to explain away her ward's moodiness. 'He's disappointed because he thought Danny was takin' him to the swimming trials tonight. I thought he was myself when I heard him put off Madge Edwards this morning.'

Once more MacTaggit was the alert squirrel, missing nothing. 'Madge Edwards? Has she also been round today?'

'Aye; she came just before twelve. I wouldn't let her go up to his room – that's how I heard what was said. She asked him to go wi' her to a party tonight, and he said he'd something else to do – I thought by that he meant his outing with Tommy. After haggling with him some time she went off in a bit of a huff.'

'And later on Clinton came to see him?'

'That's right, just before two. I heard him say he'd like Danny to help him out as he's a man short tonight, but didn't hear what Danny's answer was. It wasn't until half past four that we found out he wasn't takin' the lad after all.'

MacTaggit turned to Beris. 'There it is – we know the place is in Darntown but that's all. We'd better get along and see what we can do.'

Tommy followed them outside where the frost was fast tightening its grip. Seeing his dejection Beris pressed a half-crown into his hand. 'Cheer up,' she whispered. 'You can still go to the swimming, can't you?'

'I dunno if Ma Johnson'll let me go on my own,' he muttered. 'And anyway, it's not much fun.'

'Never mind. I'll call round for you in a day or two and we'll go out together.'

He wandered along up the street with them, a woebegone little figure in the thickening fog. Beris's eyes ached at the thought of his misery when Danny was arrested.

They decided to use Beris's car. As she started the engine Tommy thrust a doleful face through the lowered window. 'I've just remembered – it must be somewhere on th' main road 'cause Danny said something about there being a café near by where lorries called. But if you can't find it, why don't you ask the girl where it is?'

'What girl?' Beris asked.

'Madge – the girl who came round to our house this mornin'.'

Beris shook her head. 'She doesn't know Mr Clinton. Danny told me so.'

'I don't know about that, but she knows 'im now,' Tommy affirmed. 'I saw her talkin' to him in his car down Walton Street when I came back from school this mornin'. And from the way they were talkin' they seemed to know one another pretty well.'

Beris felt MacTaggit give a sudden start. She turned to him in surprise.

'What's the matter?'

He stared at her with an odd expression. 'It's something the lad just said. It made me wonder…'

Something, she did not know what, made her heart begin beating hard. 'What is it, Mac? Tell me.'

26

MacTaggit leaned forward and spoke to Tommy. 'Run along now, lad, will you? I've got something private to say to Miss Carnes.'

Tommy threw Beris a pleading glance before reluctantly withdrawing his head. Muttering good night he began tramping away down the street, throwing them a last, reproachful glance before disappearing into the fog. Giving him a farewell wave Beris then turned eagerly to MacTaggit.

'Well. What is it?'

The odd expression was still in MacTaggit's eyes. He gave a brittle, uneasy laugh. 'I don't quite know what to say, lassie. It's such a crazy notion and it's a million to one I'm wrong.' He paused, then made his decision. 'I'll make a phone call first, then if I'm right I'll tell you.'

She leaned forward threateningly. 'What made you jump like a startled cat just now? It had something to do with Danny, hadn't it? If you don't tell me I'll scream and claw your eyes out.'

He grinned. 'No; the phone call first. Then we'll see.'

They found a telephone kiosk two hundred yards down the main road. 'Don't expect anything to come of this,' MacTaggit warned her as he jumped out. 'It's one of those crazy ideas that probably don't mean a thing.'

She waited for him anxiously, watched the kiosk through the frosted side window. Five long minutes passed before he came out and jumped back into the car. She did not need to ask if his call had been a success: in spite of his efforts to conceal it, excitement hung around him like a static charge.

'I was right,' he muttered. 'By jingo, I was right...'

'What is it, Mac?' she pleaded. 'For heaven's sake tell me before I scream.'

He sat silent a full half-minute before

turning to her. 'Listen. If I tell you, will you make a solemn promise not to build up any hope on it? The chances are still a thousand to one that I'm wrong... Will you promise me that across your heart?'

'Of course I will. Now what is it?'

There was still doubt on his face. She caught hold of his shoulder and shook him, half playfully, half seriously. 'Don't worry about me. I'm not the type to fold up – surely I've proved that. Now, please tell me what it's all about.'

At that he made his decision, turning his bright, bird-like eyes on her. 'All right, lassie; here it is. It was what Tommy said about seeing the girl and Clinton together in his car that made me jump. I've always been vaguely curious about those two – you remember I asked you to find out all you could about them. You said Danny told you they didn't know one another. Do you think he believed it, or could he have been lying?'

She thought back to her conversation with Danny in the tower. 'He said they'd met for a couple of minutes once, but that was all. No; I feel certain he believed it.'

'Right. And yet this lunch time young Tommy sees them both as friendly as can be, sitting together in Clinton's car. Now why were they both there and what could they have been talking about?'

She was puzzled. 'I don't see what you're

getting at.'

'This is what I'm getting at, lassie. Mrs Johnson says Madge came to the house before twelve, and as Tommy doesn't leave school until after twelve he must have seen them together after Madge had called on Danny. Now why should Clinton be around at that time unless–'

Suddenly she saw light. 'Unless he knew she was calling on Danny and was checking up to see what had happened.'

'Exactly. Now let's take it a step further. Supposing, when he found out Danny hadn't agreed to go out with her, he went round himself later with a yarn that he needed help because his garage was a man short.'

She was still puzzled. 'But why should it matter so much that he went out with either of them tonight? What could their reason be?'

MacTaggit waggled a sharp forefinger at her. 'Has it ever occurred to you that each time there has been a robbery that girl has been involved in some way with Danny?'

Her voice trembled. 'You don't mean she is an accomplice of his?'

MacTaggit shook his head grimly. 'Not of his, lassie.'

She felt herself on the verge of a revolutionary discovery and her voice quickened as a consequence. 'What are you getting at,

Mac? Don't hedge – tell me.'

His forefinger changed its purpose for a moment, pointing at her warningly. 'Remember – this is only a theory!'

She managed a smile. 'I remember. Go on.'

'Right. Now do you remember my telling you that after the first robbery Danny claimed somebody had planted those pound notes in his mackintosh pocket?'

'Yes; but I couldn't think of an earthly reason why anyone should.'

'Neither could I at the time. But suppose someone had heard about him, knew his record – wouldn't he then have been an ideal person to frame? All the real criminal would have to do was commit the robbery so it appeared to the police like a new-comer's work, arrange for Danny to go to the Erebus, have the money planted on him there, and then anonymously tip off the police that there was gambling on the premises that night. It wouldn't take a pro-found knowledge of delinquent psychology to know that Danny would try to avoid having his name taken during the raid. That meant he would be arrested and the money found in his coat.'

'But what would be the purpose of that? They'd only lose the money – they'd know the police couldn't prove it didn't belong to Danny.'

In spite of himself, MacTaggit's voice turned triumphant. 'Aye; and that's exactly what a real criminal would want, lassie. He wouldn't want Danny to get a sentence or he couldn't use him again. The purpose would be to convince the police that they'd found the real thief so that in the future their eyes would be focused on him, leaving the real crook a free hand to do the same thing again at a later date.'

She struggled to understand him. 'And you're saying this crook could be Clinton with Madge Edwards helping him?'

He nodded. 'I'm saying it could be, nothing more. Think about the second robbery for a minute. According to what you told me, Danny said he'd been on a wild-goose chase that night, and it could be true. Madge could easily have arranged that her aunt left Merriby early so that he missed her. And as Madge would think he'd go there in the bus, he'd be left with no alibi – which meant he'd again attract the maximum suspicion from the police without them being able to convict him.'

'Yes; I see that,' she muttered. 'But you haven't explained yet why they would want him to go out with them tonight. What would the point be of that?'

His sharp eyes held her gaze. 'That shouldn't be hard to guess. Think for a moment!'

Her breath caught. 'You mean the Del-mont collection – that Clinton could be after it, and not Danny?'

'Why not? I should say it's easily the most tempting thing in the district for a crook.' Despite his caution, MacTaggit's voice became enthusiastic at the plausibility of his own reasoning. 'It would be a perfect frame-up, lassie. Who would the police immedi-ately suspect if some of that collection were stolen? Who would everyone, even you, his best friend, suspect? Danny, of course! Everyone already believes he's the current thief in these parts. He'd be guilty before a single clue was found – *provided he had no alibi*. Now do you follow me?'

The plausibility of his case astonished her. She listened in silence as he went on: 'Of course, this time the game would be over because it's almost certain Danny would receive a prison sentence. But that wouldn't matter to Clinton – he'd know it couldn't last for ever and in any case he'd make enough out of this job to set him up for life.'

She wanted to go on listening, to float along indefinitely on the warm, buoyant tide of his optimism. It was not easy to face reality again.

'But, Mac … Mac; you've forgotten my father's detective. He *saw* Danny go to Trin-bury Park – he *knows* Danny is the thief…'

She closed her eyes, not caring to see the

enthusiasm die from his face. He reached out, turned her face gently towards him. 'Beris,' he said quietly, 'why do you think I wanted to make a phone call before telling you this? I got in touch with the Station, where a friend of mine ran through a special list they keep there – a list of detective agencies giving the owners' names as well as the names under which they operate. One of these agencies is called Foley Investigations, but its owner's name is Clinton. Now are you with me?'

It was some seconds before she could speak coherently. 'Are you certain of this? There couldn't be a mistake?'

He shook his head. 'There's no mistake about Clinton being the detective. And think what it could mean. Danny returns to Lidsborough, and your father, suspicious of his motives, goes and asks Clinton to trail him. To do this he has to tell Clinton Danny's history, and that might have triggered off the whole idea in Clinton's mind. He might have already known your father intended exhibiting the Delmont collection here – after all, it was general knowledge months ago in some circles – and so, with the theft of the collection as the climax of his scheme, he goes to work – all the time drawing pay from your father while doing it. First he makes a friend of Danny and then frames him with two smallish, but still quite profitable, robberies in order to set him up as a sitting duck for the big one later. For this one he'd probably intend the police to get Danny – possibly by leaving around the scene of the crime some object with Danny's fingerprints on – he'd give himself plenty of opportunities to get them. Of course, all this time he'd be giving your father information, and by lying that he saw Danny go to Trinbury Park he'd not only make certain your father would indict Danny after the theft, he'd also get himself the job of guarding the very thing he intended to steal. Which is pretty clever.'

And her father had gone to Clinton because he feared Danny might steal the collection... Beris was not unaware of the irony. But the renaissance of her faith in Danny was a wildly exciting thing, overshadowing for the moment her father's danger.

'It's wonderful, Mac. It's like waking up after a nightmare...'

He now had the task of damping down her ardour. 'Remember your promise, lassie – you mustn't let your hopes run away with you. Things might still be as they seemed half an hour ago – Clinton might just as easily have told the truth about what he saw. The only basis for my suspicions are that Tommy saw Clinton and Madge talking together in a car at noon today. And there could be a hundred simple explanations of that. It might be, for example, that Clinton was spying on Madge just as he has been spying on Danny.'

She would allow nothing to disturb her reborn faith in Danny. 'That wouldn't explain why they both tried to get him to go out with them tonight. They're guilty, Mac – I'm certain of it. Phone the police and tell them everything.'

He frowned and shook his head. 'That's one thing I can't do. I haven't one scrap of evidence to support me.'

She remembered her father's danger. 'Then phone Daddy. We must do that or he'll be ruined.'

MacTaggit's sharp face was troubled. 'Now wait, lassie,' he cautioned. 'We must think this thing out very carefully. Let's examine the two alternatives – that Danny is either guilty or innocent. If he's guilty and he's going to Merriby tonight then your father is fully prepared for him and there's nothing we need do. If, on the other hand, he's innocent, we have to think before we act. If we phone your father about our suspicions of Clinton the chances are a hundred to one he won't believe a word of it. All that'll happen is that Clinton will be warned. I agree that might save your father's antiques but it certainly won't save Danny. He'll remain under police suspicion until

Clinton finds another golden altar to sacrifice him on. We want to find a way to clear his name and trap Clinton at the same time.'

'But how can we do that?'

MacTaggit glanced up at her sharply. 'We could do it if we could find Danny and keep him with us all night. Then, if Clinton commits the theft, we have him trapped because we can give Danny an alibi.'

'But what about my father? If Clinton is the real thief the collection is practically unprotected. Apart from Clinton's men there's only one other guard there, a Merriby policeman.'

MacTaggit scowled. 'I don't think your father would be in much danger of losing any of the exhibits. Clinton wouldn't have much time to get rid of them.'

'But there'd still be the disgrace of his having had them stolen.'

'I know that, lassie, but what can we do? With Danny in as deep as he is, I can't think of anything else that will convince the police of his innocence.' MacTaggit's voice was sympathetic. 'I know how difficult it is for you, and I shan't try to stop you if you want to warn your father. But for Danny's sake I wouldn't advise it.'

'Where do you think we could find Danny?' she asked. 'If Clinton has lied about everything else, isn't he likely to have lied about the garage?'

'I don't think so. Remember – Danny once told you he'd worked for a couple of days in a garage. Clinton, being a detective, would be no ordinary crook – he'd know how a case can be broken down by neglect of detail. I think he probably has an interest in a garage, although whether Danny is there is another matter.

Beris was thinking of her father, painfully aware that the mere recovery of any stolen exhibits would not restore his broken prestige. Then MacTaggit claimed her attention again.

'Don't be too long making up your mind, lassie. It's not likely Clinton would make an attempt before midnight, but if he did and we weren't with Danny, the lad's goose would be well and truly cooked.'

She waited to hear no more. She started the car engine, threw in the gears. 'Let's try to find him, Mac.'

27

The first garage they encountered was on the outskirts of Darntown, a huge, brilliantly lit, glass-fronted affair that stained the surrounding fog a deep orange. Mac-

Taggit made a few brief enquiries from the attendants, but neither he nor Beris were surprised at their blank headshakes.

'It's almost certain to be a small filling station,' MacTaggit told her. 'Wait here in the car a moment. I'll borrow a phone directory from them and take a list of Darntown garages from the classified index.'

He returned a few minutes later and they drove off into Darntown. As houses and shops closed in on either side so the fog grew denser, forcing Beris to slow down to a crawl. MacTaggit pulled a wry face. 'This isn't going to make things any easier, I'm afraid. It's going to be a regular pea-souper before the night's out.'

Because of the fog which made the street names impossible to read, MacTaggit's list proved of little use. It took them ten minutes to find a second garage, and fifteen more to find a third, and neither offered them the slightest encouragement. As they crawled on down the road, diffused lights, seemingly detached from the cars and lorries carrying them, drifted eerily out of the greyness and disappeared as mysteriously into it. The cold seeped through into the car, numbing their feet. As she glanced down at her watch Beris felt a hard knot of panic form in her throat.

MacTaggit noticed her movement. 'What time was your father closing the exhibition tonight? Eight o'clock?'

She nodded. 'And it's gone that already, Mac. It's eight-twenty.'

He saw the frightened look in her eyes and tried to comfort her. 'I don't think there's much danger of anything happening before midnight.'

'The other two robberies happened before midnight. Why shouldn't this one?' She stared into the fog that enveloped the car like a grey cocoon. 'Why had there to be fog tonight, Mac? Why tonight of all nights?'

'Steady, lassie,' he said quietly. 'It's not going to help him if we lose our heads. Keep going – we'll find him if he's here.'

She drove on, every muscle of her body rigid with tension as the minutes sped by. They found another small garage whose attendant told them there were at least three more filling stations on the road ahead.

They found the second of these twenty minutes later. It was a small brick building standing in front of what appeared to be a site demolished by air-raids. Being on the outskirts of Darntown, the fog was less dense here, and MacTaggit nudged Beris's arm as he pointed at two long, shadowy shapes just discernible alongside the building.

'Lorries pulled up on that waste land, lassie – it looks promising. Drive right up to the pumps.'

Beris drew up on the tarmac drive. A heavily built attendant wearing overalls and a pulled-down cap emerged from the building and approached them. He had a heavy, scarred face with jutting eyebrows and a negroid fullness to his lips. As he bent down to Beris's lowered window, MacTaggit nudged her arm and leaned in front of her.

'Does anyone by the name of Clinton own this garage or have an interest in it?'

Beris imagined a wary expression crossed the man's scarred face. He hesitated, then shrugged his heavy shoulders. 'You'd better 'ave a word with Mr Jackman, mate. He's the boss around here.'

'He looks a tough character,' Beris whispered as the man tramped back to the garage.

'Straight from Dartmoor by the look of him,' MacTaggit grinned, giving her a wink. 'Hold thumbs, lassie. This looks promising.'

Jackman proved as thin as his attendant was burly – a narrow-faced, thin-lipped man of about forty with receding hair. His black, beady eyes ran over Beris with interest before settling on MacTaggit.

'What's this about Mr Clinton?' He had a shrill, nasal voice.

'I want to know if he has a share in this garage,' MacTaggit told him.

Jackman thrust his ferret-like face a few more inches into the car. 'What's it to you, mate? Who are you, anyway?'

Nothing more was needed to bring out the quarrelsome terrier in MacTaggit. 'I'm a probation officer, and if you're smart you'll answer my questions. If you're not, then I'll soon find a way to make you.'

Jackman's eyes narrowed. 'All right – there's no need to get tough. Yes, Mr Clinton's a director of this business – has been for years. What about it?'

'Has a lad called Danny Meadows been sent here by Clinton tonight? Is he here now?'

Jackman shook his head. 'No one's come here tonight. We were promised one in place of a man that's gone off sick, but nobody's turned up.'

MacTaggit's sharp eyes were watching the manager closely. 'Are you sure of that?'

'What d'you mean – am I sure? I've only had to do some of his damn work tonight – that's how sure I am.'

'Will you let me come in and look around?'

Jackman hesitated, then gave a sour grin. 'Sure, if you want to make an even bigger fool of yourself. Come right in.'

Afraid from MacTaggit's expression that he might get himself into trouble, Beris went with him into the garage. The office was empty, and there was no one in the workshop but the burly attendant. Acutely conscious of

Jackman's derisive eyes, MacTaggit went into a small room at the rear of the building and even glanced into the toilet, but both were empty. Jackman's sarcastic remarks as they passed him on their way out were oil poured on his smouldering discomfort, and Beris had to hustle MacTaggit into the car to avoid a scene. She turned and drove a few hundred yards back into Darntown before pulling up and offering him a cigarette. When he refused it she turned his face reproachfully towards her.

He glowered at her, then gave a bashful grin. 'I am acting a bit like a schoolboy, aren't I? But, man, that thin-faced mongrel annoyed me...' He met her eyes again and sighed. 'All right – I'm coming round. I'll have that cigarette now.'

They sat smoking while the lights of lorries and cars drifted slowly by them in the fog. It was MacTaggit who broke the silence first, scowling down at his cigarette.

'On the face of it that knocks my theory cock-eyed. I believe they really are a man short, so it's feasible Clinton did go to ask Danny a genuine favour. And instead of coming to the garage he's gone to Mer-riby...'

'No,' she protested.

'You say no, but as I told you earlier it's just the thing his old childhood inhibitions would drive him to do,' MacTaggit growled.

Then he gave a snort of defiance, and jerked a thumb in the direction of the garage. 'But if Clinton employs men like that he's capable of anything. So we won't give up yet, lassie.'

She felt sick and shaky with disappointment. 'Where else can we look for him now?'

MacTaggit rubbed his chin. 'There are plenty of places where he could be hidden – too many, that's the trouble. Remember, he needn't have gone voluntarily this time: Clinton could have had him kidnapped.' Seeing her alarm he sought to reassure her. 'Not for long. They'd let him go after a few hours.'

'Only for the police to grab him and throw him into another cell,' she said bitterly.

MacTaggit gave a sudden start. 'What about this girl Madge? We might get something out of her. Have you any ideas where we might find her?'

Beris was forced to shake her head. 'No. I don't even know what she looks like.'

'That's a pity,' he muttered. 'She could be the key to everything. Wait a minute – what about the Erebus? It's a club – it would keep all its clients' addresses. She was there with Danny when he was arrested: it might be a favourite stamping ground of hers, and she'll need an alibi for herself tonight if our guess about Clinton is right.'

He grinned encouragingly as her hand leapt forward to the ignition key. 'That's the spirit, lassie. We won't give up until we've tried everything.'

But their journey to the Erebus proved only another disappointment and a further waste of time. Half an hour was spent crawling back through Darntown, another fifteen minutes finding their way through the narrow, fog-choked streets of the old town, only for them to hear in the hot, smoky hall of the Erebus that not only was Miss Edwards absent that evening but the management had no record of her address.

'I don't believe 'em,' MacTaggit fumed as they groped their way back to the car. 'It's a club – they must have their clients' addresses. If it wasn't for the explaining I'd have to do and the time it would take, I'd get the police to help me–'

Beris's dull voice interrupted him: 'That's our last hope gone, isn't it?'

MacTaggit hunched down in his seat, a fiery little gnome growling at his own frustration. After a minute he turned to her.

'Let's go back to Lambert Street and have another talk with young Tommy. He's got ears like a baby elephant and he might have heard Danny say something that'll give us a clue.'

Mrs Johnson led them up the stairs to the tiny landing. 'I let him go to th' swimming, but made him leave early,' she told them. 'Even then, because of th' fog, he only got back half an hour ago, so I don't expect he'll be asleep yet.'

Tommy made no liar out of her. He had heard their voices and was sitting up in bed, his eyes shining their welcome. Beris had never seen him in bed before, and thought how childlike he looked, with the collar of his blue-striped pyjamas making a frame for his freshly scrubbed face. She went to his bedside and knelt down alongside him.

'Tommy; I want to talk to you about Danny. It's terribly important, so listen very carefully.'

She began to tell him everything they knew and all they were guessing. On their way back from the Erebus she and MacTaggit had agreed it better, both for the boy's sake as well as their own, if nothing were kept back from him. On one point MacTaggit had been insistent – that mention be made of the possibility of Danny's guilt – and reluctantly she had seen the wisdom of preparing the boy for the worst. This she now tried to do as gently as possible, incorporating the possibility in her story.

'So you see, Tommy,' she finished, lifting her eyes briefly to MacTaggit who was standing at the bedfoot. 'We can't be absolutely certain Danny is innocent, but we're hoping he is. And we've come to ask you if you can help...'

The loyalty that is a hard-won victory in the adult is a spontaneous gift in the child. Tommy's wide, puzzled eyes had never left her face while she had been speaking. Now he interrupted her with a shrill cry of protest: 'Danny never did those things, miss. I know he didn't do 'em.' His voice turned accusing. 'And you oughter know that too. You're his friend, aren't you?'

She wanted to hug the boy breathless for his faith. 'Can you remember anything that might help us, Tommy? Has he ever mentioned any district or street in connection with this girl? Or has he ever talked of places that he and Clinton have visited together – places where he might go unnoticed if he went?'

'He's never talked about th' girl to me,' Tommy muttered. 'But I know he and Clinton used to go dog-racin' sometimes. And billiards – they used t' go to a saloon somewhere in Darntown.'

MacTaggit shook his head at Beris's enquiring glance. 'Fog would cancel all dog-racing tonight. And he'd be noticed in a billiard saloon. I want some place where he couldn't possibly get an alibi. You don't know anywhere else where they used to go?' he asked Tommy.

'There's Clinton's flat. Danny's often gone there.'

Beris started, but again MacTaggit shook his head. 'No; Clinton would never use his flat or offices – he'd be far too smart to do that.'

Beris put her arm around the boy's thin shoulders. 'You can't think of anything else, Tommy? Some little thing that might give us a clue?'

Tears of frustration welled into the boy's eyes. 'I can't, miss. I can't think of anything.'

She pressed his head against her, tried to comfort him. 'Never mind. It's not your fault and you mustn't worry about it.'

He fought back his tears with all the grim courage of his kind. 'Danny isn't goin' to be sent to prison, is he, miss?'

'Of course not, darling,' she whispered. 'Go to sleep now and everything will be all right in the morning.'

She dared not let him see her face as she hurried from the room. MacTaggit followed her downstairs. 'Don't be too disappointed, lassie,' he said quietly. 'This might be only a wild-goose chase, you know.'

For a moment her voice was harsh, condemning. 'Why can't you have faith in your own ideas?' Then she turned towards him. 'I'm sorry, Mac. It's just that things seem so hopeless. This is the end, isn't it?'

Against his black overcoat collar his

seamed cheeks looked pale and drawn. 'Not quite the end, lassie. We can still phone your father. If we're right about Clinton, that should put paid to his games for tonight anyway. And that should give Danny a day or two of grace – we might think of a way of convincing the police of his innocence in that time.'

A reprieve – she had forgotten such a thing were possible. Days, even minutes, of grace were precious now. With renewed hope she looked down at her watch, only to give a start of alarm. It was a quarter to eleven...

She was all nerves again, all urgency. 'Hurry, Mac. The exhibition's been closed for nearly three hours. It could happen at any time.'

He nodded. 'I think we're fairly safe until midnight but I won't dawdle just the same. I'll take your car if I may.'

Outside the fog choked the street like the protoplasm of some nightmare creature from outer space. MacTaggit gave it one glance and turned away from the car. 'It'll be quicker to run to the kiosk. Go inside and wait for me.'

His wiry figure vanished into the fog almost immediately, his muffled footsteps dying a second later. Shivering from the cold Beris returned into the house, leaving the front door off the latch. She went into

the kitchen where Mrs Johnson was preparing sandwiches and tea, and tried to
make conversation. After a few minutes she
roamed restlessly back into the living-room
where she finished one cigarette and lit
another. Mrs Johnson brought her a cup of
tea which she sipped mechanically, glancing
down at her watch every few seconds.

Ten minutes, fifteen minutes passed by,
and she could no longer suppress a fine
trembling that ran in slow waves through her
body. Mrs Johnson noticed her nervousness
and tried to comfort her – in turn she tried
to make conversation and hardly knew a
word of what she was saying. Another five
minutes and she could stand the suspense
no longer, going to the front door and listening while the grey fog bellied obscenely into
the hall.

Two minutes more and running footsteps
sounded on the pavement. Breathless,
coughing, MacTaggit threw back the gate
and approached her.

'I'm afraid I've got bad news for you,
lassie,' he panted.

She put a hand out blindly, caught hold of
the door.

'It's already happened. The policeman
guarding the rear of the building was discovered unconscious nearly an hour ago. A
window had been forced and a number of
valuable pieces are missing.'

The wound that numbs is the wound to fear. She felt no pain at that moment. 'Clinton?' she asked tonelessly. 'What about him?'

'He has a perfect alibi. He and one of his assistants were talking to your father at the front of the building when it must have happened. Later on they went with him on a tour of inspection and found the unconscious policeman. When the police came and made their search they found a shillelagh not far away.' As he told this, MacTaggit's eyes avoided her face. 'They've already established it has Danny's fingerprints all over it.'

Still there was no pain. 'And now, Mac. What now?'

'Inspector Greaves from the Station is on his way here. Your father is coming with him.'

'So it's over,' she said slowly. 'Nothing can save him now, can it, Mac? Nothing at all.'

He gripped her and pulled her fiercely into his arms. The rough fibres of his overcoat, wet with fog, pressed against her face. All his love for her, all his resentment against a pitiless world, sounded in his broken, tormented voice. 'Oh, lassie. I'd do anything for you – anything at all. And I'm helpless now … utterly helpless.'

The pain was starting now. First a long, vicious stab that brought her head spasmodically back. 'Prison will destroy him this time, won't it, Mac? He'll lie awake at nights, brooding about the injustice of it ... he'll grow to hate everything and everybody. And when he comes out all he'll be looking for is revenge. That's right, isn't it, Mac? That's how it will be.'

He tried to press her head down to hide the sight of his twisted face, but she caught a glimpse of his expression and from it her real agony began, a searing shock of pain that made her gasp at its brutality. She clutched at him, blindly seeking protection from it.

'There's something else too, isn't there, Mac – something that makes it even more cruel? We're never going to know the truth now, are we? We're never going to be certain he didn't do it...'

28

The police car arrived twenty minutes later. MacTaggit held Beris back and opened the front door himself.

There were four men outside, three police-men and Carnes. One of the policemen stepped forward on seeing MacTaggit; a craggy, square-set, middle-aged man whom Beris recognized as Inspector Greaves, a golfing friend of her father.

'He hasn't been back yet, has he?' Greaves asked.

When MacTaggit shook his head Greaves gave a grunt of satisfaction and turned to the two constables behind him. 'Morgan; you get the car out of sight smartly and then hide yourself in there,' and he pointed to a narrow alley that lay alongside the neighbouring houses. 'Chisholm; you hide yourself in the fog on the other side of the road. Listen for him, and remember – let him get inside the house before you make a move. Otherwise he might dodge you in the fog.'

The two constables saluted and withdrew. Greaves stood aside and motioned for Carnes to enter the house. It was then that Beris, standing in the rear of the hall, had her first clear glimpse of her father.

At first sight, in his Crosbie overcoat and white silk scarf that hid his evening dress beneath, he looked the sturdy, reliant business man she had always known, taking his set-back with grim confidence in his own powers of resilience. It was only when the light from the living-room fell full on his face that she saw the change in him. His cheeks, that in spite of their abundance had always seemed firm and healthy, now appeared to be sagging, as though the aggressive bones supporting them had suddenly collapsed. And his eyes, once so steel-blue and keen, were now muddy with the silt of despair – the eyes of a man who, after a lifetime's purposeful march down a wide, straight road, had suddenly found a cliff edge at the end of it.

Like Greaves he showed no surprise at seeing her – MacTaggit had informed the police over the phone of their presence in Lambert Street. He paused before her and his words, although low-spoken, bruised her like blows. 'Well,' he muttered. 'Are you satisfied now?' With that he moved heavily into the living-room.

She followed him in and caught his arm. With MacTaggit talking in low, urgent tones to Greaves in the hall and with Mrs Johnson withdrawing discreetly into the kitchen, she was alone with him for the moment.

'You're terribly wrong about him. It was Clinton who did it. He's been deceiving you all the time.' She saw from his expression that he had already heard something if not all of MacTaggit's theory. 'Don't turn your head away. Listen to me…'

He raised an arm in protest. 'I've heard it all – Greaves told me before we left. And it's downright madness. Do you realize I was actually talking to Clinton and one of his men when it happened?'

'But don't you see he did that to give himself an alibi? While he was talking to you another of his accomplices attacked the policeman and committed the robbery.'

'And what about the evidence – the stick with Danny's fingerprints on it?'

'Can't you see – they planted that to make certain he got the blame.'

He turned slowly towards her as if he had not heard her last words. 'Do you know the thought that came to me after it had happened?'

She shook her head.

'I knew he had ruined me, but I thought one good thing would come out of it – you'd be convinced at last that I hadn't been unkind or unjust to him. I clung to that thought all the way back from Merriby. And then I heard from Greaves of the fantastic excuses you and MacTaggit were making for him...'

Tears were blinding her. 'They're not excuses, Daddy. If only you would listen...'

But he was not listening. A sudden quiver ran through him, closing his eyes. 'I hate that boy,' he whispered, and although low his voice was virulent with emotion. 'I hate him more than I believed I could hate anybody on God's earth.'

The intensity of his hatred terrified her, yet in a way she understood it. With the desertion of his only daughter, with his ambition in ruins around his feet, it was a vital façade to conceal his failure. Without it that failure was visible, not only to the world, but to his own pitiless contempt. And so, proud man that he was, he would reinforce it with all the strength of his mind and body.

She tried to fight it. 'Can't you see what your hatred has done? If you hadn't thought the worst of him when he returned to Lidsborough, if you hadn't gone to Clinton in your distrust, none of this would have happened. You haven't only destroyed him with your suspicions, you've destroyed yourself as well.'

Not for the first time she had the feeling of being an actor in a play. The lines had to be said but nothing would change the characters and finale – both were predestined.

The hopelessness of it all became suddenly overpowering and she turned away and stumbled towards the fireplace. Putting her arms up to the mantelpiece she rested her head wearily against them. In the silence she heard MacTaggit and Greaves arguing in the hall outside. It took her no more than a few seconds to realize that Greaves, presented with a neatly sewn-up case, was doing little more than humouring MacTaggit.

'Yes, Mac; it's a clever theory – I'll give you that – but every bit of it is based on supposition. If one likes doing mental exercises of this sort, one could probably find similar excuses for any crook – why he was innocent and how all his acquaintances were framing him. But it would be just as unrealistic. Let's face it – every bit of evidence points straight at Meadows, and in addition to that he's got a criminal history sheet behind him. There's nothing against Clinton or the girl.'

'But, man, can't you see it's that very history of his that could have made him a sitting duck for these people?'

'Come off it, Mac. I know you do your best for these delinquents, and I respect you for it, but people don't automatically frame 'em because they have a police record, you know. And anyway, he's going to have a trial. He'll get a chance to say his piece.'

MacTaggit's snort of disgust was heard clearly in the living-room. 'With all the suspicion and all the evidence those two have piled against him, a trial will be a formality and you know it.' A moment of silence and then his peppery voice again. 'If you're so certain he did the job tonight, why are you expecting him back here? Surely this is the last place he'll come.'

'Crooks do odd things – you know that well enough. He came back here after the last job.'

'He came back the last time because he was innocent,' MacTaggit growled. 'And if he comes back tonight it'll be for the same reason.'

'Miss Carnes made us think he was innocent,' Greaves reminded him. 'It's just possible he might come – I thought it worth the chance. But this isn't all we're doing, you know. We've half the police in Lidsborough searching for him as well.'

'You're searching for the wrong man, Greaves. One day you're going to find that out.'

'You don't believe that, Mac – not deep inside. But anyway,' and Greaves's voice became condescending, 'don't think we won't bear in mind all you've said. Now what about joining the others. It's damned draughty out here.'

They entered the living-room, Greaves broad-shouldered and confident, MacTaggit a frustrated, angry bantam. Greaves went over to Carnes, who was sitting in a chair by the table, and touched him encouragingly on the shoulder.

'Cheer up, Vic. I think we've a decent chance of getting those missing pieces back. I've got every fence in town under observation.'

As he moved towards the fire there was a sudden commotion in the room above. There was a loud bump, followed by the rapid scamper of feet across the ceiling. Greaves glanced sharply at MacTaggit and swung round to face the door. A moment later Tommy, bare-foot and in his blue-striped pyjamas, burst into the room. His dazzled eyes, screwed up from the light, settled on Beris. He made straight for her.

'Miss; somethin's just come to me. It might be the thing you wanted.'

She knelt down, caught hold of his shoulders. 'What, Tommy? What is it?'

'It's a key, miss. One Danny lost a couple of weeks ago. It was missin' one mornin' – after he'd been out with Clinton. Don't you see – Clinton might 'ave stolen it.'

Her heart was thudding now like a madly beaten drum. 'What was the key, Tommy? Do you know?'

'Yes, miss. He had t' have another one made – he always kept two. They were keys to the lighthouse.'

It was like the distant glimmer of light to someone hopelessly lost in the nightmarish darkness of catacombs. It was every lost and buried hope in the world being given a magical resurrection, and for a moment she was stunned at the suddenness of it. Then she swung round on MacTaggit.

'Do you hear that, Mac? The lighthouse – it's the perfect place.' She grabbed hold of Tommy and almost squeezed the breath from him. 'Oh, you wonderful boy.'

The effect on MacTaggit was equally electric. His eyes were dancing with excitement as he turned to Greaves. 'Come on, man. If he's there we have to reach him before Clinton does or you'll never believe us.'

Greaves, eyes suddenly alert, looked from

Tommy to MacTaggit. 'Wait a minute. Keep cool. What are you thinking – that Clinton stole the key two weeks ago in preparation for tonight?'

'Wouldn't it fit in with everything I've already told you? We never thought of the lighthouse because we believed you people were in possession of all the keys, but this changes everything. Come on, man. I shall want you as a witness if he's there.'

Greaves, no opinionist in spite of his human desire for a sewn-up case, frowned uncertainly. Carnes broke in, his voice incredulous:

'Surely to God, Jack, you're not starting to believe there's something in this cock-and-bull idea.'

Greaves glanced at him. 'I'm not saying I believe anything, Vic. But it mightn't do any harm to take a look.'

Carnes could not control his anger. 'You're turning as daft as they are, man. You're a police inspector with a responsibility to the public. Your job is to arrest the thief who's just robbed me, not go chasing fairies all over the countryside.'

Nothing makes up the northcountry mind quicker than a taste of its own bluntness. Greaves frowned his displeasure and turned to MacTaggit. 'Ten to one it's nothing but a false alarm,' he grunted. 'He could have lost the key anywhere. But come on – we'll go along and make sure.'

'And what happens if he comes here while you're away?' Carnes asked, staring at him unbelievingly.

Greaves paused at the door. 'Taking a look at another horse doesn't mean I'm changing my bet, Vic. Both my men will still be outside – they'll grab him fast enough if he comes.'

As MacTaggit followed Greaves into the hall he caught sight of Beris's anxious face. 'Hold thumbs for us, lassie,' he muttered. 'But don't be too disappointed if nothing comes of it.'

'Hurry, Mac,' she begged. 'Make him hurry. It's a long time now since the robbery.'

He knew her fear and tried to comfort her. 'They'd first have to get rid of the exhibits, and then there'd be the fog – that would slow 'em down in getting back to him. Don't worry – we won't waste any time.'

With that he ran after Greaves. The front door slammed, leaving her with her father, Tommy, and Mrs Johnson, who on hearing the voice of her ward had appeared at the kitchen door.

Beris bent down and put her hands on Tommy's shoulders. 'Don't you think you ought to go back to bed now, Tommy? You might catch cold down here.'

Mrs Johnson took her cue, lumbering forward like an accommodating she-bear.

'Yes, m' lad, it's bed for you. Come along.'

No soldier punished for a trivial breech of discipline after an effort to save his regiment could have looked more injured than Tommy at that moment. 'But, miss, I can't go to bed now,' he wailed. 'I want t' know what happens...'

Beris took hold of his hands. 'Please, Tommy, I want to speak in private to my father. But I promise to come up and tell you everything that's happened as soon as Mr MacTaggit gets back.'

Tommy was somewhat mollified by this promise. 'You're sure you won't forget?'

'Of course I won't forget – if we find Danny we shall owe it all to you. You wait snug and warm in bed upstairs and I'll come up to you later on.'

At this Tommy even allowed her to kiss him. As he followed Mrs Johnson from the room she turned to face her father.

He was standing near the fire, his expression betraying his bewilderment at the new turn of events. He eyed her resentfully as she drew closer.

'You don't really believe they're going to find Danny locked up in that tower, do you?'

'I think there's a chance,' she said quietly.

He stared at her for a long moment, then dropped into one of the armchairs. His broad, powerful hands came together, stubby fingers intertwining. As they tightened their pressure, the muscles alongside his thumbs bunched into hard, shiny ridges. They drew her eyes, fascinating her. They seemed to symbolize his character, powerful, unyielding, yet by virtue of their very toughness oddly vulnerable to the tugs of fortune. Without flexibility, one great wrench could sunder them, leaving only ruin where there had been strength.

'It's impossible,' he gritted. 'You must have all gone mad. Stark, staring mad.'

But the merciless firelight betrayed the fear in his eyes. Until now his faith in his own moral behaviour towards Danny had remained unimpaired by all that had happened – his very ruin had been its vindication, and a certain grim satisfaction lay in it. But this new development was a hideous spectre – it not only hinted that he had been guilty of a grave injustice but also that the whole foundation of his moral beliefs was based on sand. And to one as uncompromising as Carnes, that was a threat to the innermost citadel of his ego.

Beris had an instinct of this as she stood gazing down at his straining hands. It did not make the thing she wanted to say any easier.

'Supposing for the moment that Mac and I are right and they bring Danny back. What will you do?'

His appearance suggested he had been expecting the question and dreading it. It was some seconds before he looked up at her. 'What do you mean?'

Looking down into his embittered face, knowing the laceration and disappointment that lay behind it, she had to fight back the temptation to drop down and comfort him. 'You know what I mean well enough. If they bring him back it means he is innocent of all the things you've attributed to him. It'll mean more than that – it'll mean your suspicions, however unintentionally, have caused him a great deal of suffering and nearly got him a prison sentence as well. So I'm asking what you intend doing.'

His hands increased their pressure, knuckles cracking with the strain. 'The question won't arise. You'll see I've been right all the time.'

'But if it does,' she insisted. 'What then?'

He fought off doubt with all his grim tenacity. 'It won't, I tell you. He's got a bad streak in him – he's had it all his life – and he's guilty. Won't anything convince you of that?'

'All my life I've respected you,' she said slowly. 'I've always thought you a big man. Recently I've realized you've got faults … like the rest of us have. But I still thought you big enough to confess when you were wrong. If they bring Danny back tonight it'll not only mean you've been wrong … it'll mean you've made the greatest mistake of your life. If you won't admit that – to him as well as to me – I shall never come back to you because all my respect for you will be dead.'

After that they sat in silence, each with his thoughts and hopes, while the hour hand of the clock on the mantelpiece moved like doom itself.

29

The long wait drained away all Beris's courage: when the sharp rap finally sounded on the front door she felt physically incapable of answering it. It was her father who went, rising heavily from his chair and walking past her with the slow preoccupation of a man about to receive his verdict after a long and exhausting trial.

A positive fusillade of knocks assaulted the door as he fumbled with the latch. Hinges creaked as the door opened and a cold draught of air entered the sitting-room. Hugging herself in her suspense, Beris bent forward in her chair, seconds becoming hours as the time stream of her life slowed down to a crawl.

Then MacTaggit's excited, exultant voice sounded, and for a moment the room spun like a roulette wheel before her eyes. 'Where's Beris? Tell her everything's all right. Tell her we've found him.'

Instantly time raced away with her, tossed her over a cataract, ran her into a series of whirlpools. She found herself in the hall, where MacTaggit was helping Danny inside – a white-faced, dishevelled Danny who moved stiffly and whose dark-shadowed eyes were still full of amazement at the things he had recently been told. Another giddy swirl of time and she seemed to be hugging both him and MacTaggit at once, her laughs and sobs breaking over them at the miracle of it. Through the confusion of sound came MacTaggit's voice, speeded up by time but with no essentials missing.

'Two men jumped out from a car when he was going out this evening, and when he resisted they knocked him down with a rubber hose. They took him to the light-house ... bound him and left him locked inside. Greaves has stayed behind ... sent a message with me for his two constables to join him at the double.'

Faces came into focus, blurred into shadows again. Her father's face, still struggling with the full significance of his sentence. MacTaggit's face, exultant, yet tinged with a faint wistfulness. He spoke to her again, quietly this time.

'Take him upstairs, lassie. He'll need to lie down for a while – he's had a bad night. Stay up there with him – you've a lot to talk about – and I'll make you both a hot drink.'

Halfway up the stairs she remembered... 'Don't let my father leave... Whatever happens he mustn't leave before I've seen him again. Do you hear me, Mac?'

'I hear, lassie, and don't worry. I'll talk to him.'

Then there was Tommy – Tommy to whom they owed so much. 'We must see him first, Danny. If it hadn't been for him we'd never have found you...'

A timeless moment that was centred about a small boy's bright, glad eyes and excited face, and then the current threw her forward again, this time into Danny's room. He seemed in the same vortex now, drawn like herself into its centre. Nearer he swirled and nearer ... until his white face filled the entire frame of her vision.

It was half an hour before the delirious time stream steadied down and she was reminded that some problems were still outstanding. She was sitting on his bed, one hand tightly clasped in his own. He, still feeling the effects of his rough handling from Clinton's men, was lying full-length beside her, his eyes fixed on her face. There was a shyness of belief in them, almost a fear of such unexpected happiness, and they followed her every movement and expression as though afraid the moment was a dream and had to be well remembered.

She touched his face, running her hand gently down his cheek. Her voice was low and a little nervous. 'Will you do something for me, Danny? Something that will make me very happy?'

He cleared his throat. 'You know I will if I can,' he muttered. 'What is it?'

'It's about my father, Danny. Before Mac brought you back tonight I had a talk with him. I told him that if they found you in the tower it proved beyond all doubt that he had wronged you and that if he didn't then ask your forgiveness I couldn't live with him again.'

There was a moment of silence before he spoke. 'What did he say?'

'He didn't promise anything. But I know he was terrified of being wrong. Now his conscience will never let him rest – he'll lose his self-respect and go to pieces unless he makes it up to you in some way. So he must come to you – somehow I have to make him. And when he comes I want you to help me by forgiving him.'

Old resentments, like old stains, are not easily removed. He shifted uncomfortably on his pillow. 'Do you really believe he has that kind of conscience?'

'I know he has, Danny.'

'No,' he muttered. 'Not your father. I can't believe that.'

Reality is no respector of persons, and not for the first time she realized it demanded frankness to friends as well as foes.

'Danny; it isn't only for Father's sake that I'm asking this. It's for yours too. You've got to lose this bitterness towards him. It's poison – it's the same poison that started off all your trouble when you were a child. And if you don't try to get rid of it, you're never going to be your true self again.'

A shadow lay across his face like a bruise, hiding his expression. When he did not answer she went on:

'I'm not defending him: don't think that. He treated you badly when you were a child, and his conduct these last two months has been indefensible. But think – weren't you just as suspicious of him when you returned here? Can you honestly say that if the situation had been reversed you wouldn't have done the same things to him as he did to you?'

Still he did not answer.

'I'm asking you for your own sake, Danny. Mr MacTaggit once said that he believes no one can be healthy in mind or body if they harbour rancour towards others, and I'm sure now that he's right.'

At that he stirred, brushing an arm fretfully across his eyes as though something were obscuring his vision. 'You talk as if forgiveness were just a matter of saying the words. But there's so much more to it than that.'

She sat silent, listening.

'You have to mean it too, Beeda. And that's why I don't want to see him. I don't want to be a hypocrite on top of everything else.'

She looked at him in dismay. 'But surely it isn't that hard to forgive him.'

Again he shifted, restless from the struggle within him. 'It is hard. Whether it should be or not, it is. I can't help it.'

Then she remembered his history, the bitterness that had pressed into a boy's tender mind like a sharp heel into clay, to set there as the weathering years passed by, and she was silent again.

His tone changed, touching her with its eager wistfulness. 'It isn't that I don't want to do it, Beeda. It's just that I can't feel it inside. I want to but I can't.'

It was not easy to make the admission, but honesty forced her to it. She gave a slow, reluctant nod. 'I know what you mean. I've often felt that way myself. But it was never as important as this. This is something you must do if you want to be happy again.'

While she had been speaking he had

suddenly lifted up on his elbows as if something had occurred to him. 'You don't have the same difficulty in forgiving people now, though, do you?'

She hesitated, surprised at the truth of his assertion. 'No,' she admitted. 'I don't believe I do. Not as much, anyway.'

'You don't,' he said with conviction. 'You've changed out of all recognition from what you were like when I left home – that's what I can't understand. What helped you to change – what helped you to forgive me, for example?' He was sitting upright now, staring at her with eager intentness.

'There never was any question of forgiving you,' she protested. 'You weren't the offender.'

He shook his head impatiently. 'That's nothing to do with it. As far as you were concerned I had wronged your father, and yet you found a way to forgive me. Tell me how. I want to know.' There was a deep earnestness about him that made her feel many things might depend on her answer. Although she believed she had the right one, it made her nervous and she went forward carefully, afraid of making a false step.

'It was Mac's stories about his delinquents that were the beginning of it. Until then they'd been creatures of another world to me: I'd never thought that but for luck I might have been one of them. But Mac showed me their lives through their own eyes. He told me all about Tommy, for example, about his unsympathetic mother, about the death of his father and its effects on his mind... I began to realize that if I'd been in Tommy's shoes I would probably have done just the same things myself.'

'Is that how you began to understand my trouble?' he asked.

Beris nodded. 'Yes. And later on Mac explained to me in detail what you had suffered. He did it so well that at times I was you and then I understood everything.' Her eyes were bright now as her confidence grew. 'That's the secret of forgiving people, Danny – it's one of those simple things that are often so difficult to see. You have to learn to live their lives in your imagination ... to *be* them for a little while. Then your views on them often change completely. Mac once said that that kind of imagination can and should be taught in schools. I wasn't quite sure at the time, but now I know he's right. It can be taught to people: he taught it to me ... it really works. You discover all you can about the other person's environment, their inherited temperament, the hard luck they've had – all the things they've had no control over – and suddenly you realize they're not a party, but a prisoner, to it all. After that it's easy. You ask yourself how you would behave if all these things had been massed against you, and sometimes you get a shock at the answer.'

His eyes had never left her face while she had been speaking. Now he released his breath and fell back on his pillow. He lay silent a moment frowning up at the ceiling. Then he lifted his head to stare at her again.

'Couldn't forgiveness of that kind be just sentimentality, or even complacency? Your father would say so, and he could be right for once. After all, on your argument you could probably find an excuse for Clinton.'

'You probably could if you examined his life history,' she agreed quietly. 'I know what Mac's answer to that would be. He'd say that just because we have to put criminals out of harm's way doesn't mean we can't understand and forgive them. And if he's able to do it with the people he meets, surely you can do it with Father. Think of his life, Danny. He was terribly in love with Mother ... it nearly killed him when she died. Afterwards he turned all that love on me ... there was far too much of it ... it made him blind to everyone else. Love can be selfish, you know. Then there was his upbringing – he was a self-made man in an industrial town and he had to fight his way through the slump in the thirties ... can you wonder his mind works the way it does today? – life has made it like that. Think of him that way, Danny, and you won't find it so hard to forgive him then.'

Held by her sincerity he lay motionless, gazing at her. Then he gave a sudden exclamation of distress and rolled over, hiding his face from her.

'I can't do it, Beeda. I want to but I can't.'

Startled, she bent over him. 'Surely it can't be as difficult as that, Danny.'

His voice was half stifled in his pillow. 'You don't understand. It's something quite different.'

She tried to turn his tortured face towards her. 'Then what is it, darling? What else is there?'

The dry sobs that jerked his body reminded her of his breakdown in the tower. When he did not answer she put her lips close to his cheek, her voice gentle:

'Danny; we've travelled too far together to have secrets from one another still. What else have you to tell me?'

She could feel the struggle within him, torturing his body as though it were on the rack. When he answered his words were jerky, torn away by his love for her.

'To forgive anyone you have to be in the right yourself or the thing's a mockery. I'm not. It's as simple as that.'

Her mouth was suddenly dry. 'I don't understand. You weren't involved in any way in those two earlier robberies, were you?'

His head rocked on the pillow.

'Then what's worrying you?' she asked, puzzled. 'What have you done not to be in the right?'

His face suddenly lifted and turned to her, his eyes bright with self-aversion. 'Aren't you forgetting about tonight?'

'Tonight? But you didn't do that – you were locked in the tower when it happened.' Suddenly she was frightened and gripped his shoulder tightly. 'It was true, wasn't it – the story you told Mac?'

He avoided her eyes. 'It was true enough,' he muttered. 'But what I didn't tell him was that I wasn't going to Clinton's garage when his men grabbed me.'

She felt as though someone had struck her a heavy blow, sending her mind reeling back in time ... back to MacTaggit's warning earlier that evening! *'It's quite possible, lassie ... a complex has remained with him ever since ... the danger is very real he may retaliate again.'*

His voice came through the dull, numbing mist that seemed to surround her. 'I had intended to go to the garage, but the urge to get my own back on your father grew stronger and stronger... I tried to fight it but it was no use... I didn't plan anything; I'd no idea what I intended doing. All I knew is that when I left the house this afternoon I intended going to Merriby.'

A pause, and then his bitter finale. 'But it's

389

not difficult to guess what I'd have done once I got there.'

Something inside her was both laughing and crying at the irony of it. In trying to incriminate him, Clinton had probably saved him from himself. Then she rallied her faith and dug her fingers into his arm. 'No, you wouldn't. I know you wouldn't.'

'You don't know,' he said bitterly. 'And you'll never know, because I don't know myself. But you can see how absurd all this talk is of my forgiving your father.'

Her voice was fierce. 'It's not absurd. It's more necessary than ever now. Can't you see – it was the knowledge of what he'd done to you that gave you the desire to steal … you wanted your revenge. Once you've forgiven him you'll lose that desire for ever.'

'And do you think he's likely to come to terms with me when he's heard my confession? He'll be convinced he was right all the time – as he probably was.'

She shook his arm vehemently. 'You mustn't tell him. You mustn't say a word about it, do you hear? Nothing.' Her expression suddenly changed, became thoughtful. 'Perhaps in a way it's a good thing…'

'A good thing?' he muttered, trying to understand.

She looked him full in the face. 'Yes. It should make it easier for you to forgive him.'

A pause, and then he nodded slowly. 'I

know what you mean. It's quite true.' The sudden wistfulness that came into his voice made her catch her breath. His eyes searched her face as though trying to impress it indelibly on his mind before the chance went for ever.

'You can see now why there can never be anything between us, Beeda. Whatever else it did, tonight showed me one thing – that I'll never change.'

She caught hold of him, pulling his head against her like a mother protecting a child. 'Of course you will. You've changed already. And once you get rid of all this bitterness you won't know yourself.'

'No,' he muttered, trying to pull away. 'Every time someone did us a dirty trick I would want to get my own back on him. It wouldn't be fair to you.'

Fiercely she clung to him, pressing her wet cheek against his own. 'It wouldn't be fair if you left me… You're not going, Danny. Everything will come right in time. You'll see.'

Both his voice and his resistance broke, and warm tears soaked through her dress. 'You'll always be the strong one between us, Beeda. It's as if I'd had an accident as a child and was a cripple. I'll try to run with you – I'll try terribly hard if you'll have me, Beeda – but I'll keep stumbling… I won't be able to help it. And then you'll have to pick me up. You'll have to pick me up or I'll never finish the race with you…'

She laughed at him with the tears pouring down her cheeks. 'I'll help you up, Danny. We'll get to the finishing post together.'

A few minutes later she went downstairs. To her relief her father was still there, sitting in the armchair opposite MacTaggit. Allowing herself no hesitation she went straight across to him.

'You've had plenty of time now to reflect on everything,' she said quietly. 'And I've come to ask what you intend doing.'

It was MacTaggit who interrupted her. 'It's all right, lassie,' he said, dropping a cautionary eyelid at her as she turned towards him. 'Your father's been waiting for you to come down, that's all.'

She turned back to her father. 'You are going up to him, then?'

He nodded heavily and rose. She followed him to the foot of the stairs where he paused, gathering his courage. She had never felt greater affection for him than at that moment, and she leaned forward to kiss his cheek.

'Thank you,' she whispered. 'I'm very proud of you.'

His hand fumbled at his side and squeezed her own. Then, one slow foot before the other, he started up the staircase towards the greatest ordeal of his life. Moist-eyed she watched him reach the landing. There his strength appeared to falter: he paused and turned back to her.

'Perhaps you'd better warn him,' he muttered. 'It might be wiser.'

She ran upstairs and past him. Entering the bedroom she found Danny standing beside the wardrobe, facing the door like a man at bay.

'Father wants to see you,' she panted. 'He's waiting outside now.'

'I know. I heard him.'

She caught hold of his hand. It was clammy with nervousness. 'Remember all you've promised me. Be patient with him and be forgiving – for my sake.'

'I'll try,' he muttered. 'I'll do my best.'

There was no time for further reassurance. She kissed him, threw him a last pleading glance from the door, then crossed the landing to her father.

'It's all right. He's waiting for you.' As he nodded she went on: 'Will you remember something when you're in there? Will you remember I love you both very much?'

She went with him as he moved heavily forward. 'I'm very proud of you,' she told him again. 'You're all the things I always believed you were.'

At the door he turned to her, his voice hoarse and unsteady. 'Don't wait here for me, Beeda. Go downstairs.'

It was an urgent plea for her not to witness his shame, and she wanted to obey him. But the door had already swung open; he and Danny were suddenly face to face; and the drama of the moment held her paralysed.

Danny was standing utterly motionless, staring at her father with eyes that were dark holes in his chalk-white face. With his features expressing dislike – his first instinctive reaction – his very immobility suggested he was now waging a desperate personal battle, and Beris hardly dared watch the outcome.

Her eyes turned to her father. Standing in the doorway with bowed shoulders and lowered head, he looked an abased and broken man, and pity made her suddenly wonder if she had been right to bring him to such shame, if the experience might not leave him permanently disabled. His silent agony as he sought for words was a refinement of torture to her, bringing out the sweat in her clenched hands.

The silence and the struggle seemed interminable, giving her an almost overwhelming desire to run forward and help him. Then, just when she believed all was lost, in that moment of choice between pride and equity, the true quality of Carnes's character became evident.

Grimly his bowed shoulders came back, back until his set face was lifted up to

Danny's. 'Lad,' he said, and the gritty strength of his voice was unrecognizable from the one that had spoken to Beris a minute earlier. 'You know why I'm here. I've found out tonight that I've wronged you, and I've come to ask your forgiveness. Will you give it to me, lad?'

Danny did not answer immediately, and when his lips did move his voice was too low for Beris to overhear him. But his turbulent face had already given her his answer. In place of the initial dislike mirrored there had come a reluctant pity at the sight of Carnes's humiliation. It had come slowly, over the dragging minute or more in which Carnes had struggled with his pride. But there had been no reluctance in the emotion that had superseded pity.

It was unqualified admiration. For, in his conquest of pride, with his courage expurgated by humility, Carnes had unknowingly found his true strength, and that strength had turned a defeat into victory, a victory for them all.

The door closed then, hiding both of them from Beris. Blinded by tears, she went down the stairs to find MacTaggit waiting in the hall for her. His anxious eyes lit up with relief at her expression as she approached him.

'You're radiant,' he told her with admiration. 'Beautiful. That means things are going well, doesn't it?'

She tried to laugh but only managed a sob of thanksgiving as she flung her arms around him. 'I think so, Mac. They'll have a great deal to say to one another, but I believe everything will be all right now.'

His hand touched her hair, stroked it gently. 'I'm glad, lassie. So very, very glad.'

Holding him tightly she explained what had happened. He was silent a moment, then said quietly: 'What about the future – about you and the lad, I mean? Are you going through with it?'

She pressed her wet face against his cheek to avoid meeting his eyes. 'Yes, Mac. I'm going through with it.'

His arms tightened around her for the last time before gently relinquishing her. 'Good girl,' he smiled. 'Then we needn't worry any more about him. He's in excellent hands.'

Remembering what Danny had confessed she could not keep apprehension from her question. 'Have you any advice for me, Mac?'

He glanced at her under his bushy eyebrows. 'Just think of the lad as someone who's had a chronic illness in his youth, and has been left a bit prone to the same kind of germs. Keep him clear of 'em and you shouldn't have any further trouble. Or, if you'd like another metaphor, be a good shepherd, lassie. Then the wolves won't get at him again.'

'Be a good shepherd,' she repeated slowly. 'And then you think everything will be all right. You wouldn't lie to me, would you, Mac?'

His eyes paused on her face for a moment. 'No, lassie,' he said quietly. 'No; I wouldn't lie to you.' Then he turned to the hallstand and reached for his overcoat.

'Well; I suppose there are plenty of morals one could draw from this affair but it's too late in the night for me to work 'em out.'

She stared at him as he shrugged on his coat. 'You aren't going yet, are you?'

'Yet?' he grinned. 'It's gone two o'clock – I've got a fresh batch of delinquents to face in seven hours' time. And we can't occupy Mrs Johnson's house all night.'

'Where is she now – in bed?'

'No; she came down a few minutes ago to make another cup of tea – she's in the kitchen. She's all right – she's only too glad things have worked out this way.'

'Thanks to you, Mac. Everything is thanks to you.'

He laughed. 'You haven't done such a bad job yourself. I wouldn't mind a couple of assistants like you.'

She saw he was going to keep the moment light and loved him the more for it. 'I wish there was another like me, Mac. I'd be waiting all night outside the office door for you to open it.'

Their eyes met and held for a second, and then he was grinning again. 'It's just as well – I'd never get any work done with you around. S'long, lassie. Give me a ring one of these days – I shall miss those little talks of ours.'

Before she could answer the door had opened and he had gone. And she was standing alone on the porch, blinded by the fog that seemed to burn her eyes like acid.

The publishers hope that this book has given you enjoyable reading. Large Print Books are especially designed to be as easy to see and hold as possible. If you wish a complete list of our books please ask at your local library or write directly to:

Dales Large Print Books
Magna House, Long Preston,
Skipton, North Yorkshire.
BD23 4ND

This Large Print Book, for people
who cannot read normal print,
is published under the auspices of

THE ULVERSCROFT FOUNDATION